"W'at do you want from life, Jessica?"

Armand's hands were on her shoulder and his gaze demanded honesty.

"I want to do my work," she said evenly. "My . . . my career is important to me."

"Don' you want love? And chil'ren?"

He was standing so close that she was aware of his presence in every cell of her body, and they were trembling with need. Closing her eyes, she whispered, "Someday . . ."

"Look at me, *chère*."

Forcing her eyes open, she shivered. His lips were inches from hers. A second later his tongue traced the shape of her mouth, leaving a quiver of response wherever it flicked.

Sighing, Jessica moved her hands over his chest, feeling the taut muscles. Then their mouths were seeking and tasting with such ardor that their passion blotted out the kitchen with the books lying open on the table, the coffeepot burbling on the counter and the night songs from the bayou drifting through the window.

Everything was blocked from their minds but the magic of feeling. . . .

ABOUT THE AUTHOR

Virginia Nielsen has enjoyed a long and prolific career as a writer. She's penned more than 250 short stories and over thirty novels. Some years ago she received the Golden Treasure Award from the Romance Writers of America to mark her contribution to romance fiction. Virginia and her husband, Mac, live in Sacramento, California.

Books by Virginia Nielsen

HARLEQUIN SUPERROMANCE

110–TRUSTING
159–MOONLIGHT ON SNOW
226–CRIMSON RIVERS
279–ROOM FOR ONE MORE

Don't miss any of our special offers. Write to us at the following address for information on our newest releases.

Harlequin Reader Service
901 Fuhrmann Blvd., P.O. Box 1397, Buffalo, NY 14240
Canadian address: P.O. Box 603,
Fort Erie, Ont. L2A 5X3

Jessica's Song

VIRGINIA NIELSEN

Harlequin Books

TORONTO • NEW YORK • LONDON
AMSTERDAM • PARIS • SYDNEY • HAMBURG
STOCKHOLM • ATHENS • TOKYO • MILAN

Grateful acknowledgment is extended to Mildred and John Teal for permission to quote from pages 1 and 168 of *Life and Death of the Salt Marsh*, Audubon/ Ballantine paperback edition, 1972.

Published March 1990

First printing January 1990

ISBN 0-373-70397-X

To our many friends in Houma, Louisiana, who have been so helpful in our research in modern Acadiana, especially to Frances Dansereau and her family. A special thank-you to Mr. and Mrs. Thomas J. Cobb, and to J. W. Moss, who introduced us to "Sonny" Hailey, the real-life "company man," whose life jacket failed to inflate when his helicopter ditched in the Gulf

CHAPTER ONE

THE BOAT WASN'T READY. That was the first thing Jessica noticed as she walked down the dock with Dr. Chris in the clear Louisiana dawn. Her students, a group of young men all clad as she was in shorts and T-shirts, were watching the approach of an unfamiliar fishing craft.

"I've engaged a shrimper to take you out this morning," Chris said. "They're still working on that engine overhaul on our shallow-draft boat."

The man who stood at the helm of the small trawler was shirtless and deeply tanned. When he came out on deck the rising sun threw a mantle of gold on his powerful shoulders and arms, and illumined the white of his teeth as he smiled. He raised one arm and shouted above the throb of his idling engine, "*'Allo!*"

"*Bonjour*, Armand," Chris called back.

A young crewman, also shirtless, had leaped to the dock and was tying up, but Jessica's gaze lingered on the trawler's skipper. She was struck by his aura of vitality and bonhomie. He looked so *alive*. And he was so obviously enjoying life. Even his hair, thick and black with a tendency to curl, had a bounce to it. Intriguingly, the tendency was more pronounced on his muscular chest where the wedge of black hair formed tight little coils.

"Who is he?" she asked Dr. Chris. Chris Weigel was the visiting research scientist she was assisting in his study of the insects found in the salt marshes that stretched from this last bit of dry land to the Gulf.

"A local fisherman. One of those native Cajuns whose family has spoken French for generations—or what passes for French down here in the wetlands."

"He speaks English, doesn't he?" Jessica asked in some alarm.

"Oh, yes. You'll be able to communicate. And you can't lose him in the marsh. He knows it far better than we do. Just tell him what you want and he'll find it for you."

Jessica drew in a deep breath, reveling in the balmy tang of salt and marsh vegetation. It was an odor that in her girlhood had been associated with treasured excursions into the New Jersey marshes with her father, and now was an inextricable part of her own career as a marine biologist. This morning she was putting her students to gathering specimens for Dr. Chris's project.

"You'll have to bring your samples back to the lab to label," Chris was reminding the students. "Try to get them back to me in good shape."

"Sure, Dr. Chris."

"I'll see that the teaching lab is set up for your teams," he told Jessica.

She nodded. The facility's two research vessels were equipped with laboratories, but she and the students would lack that advantage today.

"Let's get the gear loaded," she suggested to her students, and they began picking up their backpacks of specimen containers and the wooden quadrats, the one-half-square-meter frames they would use to mark their collection area.

These were upperclassmen from various Louisiana universities, who were at the Marine Biological Laboratory for a three-week course of field instruction. Some had probably never seen a salt marsh before coming to the laboratory, but she would have wagered that all of them had heard horror stories about people who perished because they lost their way in a marsh's characteristic maze of lakes and interlocking bayous, or were sucked down into bottomless mud.

These students were all male—tall, agreeable young men who were clearly intrigued with the prospect of spending three weeks in the company of a blond field instructor. But to Jessica, still standing with Chris on the dock, they appeared callow beside the bronzed, hard-muscled man who directed the placing of their equipment, talking to them and making them laugh as they worked.

She was eyeing the bare-chested fisherman speculatively, and Chris teased, "Would you classify him as a hunk?"

"Oh, definitely a hunk!" Jessica said with a grin. But her cheeks felt warm. Chris had come close to guessing her vagrant thoughts. The fisherman was an intriguing specimen. He was so very different from the men in her family—in fact, from any man she had known. He was so blatantly...the only word for it was *physical*.

His background was intriguing, too. Jessica had been hearing Cajun stories ever since arriving in Louisiana from the northeast a few short months ago to take her first permanent job as one of the facility's teaching faculty. What she had known about Cajuns before accepting the position came from *Evangeline*, a poem of Henry Wadsworth Longfellow's studied by most high school students that told the sad love story of an Acadian girl, and of course she'd heard of Cajun cooking. She had known a French flavor was still lovingly nurtured in New Orleans. What she had not expected was that Louisiana's wetlands would seem like a foreign country.

She walked across the dock toward the boat, and Dr. Chris followed her. Most of the vessel's deck was taken up by the low-walled hatch located aft of the small cabin. The hatch served to contain the boat's shrimp catch.

"Armand!" Chris called.

The fisherman looked up and smiled, and the effect was dazzling.

"Jessica, this is Armand LeBlanc, who will be your skipper. Professor Owen is the instructor today, Armand."

"'*Allo*, Miss Jessica!"

She nodded with reserve. His use of her first name was disconcerting, but she reminded herself that she was in the South now, and had heard "Miss Jessica" more than once. Two of her students left what they were doing and started for the rail to help her board but Armand leaped ahead of them, his brown eyes sparkling.

Armand had noticed her when she walked down the dock with the sun on her golden hair. It was caught back in a ponytail, a severe style his sisters scorned, but Armand decided he liked it. It exposed her face, and her features had an aching beauty—like the flight of a lone blue heron above the marsh, he thought—but it was a face full of secrets. Her yellow shirt outlined small breasts that pointed to the paling moon. He wagered he could span her waist with his fingers. And then there were those long golden legs revealed by shorts as white as Sister Catherine's wimple.

She was like a glass of chilled white wine, that one, he thought admiringly. And she was the instructor?

He offered his hand and she took it. For a few seconds Jessica hesitated, and they looked into each other's eyes, his smiling, hers cool and questioning.

It was a curiously measuring look they exchanged, Jessica realized, and wondered why on earth she had prolonged the moment. She jumped lightly down to the deck and he released her hand.

He went to stand at the wheel, just aft of the low engine housing and protected by a wheelhouse, and shouted cheerful orders as his engine roared to life. A couple of the students went to help the young crewman untie the line, and the boat began backing away from the dock.

Dr. Chris waved and started for the lab. Jessica stood on the deck and watched him go.

The sandstone walls of the Marine Biological Laboratory seemed to float in the air as the boat moved out of its harbor on the marsh lake. The illusion was created by the eight hundred or so pilings on which the sprawling building stood, bringing its floor eighteen feet above mean sea level to protect it from hurricane tides.

It was a new facility with two well-equipped modern laboratories, one wet and one dry in its separate wings, and housing facilities for students and visiting scientists. Jessica was inordinately proud to be sharing an office in it.

She turned her back to the building, which faced south. To the east, a small lake lay like a golden platter reflecting the light of the rising sun. Directly ahead, the bayou cut a southward water path into the salt grasses that surrounded the lake and stretched as far as she could see.

Armand was thinking of the woman as he steered his boat. The look from Miss Jessica's eyes had been as gray-blue as the Gulf in winter. He glanced at her when he could take his eyes from his course. She walked over to the group of college students and began separating them into three teams of two each, and telling them what she wanted them to do. A pretty little marsh hen to be so cool and serious about her work. *Professor* Owen, if you please!

He felt suddenly exhilarated, and burst into song, earning a surprised look from the professor and the young men surrounding her. Her students grinned. The whole mood on the deck lightened. Jessica stared thoughtfully at Armand LeBlanc.

Presently she came into the wheelhouse to stand beside him. He thought her skin was as fair and smooth as a swamp lily. "Mr. LeBlanc," she began, in the low-toned Northern voice that he found deliciously different.

"Armand," he corrected her with his infectious smile.

"Armand," she parroted, realizing that she was not pronouncing the name quite right. "What we're looking for this morning is a small slough where the saltwater mixes with the fresh. About eighteen parts per thousand, er, fifty percent salinity. Do you understand?"

"Ah, *oui*," he said cheerfully. "You want the middle oyster beds."

"The middle oyster...?" she repeated uncertainly.

"The next to last bed before the farmer moves him to market, no?" When she did not immediately answer, he elaborated. "The last one is just briny enough to season him for the table."

He cupped his fingers to his mouth and pulled them away with a kissing sound in the exact gesture she had seen in a fishing village in Brittany on a summer spent in France. His accent was slight, but disconcerting. His "the" had come out sounding almost like "duh," with a very soft *d*.

But his eyes were lively with intelligence as well as a hint of humor and a disturbing admiration. He was smoothly shaved and his tan was even except for little laugh lines where his eyes had crinkled. They were lighter in color. He had a proud nose between eyebrows that tapered at the outer ends, and his eyelashes were black and very thick.

"You understand?" he asked gently, an enigmatic look in his dark gaze.

Her cheeks warmed as she realized she had been staring. She wondered if he could possibly be teasing her. "I'm not that fond of oysters," she said in cool retreat, and he grinned.

He changed their course slightly to enter the bayou. Grassy banks soon hid the lake from their view. "We take 'Tee Caillou," he told Jessica.

She nodded. Petit Caillou was the little bayou on whose banks she lived, a few miles north of the lab where she rented a modest house. It was the bayou bank she followed northward when she wanted to go to a shopping center, or to take the highway to New Orleans. But from here to the Gulf, there were no roads—just waterways and saltwater grass.

She raised her voice to carry over the sound of his engine. "I want to get away from a navigable bayou. This one is heavily used, isn't it?"

"Many fishing boats take this way, yes."

"We want samples of marsh habitat as free from human waste as possible."

"As free as possible," Armand agreed readily. "But the tides that sweep it out, they wash it back, anh? And not always to the same place?"

That rising inflection that gave his speech a certain lilt came from his French origins, Jessica knew. She found it very attractive. She eyed him, her glance dipping to his beautiful bronzed shoulders and pectorals, and coming back to his smiling eyes. He understood very well what she was saying—and probably what she was not saying, as well.

She moistened her lips. "True, Armand. But I want to get away from the main water thoroughfares to the Gulf.

Can you find us a slough shallow enough so we can wade? Or with mud banks solid enough to walk on?''

So she intended to wade with her students, Armand thought. That should be interesting. "The oysterman's pirogue, that one can ride on the dew! He's been everywhere." He laughed. "But we try, Professor, anh?''

"Thank you, Mr., er, Armand.''

"For w'at?'' he said, shrugging those magnificent shoulders and showing those beautiful white teeth in the grin that invited everyone to join him. She could not have prevented herself from returning his smile, and his eyes danced with pleasure.

Jessica returned to her students, bemused.

"What's a pirogue?" she asked them.

They chuckled. All were Louisiana born, though none was native to the wetlands. "It's one of those little flat-bottomed boats you see being poled up and down the bayous,'' one of them told her.

"You mean a canoe.''

"A Cajun canoe.''

Another student offered, "It was modeled after the Indian ones.''

The trawler was moving steadily through the bayou, which now curved east and now west, but always toward the Gulf. Behind them the sprawling laboratory had disappeared, and they were surrounded by the lonely marsh. Jessica returned to Armand's side at the wheel to watch through the protective windows for the landing she wanted.

She could discern no current in the winding water road, but Armand said, "Ebb tide." He glanced at the sun. "I give you two, t'ree hours? No more.''

"Perhaps we should have started earlier," Jessica said with concern. The air striking her cheeks and bare arms and legs was cool and heavily laden with moisture. The *Spartina* grass on each side of the bayou was the fine variety, six feet high; it had fallen over of its own weight, and lay in swirls and ripples, looking like a dark sea.

"Some say it's lonely, the marsh," Armand observed, "but they haven't seen that, anh?" He gestured toward the gulls fighting a big osprey for the minnows left in a shallow pool by the outgoing tide. He grinned at her. "Or a flock of baby fiddler crabs runnin' for cover in the grass?"

"There's a lot of life in the marsh," Jessica agreed, looking at him with increased respect. "Young life." It was a marine nursery, she often told her students.

He nodded. "No marsh, no shrimp. That'd be a great pity, anh?"

Their eyes met in a shared appreciation. Dr. Chris was right, Jessica thought. Here was a man who knew and understood the salt marshes as her father did. Armand was no scientist, but she guessed that in his own way he had made a study of the abundant marine life of the marsh.

You can't lose him, Dr. Chris had said. Getting lost was an ever-present danger in this strange low country. Jessica had flown over the Louisiana wetlands and seen the region's serpentine grid of interconnected sloughs and little lakes, dividing it into irregularly shaped grassy islands, but all that water was hidden from them now. An intersecting waterway simply appeared as an opening in the sea of *Spartina* grass and was immediately hidden as the boat glided on.

Armand LeBlanc, standing confidently at the wheel, looked as if he knew exactly where he was and where he was going. He slowed the boat and nosed up to the bank just where a small slough joined the bayou, keeping the engine idling.

He said something in French to his crewman, and the lad—only a boy—lowered a bucket on a rope and pulled up water from the junction of waterways. He brought it to Armand who dipped a finger in it and raised the finger to his lips. "There's fresh water," he told Jessica. "But still too briny for alligators."

She had seen her father test the salinity of the water that way. With a surprised pleasure, she dipped her finger into the bucket, then touched her tongue. "We'll stop here, I think."

The crewman grinned happily at her, and Jessica was struck by his resemblance to his skipper. "Armand, your crewman looks like you."

"He's my brother, that one. Etienne, say *bonjour* to Miss Jessica."

She was pleased that he remembered her name instead of calling her "Professor" again. She found herself saying *bonjour* to Etienne, who blushed with pleasure but said, "My name's Steve, Miss Jessica."

"He's too proud, that one, for *bonjour* and *au revoir*," Armand said.

"Old stuff," Etienne muttered.

"He goes to school," Armand bragged. "But he wants to be a shrimper, too."

"Is that what you do for a living, Armand?"

"Sometimes I catch crab, and crayfish in season? But mostly shrimps. My father, too. And *Pépère* and his *grandpère* before him. All shrimpers." He moved the boat into the mud bank, letting his engine idle just enough to keep the bow there. "Me, I go no closer, Miss Jessica."

Etienne picked up a long pole and leaned over to check the solidity of the bank. "Okay," he pronounced.

"All right, load up," Jessica told her students.

Armand watched as they picked up their backpacks and the wooden frames, one to each team. He was grinning to himself, visualizing what they would encounter: the black mud that would suck at their bare feet, the bugs that would hover over them. It was too salty here for alligators, or for saw grass, but the cordgrass could be scratchy.

And this yellow-haired slip of a woman was going to lead them? Pretty little foot she had, with long slender toes, dainty as a raccoon's.

"When I've selected the spot, you will put down your frames and start collecting every living thing you find within that space of air, water and mud," Jessica reminded her students. "Both insects and mollusks. All the grasshoppers, periwinkles—"

"And the *mostiques*?" Armand inquired slyly.

The students laughed, but she shot back, "All the mosquito larvae," and they groaned. "Be sure to take samples of bottom mud, with the tiny creatures living in it. And don't forget your samples of water. All right, let's go. Keep close to the bank, and stay out of the soft mud. It has a suction almost like quicksand."

Armand tapped the waterproof watch on his wrist. "Two, t'ree hours," he warned. "No more or my boat, she is maybe stranded."

"Right." Jessica whipped a kerchief out of a back pocket in her shorts and tied it peasant fashion over her hair, while Armand watched in fascination. She climbed over the rail and dropped into the bayou. Her students followed her. She waded to the bank and started working her way up the creek, staying close to the grass. A white heron flew up out of the cordgrass, which was tall and tough here, and Armand heard the splash made by a muskrat diving for cover.

He watched them go, two by two, on muddy feet, all with packs on their backs, carrying the wooden frames between them, with the blond professor alone in the lead. Clouds of mosquitoes swirled above their heads.

Mon Dieu, but she was some woman, he thought, shaking his head. Some woman, that professor!

THE SUN CLIMBED HIGHER. Armand's passengers were all out of sight, working in the tall grass. He broke out some poles and he and Etienne passed the time fishing. They caught several flounder and a sea bass that had come in with the tide. Fresh fish for supper, he thought. Perhaps he'd give one to the professor.

"I shoulda brought my accordion," he teased Etienne. "I could show you how to play it."

"Don't you start, too, Armand. Papa's always after me with his old squeezebox. Who needs that old-time music?"

"Zydeco isn't old-time."

"It's just Cajun jazzed up by the blacks. I'm bored with all that Cajun stuff."

Armand laughed. He could always get a rise out of Etienne, who thought B.C. meant before he was born, about sixteen years ago. But the kid did like to fish.

Armand tuned in some music on his small radio and occasionally sang along. His ship's radio crackled with conversation, mostly in French, between larger boats out in the Gulf, where there was no season on the mature shrimp. Once he answered his call to settle an argument between two older fishermen.

"Those cabbage heads," he told Etienne. "Friends all their lives and never could get along!"

The tide was going out, and a wind had come up, a north wind that encouraged the ebb of the tide. Armand kept an eye on the slough, which was getting so shallow that he could see patches of bottom in it. He began to worry about the professor and her students.

"Toot the horn," he told Etienne. "If they're much longer, we'll have to wait on the tide, and we'll carry back a load of dead bugs, anh?"

Etienne laughed and pulled enthusiastically on the cord that blew a warning blast. Who needed bugs, dead or alive, he wanted to know. The whole idea was humorous to him. The sonorous horn, its noise all out of proportion to the size of the boat, brought a cloud of blackbirds and a half dozen white egrets flapping up from the salt grass.

That should bring them back, Armand thought. The ebb tide had already moved his boat out from the bank so that a strip of muddy bottom showed between the water and the salt grass. He started his engine and moved out to deeper water so his keel would not hang up on the bottom. That meant the biologists would have some mud to wade through.

"Lay your hand on the horn again, Etienne."

Again the deep sound filled the empty marsh, and another flock of waterfowl rose in panic, fluttering over the grasses. This time Armand heard an answering shout. Presently the study group came into sight, carrying their bulging backpacks, walking single file on the narrow firm bank of the slough close to the grass. The woman came last.

"Make tracks, you!" Armand shouted. "If I don' get to deep water, we stick here 'til high tide!"

Jessica waved to signal that she understood. She was alarmed to see that the fishing boat had moved out into deeper water. Too absorbed in trying to urge her students to complete the sweep of the framed sections of grass, she had failed to keep a watch on the slough. Now she noted with dismay that it was very nearly at low tide. Gary, the young man walking just ahead of her, was casting worried glances at the muddy bottom of the slough beside them.

In Dr. Chris's orientation talk to the students, he had tried to impress on them the dangers they would face working in the marsh. "*La prairie tremblante*, the natives call it—the trembling prairie. It is virtually bottomless, the only solid earth being the soil and detritus that gather around the roots of the *Spartina* grass."

Jessica knew the dangers. Her father had trained her well. "Never go into the marsh alone," he had told her. "Never take a boat out without checking to see that there is a rope and a long pole in it. And never jump into the mud to help someone out of it."

"Dad!" she had protested.

"*Never*, Jessica. You'll only succeed in endangering two persons and making a rescue more difficult. If you sink into the mud, keep calm. If you struggle, you'll only sink deeper."

So how could she have failed to watch the time this morning? She understood why the fisherman had moved his boat, but it meant that her students would have to wade across a strip of the bayou's exposed bottom, fighting the suction of its soft mud, and then perhaps swim a few yards of the dredged channel to reach the boat. She had checked the students' swimming skills the day they arrived and so wasn't concerned on that score. Her chief worry was crossing the mud. And how could they get the backpacks on board without losing them or ruining their contents?

She thought Gary, the student just ahead of her, looked pale. She knew how frightening the mud's powerful suction could be. She foresaw a difficult boarding, and tried to keep her voice calm as she called, "Armand! Can you lower a net or a hook for the backpacks?"

"Sure," he said. "Etienne, bring the long oar."

"Why is he so far from shore?" Gary asked nervously.

"Because the tide is out," she said matter-of-factly, but she was aware of his growing fear.

Armand watched as she directed her students in the operation. They were no longer the immaculate crew that had boarded at the Marine Laboratory dock. Their legs and hands were black. The professor's, too. But she was directing her troops like a female Napoléon.

She sent two students wading through the mud and shallow water holding backpacks above their heads. Each team had carried a backpack and a wooden frame. The first young man came near enough to the boat to be thigh deep in water. Armand lowered the long oar and the student hooked the pack's straps over the paddle. Carefully Armand raised the oar and deposited the pack on deck.

"Great!" Jessica called from shore. "Now the next one."

The second student passed his frame to the first, and a third young man waded out from shore. He tossed his pack to the next in line. Armand noted the way they had roiled up the bottom and thickened the mud. That could only get worse, he knew. And the professor was sending her students ahead of her? *Oui,* he thought, it was the thing she would do.

He looked up and down the bayou. Only here at the mouth of the slough could he get this close to the bank. They would all have to come aboard here.

He sent Etienne for a coil of rope, and when he came with it, told him to put a good solid knot at its end.

With Jessica directing them from shore, the other three students were positioning themselves a few feet apart, standing thigh deep in mud and water. Working as a team, they tossed the rest of the gear from one to the next until it was all on deck.

Jessica drew a breath of relief. Now to get everyone on board.

Before she could issue an order, Armand shouted, "Now, man, one at a time. Come on! We help."

In the past few minutes the water had completely drained from the slough. In the bayou, a river of mud extended for several yards between the bank and the boat. The exertions of the men getting their specimens aboard had stirred up the bottom, thickening the mud and giving it more suction. As they tried to advance, they began sinking deeper into the muck.

Gary, standing nearest the bank, turned and started back to where Jessica stood on the narrow strip of firm bank. His face had a greenish cast and she wondered if he were going to be ill. "Miss Owen, we'll pass you to the boat like we did the packs. Then they can haul you up in the net, okay?"

"No, man!" Armand called out sharply from the boat. "The mud, he's too deep. You'll sink for sure with her weight. We pass a rope to Miss Jessica." He tossed the knotted end to the first student, and it went back from hand to hand until it reached Gary, who carried it to Jessica. Then Armand extended the long oar over the patch of mud and water to the first student. "Grab the pole and hold on."

As soon as the young man tried to walk in the muddy water, he sank deeper into the bottom with each step. From the bank, Jessica could sense his rising panic, and that of Gary, watching beside her. She realized that Gary had been trying to deal with his fear by expressing it as concern for her.

She was beginning to grasp the seriousness of their situation. She was responsible for the safety of her students, after all, even if they were young men of twenty and twenty-one. She should have noticed the tide was emptying the slough and called a halt earlier. If Gary panicked when he experienced that suction of soft mud, a terrible tragedy could occur.

"It's a frightening thing to walk in mud that has no firm bottom, Gary," she said as calmly as she could. "But there are ways to minimize the danger."

"I can't do it," he said in a sick, embarrassed voice. "Miss Owen, I just can't do it." He had lost control. He was trembling so violently, his lips were quivering.

"You've *got* to, Gary," she said baldly. "This is something no one can do for you."

He looked at her out of stricken eyes.

"I mean it!" she said forcefully. "The first rule in fighting quicksand is that no one jumps in it to save someone else. That could mean two tragedies. Do you understand what I'm saying? It's up to you."

"Hang tight," Armand was warning from the boat, in a cheerful voice, as he extended the pole to the first student. "*Above* the paddle, man! That pole, he's slippy as an eel."

His cheerful tone said it was all in a day's work and his good nature was enormously uplifting. Jessica told herself if anyone could get them all safely aboard, this man could. The first student reached the boat. Armand threw him a short rope and together he and Etienne helped pull him aboard, leaving a trail of dripping black mud down the boat's white side.

"Look at the mess you make on my nice clean deck!" Armand gave a great laugh and shouted, "Next!"

One aboard, and five to go, Jessica thought, praying nothing would go wrong. Gary had sunk to a squatting position at her side. "I think I'll change my major," he said in a feeble attempt at humor.

Armand was inwardly praying he could get them all aboard before the outgoing tide grounded his vessel. He was dangerously near the bank, but if his calculations were right, he was in deep enough water so that would not happen. It would be close, goddamn.

"Okay!" he cried, extending his oar to the second student, who was making his way toward the boat. "Snappy, now, anh?"

One by one the men gained the boat, but each one sank a little deeper, and each rescue left the churned-up mud stickier and harder to move through. Jessica saw that it was going to be more difficult for Gary, who was least equipped to handle the experience.

The fifth student walked into the mud and was soon bent over, making swimming motions with his arms to try to propel himself forward, only his head, shoulders and upper arms out of the muck.

Gary, squatting on the narrow bank, covered his face with his hands. "I can't do that, I just can't."

"Gary, you are going to take this rope in your hand," Jessica said in level tones, "and you are going to walk into that mud and let Armand *pull* you aboard the boat. All you have to do is grasp the rope tightly and not let it go. You can do that. I know you can."

"He sent the rope for you, Miss Owen," Gary said miserably.

"So he can throw it back to me."

"Come, man!" Armand called. "I'll give you a little prop wash to soften the mud."

Gary took the rope Jessica held out to him, and with trembling fingers began trying to tie it around his waist.

Armand roared his disapproval from the boat. "No, man!" he shouted. "It must be loose so you can drop it if I pull too fast. Come, come!" he ordered the student. "You waste time!" His engine roared into life, and he shouted, "Hang tight!"

His prop wash sent a small wave of water under the boat to flood over the mud. Gary looked as if he faced death.

"Go!" Jessica ordered. "Keep your head up and your toes down." With a silent prayer, she gave Gary a little push and he stepped into the watery mud. She watched him, sensing his terror and fighting her own rising panic. What if he completely lost his head out there? What could they do, Armand trying to hold the boat nosed toward him, and she left standing on the narrow strip of bank without a rope?

And if Gary made it, could *she*?

She had to.

Gary yelled as Armand changed gears and the boat moved backward and jerked him off his feet. He threw his head up and back, his eyes wild with terror, as the boat pulled him through the mud and into deep water, but he hung on to the rope with fingers that Jessica guessed were frozen by panic.

Armand stopped the boat and Gary's companions on the other end of the rope pulled Gary aboard, where he collapsed on the bow in a shaking heap.

Armand changed gears and brought the boat back as close as he dared to the bank. "Now you, Miss Jessica! Catch the rope."

She missed it twice.

Armand said nothing, just cheerfully tossed it again. His confidence in her, and her great relief that Gary was aboard, helped her to relax, and on the third toss she caught the heavy knot tied at the rope's end.

"Now I give you a prop wash before I start up," he warned. "When I start to pull, point your toes straight down so your foot, he don't drag. If I pull too fast, drop the rope so I don't pull you under."

Oh, great! Jessica thought. That was all she needed—to be reminded that she could be pulled under. She had carefully avoided telling Gary that.

Armand's beautiful white smile flashed. "I can always throw the rope to you again. I'm not letting anything happen to you, okay?"

Oddly enough she believed him. "Okay!" she called. She grasped the rope above the knot with both hands and waded into the mud.

When he changed gears and the boat moved backward, it pulled her down on her stomach with a jerk. The sensation of gliding through the liquid mud was indescribable. And people paid good money for mud baths? She tried to point her toes as he had instructed. Her heart was beating hard, her adrenaline pumping. It would never work. She had been crazy, absolutely crazy to trust her life to him!

But he had a gentle touch on his throttle. In minutes she was out of the muck and into welcome water. He cut the propeller and a dozen hands were on the rope drawing her alongside the boat, then helping her up over the low rail.

When she collapsed on deck, her arms aching from the strain, she was dripping black goo from her breasts down. Her grinning students were all a mess, tracking muck on Armand's once-immaculate deck, but she and Gary, who still lay shivering on the deck, were the blackest of them all. There was not an inch of white showing on her shorts, spotless that morning.

Armand burst into laughter, an infectious roar that rolled over the deck and expressed for all of them their relief at their deliverance.

Jessica looked up at him. Her eyes betrayed her effort to conceal her relief from fear and her exhaustion. There was a black smear across her patrician nose and down one cheek.

Armand felt a peculiar tenderness invade his chest. "What a pretty little mud hen you are!" he cried.

She raised a hand to switch her ponytail over her shoulder and left a streak of black on its golden fall. With a cool little grin, she said, "Go to hell."

CHAPTER TWO

"BREAK OUT THE HOSE, Etienne!"

The teenager obeyed with alacrity.

"Softly, softly," Armand warned, as his brother turned a stream of water on the muddy students with devilish glee. They yelled and laughed, peeled off their T-shirts and used them to scrub themselves clean.

At the wheel Armand watched as the professor's sleek wet arms and legs emerged from the black muck, shining like pale gold. The water molded her T-shirt even more closely over her breasts, causing Armand to suffer a sudden loss of breath.

She loosened her ponytail and tossed its golden strands in the spray of water, then when Etienne moved on with his hose, twisted it into a coil to squeeze the excess water out of it and spread it like a shawl around her shoulders to catch the sun.

Watching in fascination as he steered a course up the center of the bayou, Armand found his head filled with delightful fantasies about mermaids. He felt another irrestible urge to sing, and let go with a song. He was singing "Jolie Blon'," "Pretty Blonde," but when he saw his brother's amused eyes, he switched to another tune.

Armand was a natural baritone, Jessica thought, listening as his voice soared above the sputter of the engine and the splash of the wake and Etienne's hose as he washed down the deck. She relaxed with the tremendous sense of well-being that followed their escape from a frightening danger.

When she had dried sufficiently, she got to her feet and walked into the small wheelhouse to stand beside Armand. "What were you singing just now?"

"Just an old song I learned from *Pépère*."

His father? she wondered. She raised her voice to carry over the noise. "A Cajun song? What about?"

"Love, w'at else?" he said, keeping his eyes on the horizon where the observatory tower of the laboratory was rising into view. He cut down the motor, making it easier to hear her cool Northern voice.

"It sounded very sad for a love song."

"Most all our love songs are sad."

"Why is that?"

"I don' know, me." He turned and smiled at her. "Love's one thing we don't laugh about, but sometimes it's a joke, too, anh?"

She felt an intense curiosity about him. "Are you married, Armand?"

"Me? No."

"But there are many women in his life," Etienne volunteered. He had finished washing all the marsh mud into the scuppers and came into the wheelhouse to stand behind Armand in time to hear Jessica's question. She looked at his unformed young face, with Armand's wing-shaped eyebrows and the same dent in his chin, and saw the teasing mischief in his eyes.

"He has Marie and Danielle and Claire and Sister Catherine—she's a nun."

Jessica looked questioningly at Armand, struggling with her impulse to laugh.

He shrugged. "My sisters, all younger than me."

"But I'm the youngest," Etienne said cheerfully.

"And the orneriest," Armand said.

Etienne laughed.

"What a large family!" Jessica commented, wondering what it would be like to be surrounded by siblings instead of growing up with one brother.

"A large responsibility," Armand said, his pronunciation very French.

"My father's boat was bigger than this one," Etienne bragged. "It was lost in a storm. Now Armand's building a fine big one, but he needs more money to finish it."

Armand said, "Etienne, you talk too much."

"My name is Steve," the boy said defensively.

"Go bring a plastic bag, Etienne, so Miss Jessica can take that little flounder home with her." He pointed at the fish they'd caught earlier.

"You were great back there at the slough, Armand," she told him, "getting us all safely aboard the way you did."

"Hey, it's all in a day's work."

They were approaching the laboratory dock. Directly in front of it was a seafood restaurant, which stood on high poles like all the buildings in the fishing village of Cocodrie at the end of the road into the marsh. The students were picking up their backpacks.

Jessica felt a reluctance to leave. "Will you be taking us out again tomorrow?"

"I think yes, but we start earlier, anh? Then the ebb tide don' catch us."

"An hour earlier?" she suggested.

"Okay."

"Okay," she repeated. "See you tomorrow." She went to the rail, where one of her students gave her a hand up to the dock.

THERE WAS WORK TO BE DONE in the lab before the field study group could call it a day. But as Jessica left the building that evening to drive her Volkswagen Rabbit along the bayou road to Chauvin, the village on higher ground where she had rented a cottage, her thoughts returned to the fisherman. Chris Weigel had just told her that the facility's small boat would be ready to take her and her group out in the morning, and she was surprised by the sharpness of her disappointment.

She was somewhat mystified as to why she had found Armand LeBlanc so enormously appealing. Granted, he was an attractive man, but so were some of the unmarried research scientists she worked with at the lab—and none of them had been able to distract her from her work.

It must be his novelty, she decided. Armand was from a completely different world; she could not imagine two backgrounds more diametrically opposed than that of a commercial fisherman raised in this community of French descendants on the edge of a salt marsh, and her own background of scientific training in the colleges of Eastern academia. He was the product of a pocket of Americana about which she had become intensely curious since coming to her new position.

Yet she knew it was Armand's outgoing personality that strongly appealed to her. He was a man who enjoyed life with a complete lack of self-consciousness. Look at the way he had burst into song with no thought, she could swear, of any audience he might have! She could never have done that. He was an extrovert, and she had always envied such people. She was more tightly controlled.

It was a family trait. All the Owens were very controlled. "Looking at things objectively," her mother called it.

"A simple man, with simple pleasures," she could hear her father summing up Armand.

But was he?

It was a short drive to her house, one of a row of modest cottages strung along the bayou bank where, her Realtor had explained, the most solid earth was found. That was why the villages in the wetlands were not laid out in squares but had been built up and down each bank of the waterways.

She pulled up in her crushed shell driveway; there was neither garage nor carport. Although her landlord had assured her it was not necessary, she locked her car before she left it. It was early in the season and the temperature was delightfully balmy, but the air in the closed house was stale. She left the front door open and walked through the living room to the kitchen to open the back door so the air would circulate.

While she prepared to cook the fish Armand had given her for her dinner, she thought about him. No, he was far from a simple man. A couple of things he had said stirred her curiosity.

But love is sometimes a joke, too. Why a joke? What had he meant?

And there had been the gentle way he'd turned her *Do you understand?* on her, as if chiding her for judging his understanding of English by his fractured speech.

That didn't disturb her, really. The way he often ended his sentences as if leaving a question mark hanging in the air gave his conversation a lilt that, combined with his musical voice, was very appealing.

Her father was a complex man, but he was also a marine biologist and she was enough like him to understand him. She did not understand Armand LeBlanc at all.

He was certainly a competent man in his own environment. He had demonstrated that in the way he got her and her students safely out of the marsh after she had allowed them to become stranded by the tide. She wished the mechanics had not finished their overhaul of the facility's shallow-draft boat so quickly. She had looked forward to seeing Armand again.

It had been an adventurous day. She decided she would write Russell about it after dinner. No, maybe not. Russell Brant was her oldest friend, her only lover and the man she would someday marry, but he was fastidious enough to be slightly repelled by her story of being literally dragged through the mud in her dedication to her career.

She fried Armand's fish slowly in a mixture of olive oil and butter, with a sprinkling of herbs and lemon juice, and marveled at the superior flavor of fish that was eaten the day it was caught.

ARMAND WAS DISAPPOINTED when Dr. Weigel told him that his services would not be needed the next morning. His head was filled with visions of the blond professor. Those cool eyes and sweet apple breasts and the hint of passion in her lovely Northern-talking mouth.... It was not often he met a woman who excited his imagination as she had, and he had never met a woman quite like her. He had been looking forward to seeing her again.

He had sensed her interest, a certain response that told a man when a woman was thinking, *Who are you? What are you like? You're something new to me.*

He was curious about her, too. There was no mystery in the local women to a man who had grown up with four chattering sisters. Nance Marie, for instance. She was a good friend, no? Singing with her was great. But she came from a family just like his. He always knew what she was thinking. He knew that she went to early Mass even when he kept her up all night, that she regularly confessed her sins and made promises for Lent that she couldn't keep. Very like his sisters.

The professor was a woman who excited him because she was different. She was withdrawn, yet not shy. A woman who was not afraid to enter his hard, desolate but beautiful marsh.

He grinned as he remembered how she had looked covered with mud...and how coolly she had told him to go to hell when he teased her.

She was smart, that one. A colleague of those scientists who ran the research center and told the industry what was happening in their fishing grounds. With a college degree, no less.

He suspected that the *jolie* professor was out of his league. But she was a woman, anh? He had seen the way she looked at him.

Why shouldn't they be friends?

WHEN JESSICA ARRIVED home the next evening, there was a letter from her mother in the mailbox. She took it into the house with her, poured herself a glass of white wine and sat down to read it. She had showered at the lab, then joined Chris Weigel for a cup of coffee before coming home, so she was in no hurry to prepare her evening meal, which would probably be warmed-up fried flounder.

Patricia Owen was a pediatrician and a good one. Jessica and her brother had always felt somewhat excluded by their mother's intense interest in her small patients, and the stories she brought home about them.

"If we only had a disease," Norm had joked once, "we could compete."

Typically her mother's letter today included news about her latest most challenging case as well as family news.

After describing her satisfaction at an early diagnosis of cancer that would probably save a youngster's life, her mother had written, "I lunched with Russell last week. He is such a thoughtful young man. He brought me a single salmon-colored rosebud—imagine him remembering my preference! He also remembered my favorite white wine. He misses you and is worrying that you are liking Louisiana too much. Says your letters make it sound like Eden. He likes Wall Street, and seems to be doing very well at his firm."

Jessica thought of Russell's beautiful body and his crisp mathematical mind with a guilty realization that in the past two days she had probably devoted more vagrant thoughts to the Cajun fisherman than to what Russell was doing. It was too long, far too long, since they had been close....

She read her mother's last paragraph with delight. "Your father and I are hoping to make a visit to Louisiana this spring before it gets too hot in the south. He is eager to see the new facility. As you know, he once worked with your director. We both look forward to a visit with our old friends, the Tarbells, as well as with you. If Russell can get away, he may join us."

Jessica's heart gave an alarming thump. She read on.

"You might inquire about a good hotel in the nearest town of any size. I know you don't have room for houseguests, and we don't want to impose on the Tarbells."

Her mother was right. Jessica's life-style in the rented house on the bayou was extremely informal compared to that of her parents. A hotel would suit them better. She looked at her living room furniture with her mother's eyes and for the first time saw the ugliness she had been busy enough to overlook. Hers was a simple bayou cottage with one bedroom, one bath and an attic dormitory "for the chil'ren," her landlord had explained. Her mother and father were accustomed to their own bedrooms and private baths.

But her father would be overcome with envy when he saw the facility's laboratories, and the research vessels. She would take him out in the marsh with her students, she thought happily, a trip that would bore her mother. But she could safely leave the entertainment of her mother to the director's wife, Louise Tarbell. They were old friends. And if Russell came—!

She heard the crunch of shoes on the shell walk. She looked up, expecting to see her landlord, who was a neighbor, and was stunned to see Armand LeBlanc walking up to her door, carrying a white pail. She jumped up to unhook the screen door, taken aback by his appearance at her house in what was apparently a social call.

"Armand!" she exclaimed awkwardly. "How on earth did you find me?" She realized at once that she must sound as if she felt her privacy had been violated, which was partly true.

But he only laughed. He appeared freshly showered and was wearing pressed slacks and an open-necked knit shirt with short sleeves, and although his hair still sprang up in unruly curls, it looked very well brushed.

"I can ask any child in the village where the yellow-haired professor lives," he told her. "You didn't know that, anh?"

"Come in." She eyed the white pail suspiciously.

"It's crayfish season," he explained. "You ever eat crayfish?"

"Of course," she said stiffly. "I ordered crayfish bisque at Antoine's in New Orleans. It was delicious."

"Only way to enjoy crayfish," Armand corrected her gently, "is boil 'em and peel 'em."

"I'm not sure..." Jessica began. At work she had dissected the tiny freshwater crustaceans that were mostly scorned as food in the north. The thought of boiling and peeling the little creatures didn't appeal to her.

"You'll like them, I guarantee," he said with a companionable grin that she responded to in spite of herself. He was thinking that most any Cajun woman would have greeted his offering with soft cries of pleasure. But the professor was a cool one. Or had she never tasted crayfish?

She stiffened with surprise as he walked straight through her small living room into her kitchen, just behind it.

"Don' say anything until you taste 'em, anh? I'll boil 'em for you, and then I show you how to enjoy. Now, fin' me your biggest pot. This bucket's plastic."

His calm mastery of the situation struck her as outrageous, but she was intrigued, too, and her innate good manners prevented her from saying anything but "You want to cook *all* of those?"

"You'll fin' there's little meat in him."

"I know." She grimaced, and looked into his pail. The crayfish were all red legs and antennae and curled-under lobsterlike tails, which she knew contained the only edible meat.

"Look, Armand, these are old friends in the lab, but they don't belong in my kitchen. I'm sorry."

"Anh, you'll see!" he said with sublime confidence.

"I don't know whether there's a pot that big," she protested. "I don't do much cooking—"

"Every house on the bayou has a crab pot, no? Look for it."

She gave him one incredulous stare, then obeyed, squatting on the floor to open a low cabinet door, hiding her face from him while she tried to come to terms with her mixed emotions. He was making himself quite at home in her kitchen, she thought, as she rummaged among the cottage's furnished cooking utensils.

Sure enough, tucked away in the back of the cabinet was a huge pot. She pulled it out and handed it to him. He filled the pot with water at her sink, then set it on a burner on her small stove and turned up the gas to high. He dominated the small room, his overpowering masculinity both alarming and surprisingly pleasurable.

Out of a back pocket in his slacks, he took a cheese-cloth bag filled with what looked like dried herbs and dropped it into the water.

"What's in it?" she asked.

"My mother's mix. Mustard seed, dill seed, coriander, red pepper..."

"I knew it," she said ruefully.

"How did you cook the flounder?"

She told him.

He seemed genuinely interested. "Sometime you mus' taste him the way Mama fix him."

"With hot sauce?"

He grinned. "W'y not?"

He moved about her kitchen in a competent but non-aggressive way that made him easy to be with. She liked having him there, liked being near him in the small work space. She even enjoyed sparring with him over the tiny crustaceans, pretending more reluctance than she felt.

The water heated rapidly and the fragrance of spices filled the air. He picked up the bucket and dumped its contents into the pot and a wonderful aroma enriched the spicy steam rising from the stove.

Jessica inhaled it appreciatively. "This might be edible, after all."

"Anh!" he said. He picked up the newspaper she had brought in with her mail and spread it over her kitchen table, several sheets thick. "Makes cleanup easier," he explained.

"That's tonight's paper," she reminded him.

"What news is worth more than a pot of boiled crayfish?"

In a surprisingly short time he turned off the gas, lifted the pot from the stove and emptied its contents into the sink. The hot water drained away and Jessica had a sink full of cooked crayfish.

"What now?" she asked.

"Now we eat."

He took two deep bowls from her shelves, dipped them into the boiled crayfish until they were filled and set them on the kitchen table. He waved her to a chair and, sitting opposite her, began peeling crayfish and popping the tasty flesh from the lobsterlike tails into his mouth, throwing the empty shells down on the newspaper.

Jessica tried one. The shell had turned a deep dark red and it was very hot. She cracked it gingerly and put the steaming morsel of seafood into her mouth while the aroma of spices filled her nostrils.

"Very tasty," she admitted, and he grinned. Then they dug in and the pile of empty shells between them grew rapidly.

At last, Armand said, "I don' believe you have a beer?"

"No, but I've got an opened bottle of white wine." She jumped up and handed him a pencil and a memo pad. "While I get it, write down the herbs in that bouquet you used, will you? I may want to do this again."

"When you do, jus' let me know," he said with his in-gratiating grin.

"No, really, I want to know," she said. "My family's coming for a visit." She went to the cupboard for two glasses, and took the wine out of the refrigerator. When she brought them to the table, the pencil was still lying be-side the pad, "Please, Armand."

"Jus' go to the store and ask for crab boil." He tossed a piece of meat into his mouth.

"Come on."

"I'll tell you and you write it," he suggested.

She stopped still beside her chair and looked at him, sensing something he wasn't saying.

The gaze he raised to her was sheepish. "Me, I can't spell coriander."

"Never mind," she said impatiently. "I'll know what you mean."

Still he made no move to pick up the pencil. "I don' write English very good, you see?" he confessed. "Or read much."

"But you read French? Isn't French your first lan-guage?"

"Cajun patois is spoken. Or sung," he added thought-fully.

"But you must have gone to school," Jessica insisted. Her stomach nerves had tightened painfully. She found what he said incredible. For some reason she didn't want to believe him.

"My teacher taught in English, and me, I didn't under-stand much English."

They studied each other. This was important to her, Armand realized. That was natural. She was a professor, wasn't she? But she was so much more than a school-teacher, he thought, remembering how she had kept her students from panicking and how she had come through that frightening mud that even the wild animals feared.

Jessica didn't speak. She didn't know what to say.

"I couldn't keep up," Armand told her. "*Pépère* and *Mémère*, they still speak French. Papa speaks both, but he was always out fishing or trapping when I was young. I kept failing in school. And Papa, he need me, so I quit school to go shrimping."

She was trying to understand. "Who are *Pépère* and *Mémère*?"

"My *grandpère* an' *grandmère*. They were poor Cajuns. Lived off the marsh, trapping and fishing."

"But . . . but the oil brought such prosperity!"

"Not to Papa, or *Pépère*. They're *fishermen*."

Her thoughts had veered back to him, the boy who had quit school. "But there must have been a truant officer—"

Armand shrugged. "How can he fin' me in the marsh? It's a place made for a man to lose himself, anh? Times were hard after Papa los' his boat in a storm an' had a heart attack, too. So I quit school and work on my coozanne's—cousin's trawler to help my father feed the family."

"Your mother? Does she speak English?"

"She tries," he said ruefully.

She was still almost speechless, her mind trying to assimilate what he was saying while something powerful in her was protesting it. This good-looking man, who was so vital, so full of the joy of living—he was in his physical prime!—was *illiterate*?

The gulf that her education and lifelong habit of reading had put between them yawned before her. What was passing through her head was a startled cataloging of a world of things that interested her intensely and that could not even exist for him.

He had his special knowledge, too, she reminded herself, to be fair. Hadn't he just introduced her to something quite new in her experience?

He was looking at her with perception. "You're a very smart woman, no? It shocks you that I have thirty years and don' read?"

Jessica sat down in her chair across from his. "I can't imagine not being able to read a book, Armand," she confessed. "I grew up in a house where reading was the most important thing in our lives—reading and study."

They were both silent for a moment.

She was reviewing the achievements of her family. Her brother was an electronics engineer, a *research* engineer, and a whiz at it. Her physician mother's *hobby* was collecting butterflies! And her father—she had grown up in her own discipline of marine biology under his tutelage. Reading was her family's life. Even their hobbies involved study.

And Russell. Well, he didn't read the same things she did. But the gulf between Armand and Russell was even wider. Russell's hobby was esoteric mathematical equations!

Armand looked with yearning at Jessica's small round breasts and the sheen of her skin, not magnolia-petal thick and slightly pale like that of his pretty dark-eyed sisters, but pale gold with the tiniest spatter of freckles. He wondered again what lay behind those cool gray-blue eyes that appeared to be judging him.

"I can read the marshes," he said hopefully. "I read the skies. The color and the shape of clouds tell me things. I watch the tides, listen to the winds. A flock of birds tells me where is a school of fish, anh? The egret, he leads me to where the shrimp come up with the tide. If I see a fat raccoon, he tells me the shrimp harvest will be good. That's my world.''

"I know," she said softly. "It's a large part of my world, too.''

"Isn't that as important as books?" His "that" sounded faintly like "dat."

Her throat tightened with an odd feeling, a pity so strong it was almost like grief. "What do you want out of life, Armand?" she asked, reaching for another crayfish and peeling it. She was not really hungry anymore, but they were like peanuts—once you got started on them it was hard to stop.

"A big boat," he said promptly, with a gleam in his eyes. "One I can take offshore for the big, big shrimp. Me, I'm building it now."

"You're saying you want to be a fisherman all your life?"

"W'y not? I'll make money," he said confidently. "I'll learn English, too. I need to read and write so I can borrow money for all the *chu chuts* I need."

"All the what?"

"W'at-you-call-'ems. 'Lectronic gadgets for my new boat. Someday I'll have a fleet of shrimp boats, I guarantee."

She met his gaze, surprised again, this time by his ambition. Her mind played around with what he had said. There were literacy programs. If he really wanted to learn . . .

He popped a final crayfish tidbit into his mouth with obvious relish. "It's the life I was born to, anh? My ancestors who came here from Acadia in *le grand dérangement*—when the British moved them out of Nova Scotia, anh?—they were fishermen, and all my ancestors since were fishermen. For me, there's no better life." His eyes glowed. "We work hard, and when the fishing season, he's over, then *laisse les bons temps!*"

She looked at him blankly, and he asked, "You never learned to let the good times roll?"

She thought about the Cajun phrase, which she had heard repeatedly since coming to the lab. *Laisse les bons temps rouler!* No, she thought. She had never learned to let the good times roll. Life was serious business in the Owen family; achievement was everything. To Russell, too. Making money was important to Russell. A mysterious and powerful yearning was building inside her. For what? To let the good times roll?

A question popped into her mind and she asked it before she stopped to think. "Why did you say love was a joke? That was an odd thing to say. What did you mean?"

"Just that love's sometimes sad and sometimes funny."

"But why funny?" she persisted.

"Because people always fall in love with the wrong person, anh? The one sure to make them unhappy? That's w'y our love songs are sad, no?"

He stood up. "We'll put the leftover crayfish in your refrigerator. You'll fin' a use for them in a salad or a bisque?" He rolled up the newspaper with the shells inside, and took it out the back door to her garbage can, quite as if he knew her house as well as his own.

And quite as if wrapping up crayfish shells was what newspapers were made for, she thought, amused.

When he came back he said casually, "We can be frien's, anh?"

She really did want to satisfy her curiosity about this intriguing man, formed by unfamiliar traditions in this backwater of America's past. "I'd like that, Armand."

"You want to hear some Cajun music? I can show you how we enjoy life on the bayou." His eyes glinted with mischief. "Or do you want another swim in the mud?"

She shuddered. "Once was enough."

"Me, I enjoyed that," he said with a grin so meaning-ful that she could feel a flush sweeping up her body.

She wrinkled her nose at him, and he laughed aloud, a rich, joyous sound. She could be getting into dangerous waters. He was far too attractive.

But his tone was merely friendly as he said, "Friday night, anh? I show you a *fais-do-do*."

She nodded, a little vague about what a *fais-do-do* was, but aware that she was probably agreeing to go with him to a country dance hall where she would be like a fish out of water. But she knew that if she refused him, she would always regret it.

His eyes shone. "You are some woman, Professor." He put his arms around her in a very natural embrace, and she immediately stiffened, alarmed by the way her whole body came alive at his touch.

"You take too much for granted, Armand," she stated in her coolest voice. "I said we could be friends."

"You know w'at I t'ink? I t'ink you like me more than you can tell me, anh?"

Before she could deny it or draw away, his smiling lips made the shape of a kiss and came down to close over hers. It was a soft and lingering kiss, not making any demands at all, but surprisingly seductive.

"*Bonsoir*, Miss Jessica," he said, and the screen door banged shut behind him.

She watched him go, aware that she had taken a signif-icant step out of character in accepting the invitation he had given with such ingratiating self-confidence. She was confused, not only by Armand, who was like no one else she had known, but by her uncharacteristic behavior.

You never learned to let the good times roll?

No. She never had, really.

She wondered what her family would think of Armand, a man who was surely the complete opposite of the only other man who had appealed to her sensually, a man who for two days had filled her head with the most delightfully erotic fantasies, but who couldn't read a book?

ARMAND DROVE AWAY with a song in his heart, and the silken feel of Jessica's soft lips lingering in his memory like a melody. He did not want to go home because he didn't want the edges rubbed off this extraordinary way he felt. He was not ready to share it yet.

His sense of discovery was strong. He had found a treasure of a woman. She had fit into his arms as if made for them. And she was not afraid of the marsh, understood it in ways that complemented his knowledge.

They were absolutely right together. She didn't know it yet, but he did. He smiled, remembering how the same intoxicating lips that had declared she wanted only friendship had revealed her passionate longing to be close to him. She was educated and he was not, but a man did not need schooling to know when a woman wanted him.

Soft as silk and sweet as honey, her lips were. And warm with a surprising passion. How cool she could be on the outside, eyes frosty, hiding that sensual response that had risen so sweetly and naturally to meet his suggestion of passion. It had been a wonderful surprise.

And her hair! He ached to run his fingers through that silk floss. He pictured her again on the deck of his boat with her hair spread out to dry and her wet clothing revealing every curve of her high-breasted, long-legged body, and he felt an excruciating ache of desire.

Words of love and desire bloomed in his mind. *Her hair blowing in the wind wraps gold strings around my heart....*

He drove on, feeling his need pulsing with the rhythm of his heartbeat. It was so strong that he was tempted to turn around and go back and knock on her door. He saw her opening it in something so fragile and silky that he could see all her luscious curves through it...she would hold out her arms....

Armand laughed aloud. She wouldn't even open the door!

You don't know it yet but you were meant for me, my little mud hen. It's our fate.

He kept on driving, conscious of the ache in his loins, up and down bayou roads, plotting his strategy to win the woman he had to convince belonged in his arms.

CHAPTER THREE

ARMAND CALLED FOR JESSICA on Friday night driving a vintage Chevrolet, whose dents and scratches had obviously been washed and lovingly polished.

She had debated for some time what to wear and had finally gone next door to consult with the wife of her landlord. Mrs. Thibault, a down-to-earth Cajun housewife, barely five feet tall and generously curved, said, "You're going to a dance? Where?"

"I don't know," Jessica confessed. "What's a fay-dough-dough?"

"Ah, a *fais-do-do*!" Estelle Thibault said, with tones of rich appreciation. "A real Cajun country dance. You'll see anything on the floor, *chére*, from flowered skirts to cut-off jeans." Her merry black gaze traveled up Jessica's ivory silk shirtwaist and stopped at her hair, brushed up into sophisticated loops and swirls of gold.

"You look too elegant," she said, and reached up to pull out some pins, ruining a good thirty-five minutes of Jessica's careful work. "Let it fall, *chére*."

Jessica thanked her and ran home, but when she saw her reflection in the mirror, she grimaced. She looked absurdly young. Like an awkwardly tall teenager, she thought, and muttered, "It could be a dozen years ago and me meeting my grandmother at the Waldorf for tea."

Seizing her brush, she swept her hair up to her crown and tied it tightly with a ribbon as she usually did before going to the lab.

Armand appeared at her screen door just as she finished. His eyes lit with unmistakable approval of the insouciant switch of her ponytail as she threw open the door to let him in.

"You're ready? *Bon!*" He was dressed casually in creamy light slacks and a knit shirt that was open at the neck but fit closely over his chest and shoulders, revealing their handsome proportions.

They walked out to his car. He smiled warmly at her as he turned the ignition key. In the close quarters of the front seat the aroma of his toiletries added spice to the warm fragrance of the evening air.

The quiet water of the bayou reflected the orange and lavender of the setting sun as they drove the road that followed its banks to the north. A shrill buzz of cicadas accompanied the purr of the Chevy's motor. Jessica felt a strong male magnetism from the man beside her. He was more intensely physical than the men she had known in her own world, men who were her equals in education. The novelty filled her with a sense of adventure.

"You'll have to show me how to dance a *fais-do-do*," she said, and was piqued when Armand burst out laughing.

"It's not a dance. *Fais-do-do* means 'go to sleep.'"

She stared at him.

"With us, a dance is a family thing. Cajuns have always had lots of *bébés*," he added, with a glance so unmistakably tender that she looked quickly away from him. She found his total lack of reserve unsettling. "The *bébés* used to be laid to sleep on the chairs around the walls while *Maman* danced," he explained.

"Surely they don't still do that!"

"My sister usually hires a baby-sitter," he reassured her. "I want you to meet my sisters. They'll be there."

"All of them?"

"No." His grin teased her. "Sister Catherine, she don' attend dances."

The nun. He was truly outrageous!

Dusk descended as Armand drove, and it was quite dark when they came to a clearing on the edge of a cypress swamp, and a large unpainted barn of a building. Faint light from the windows illuminated cars parked randomly among the moss-hung trees. Neon signs across the front of the building glowed meagerly against the blackness of the surrounding oaks, proclaiming on one side, *Bons Aliments, Bons Temps* and on the other, Good Food, Good Times. The aroma of frying chicken lay thick and tempting on the moist swamp air.

A burst of loud music spilled out of a suddenly opened door that threw a spotlight on a group of young men, some little more than boys, loitering around the entrance. They watched in an absorbed shy silence as Armand touched Jessica's arm and led her through their ranks to the door.

Armand spoke quietly to someone, and she heard a few murmured "Heys!" in return. The music had a strong beat, but it was not rock. It was not like anything she had heard before, but there was a melodic theme in a minor key that spoke intimately to her. The wheeze of an accordion was unmistakable.

She was suddenly filled with excitement at the prospect of a totally new experience, something like what she had felt when she first set foot in Europe during a summer vacation from college.

Inside, the air conditioner hummed, the lights were low, and the floor was crowded with energetic dancers of all ages. To the left was a door through which she could see a bar, with a dining room beyond that.

Armand put an arm around her waist and swept her into the thick of the crowd. He was a masterful dancer, now holding her close so that she felt the rhythm through his body movements, and now holding both her hands so that she faced him as in a folk dance. Sometimes he turned her loose to let her match her own interpretation of the beat to his. But his dance steps were fast and new to her, and Jessica felt stiff and awkward, unsure of herself.

Armand sensed her self-consciousness. He didn't talk, giving himself entirely to the music and to the feel of her tense body in his embrace, enjoying the sweet flower fragrance of her hair.

Jessica heard other dancers speak to Armand and his responses, and she imagined they all looked curiously at her. Gradually the insistent rhythm and the light pressure of Armand's hands began working a kind of magic on her. When the dance ended, she was warm and excited.

Immediately several couples crowded around them. Armand introduced his sisters, two friendly dark-haired women, and their husbands and another couple he called "coozannes."

"So you are Armand's professor?" said the sister he had called Marie. She threw an arm around Jessica in an impulsive hug.

Caught by surprise, Jessica was stiff and unyielding. A moment later she was being warmly hugged by his sister Danielle, who asked, "He's showing you a good time?" Their soft Southern voices echoed the French lilt of Armand's accent.

In a similar situation in New York City, a woman's most intimate greeting would have been kissing the air near her cheek. Jessica was not sure how she felt about this exuberant affection from strangers.

She had barely acknowledged the introductions when a very pretty younger girl ran up to her, crying, "You must be Armand's little mud hen! He has talked of nothing else for three days." She seized Jessica's arms, turning her around as if she were a mannequin. "Armand, she is all you said, *cher*."

"My baby sister, Claire," Armand told Jessica. "Like Etienne, she talks too much."

Jessica's cheeks felt hot, but the laughter surrounding her was so warm and friendly that she could not resent it. She sensed a loving intimacy in this family group that was new in her experience, and her reactions to it were mixed. Her innate reserve made her instinctively withdraw, yet their warmth touched a hunger in her that she had been largely unaware existed until now.

She smiled at the younger girl. "Where is Etienne?"

"Steve? Oh, he's too sophisticated for a *fais-do-do*!" Claire exclaimed. "It's nothing but modern jazz for that kid. Papa wanted to teach him to play the accordion, but he said 'no way.' It's 'uncool,' you know? French is 'uncool,' too, according to him."

The little group on the dance floor had been swelled by the addition of several young men, all wanting to dance with Claire. With teasing glances and tosses of her dark hair she flirted with all of them before making her choice.

"What a coquette she is!" said Danielle, as Claire's partner whirled her away, and her husband, Maurice, said fondly, "Your baby sister'll get herself into the soup pot yet."

"That girl!" Marie said with a sigh.

The band swung into another rollicking tune, and Armand put his hand on Jessica's waist. Dancing came more naturally to her this time. She was more at ease with the lively rhythm. By the third dance she was tingling clear down to her toes, not sure whether it was the music or Armand's charisma, and not really caring because she felt more alive than she could ever remember.

A stunning girl was singing with the band, singing jazz rhythms in a low sexy voice. Like the other musicians, she was not dressed as an entertainer, but as casually as the dancers on the floor. Her full skirt was blocked with large flowers and her peasant blouse showed off her creamy shoulders in a low décolletage. Her dark hair fell in riotous curls around a beautiful face with high cheekbones and incredibly large black eyes. Calls and whistles from the dance floor applauded her chorus, and she answered them with a wide natural smile that was very attractive.

"Arman'!" someone yelled, and others took up the call. "Hey, Arman'! Zydeco!"

"They're calling you?" Jessica exclaimed.

"Sometime I sing wit' this band. They want some zydeco."

"Isn't that some kind of rock?"

"Cajun rock, jazz, blues—the new sound. It's got a snappy rhythm, like snap beans."

"Beans!" Jessica was not sure she'd heard right.

Armand laughed, enjoying her puzzlement. "Zydeco. That's the way we pronounce *les haricots* down here. It's got a click, like snapping beans."

Jessica examined the band more closely. The four musicians ranged in age from the pretty young singer and slightly older black drummer to the grizzled accordion player, who was clearly more than fifty.

"Armand?" It was the songbird, calling him through her mike.

"Will you excuse me?" Armand said, and left Jessica standing with his sisters, who had again come up to them.

She watched as the accordion player handed Armand his instrument and left the dais. He suddenly appeared beside Jessica, a weathered man as tall as Armand and looking remarkably like him. Armand's sisters laughed as he seized Jessica around the waist. "You dance wit' Armand's papa, *no*?" he announced, and swung her vigorously into a rapid two-step as music filled the room.

Jessica shook her head, laughing, as her feet flew. This was incredible, it was crazy, but she was having the time of her life.

Armand's father was a remarkably good dancer, but Jessica could understand little he said to her. The beat was a fast two-step with a decided accent on the second beat. When she could, she allowed her gaze to return to the two standing before the mike. Armand and the girl sang incomprehensible lyrics while, with his accordion, he backed up the drummer leading the rhythm, which seemed to Jessica to have both the strong beat of rock and the excitement of jazz. It was irrestible. Armand and the girl sang not so much in duet as in a musical conversation that seemed to delight their audience.

"*Bon, non?*" said Armand's father, with a nod of his head toward them.

They were indeed good together. She knew it instinctively even before the crowd erupted in loud applause, demanding more. Most of the dancers had stopped and stood listening. Armand and the girl were obviously enjoying making music together, and there was something more than music between them. Jessica saw it in the way they sang to each other, each seeming to anticipate the other's movements, and in the luminous eyes the young woman kept turned to Armand.

His expression was one of sheer enjoyment. They did three numbers before Armand put down the accordion and returned to Jessica, bringing the singer with him. Marie and Danielle each hugged her. Jessica felt very much on the outside, looking in at something she sensed but that seemed beyond her reach.

Armand's eyes were glowing. "Miss Jessica, this is Nance Marie, an old and dear friend."

"We grew up together," Nance Marie said fondly.

Jessica's voice sounded stiff in her own ears. "You sing beautifully. Both of you."

Armand's father patted Nance Marie's shoulder. *"Magnifique, chére!"*

"Miss Jessica likes to wade in mud," Armand said, trying and failing to keep the laughter out of his eyes, "and collect bugs."

"Armand is a big tease, no?" Nance Marie said, laughing. "Pay no attention. Did you know that he is telling everyone you are an important scientist?"

Just then a loud disturbance broke out near the musicians' dais. "Hugh Broussard, *non?*" asked Armand's father, and beside Jessica, Armand tensed.

Marie turned, standing on tiptoe. "I believe it is Hugh."

"Pardon me," Armand said grimly, and left them. His father followed him.

As the dancers parted to let them through, Jessica glimpsed Claire standing between two Cajun youths who were apparently shouting insults at each other. Suddenly Claire put her hands to her mouth, as they began swinging at each other. There was an explosion of sound from the dancers. Then Jessica's view was blocked as everyone left the floor and surged around the two who were fighting.

Jessica thought she recognized Claire's shrieks over the shouts, and then she heard Armand's authoritative voice, "Hey, cool it, you guys!"

A woman screamed, "*Là*, he's got a knife!"

Jessica could no longer see Armand, but she saw what surely was his hand and arm. His forearm was heavily corded with strain, tightly grasping the wrist of a hand that held a shining blade high above the crowd.

She pushed through the spectators in her way, scarcely aware of what she was doing. When she reached the dais, the two youths standing below it had been separated. Two men were holding one of them. The other, the one with the knife, was locked in a struggle with Armand for the weapon.

Jessica's heart was beating frantically. Armand's back was toward her. She reached the combatants just in time to see Armand slowly force his opponent to drop the knife. The youth immediately buckled his knees and Armand let him fall. Swift as a striking snake, he reached across the floor for the weapon, but Armand stepped on his hand.

Now others moved forward to grab the crouching youth's arms from behind and pull him to his feet. With the strength of fury, he swung the men holding him around until he faced Armand.

"I'll kill you for this, LeBlanc!"

Jessica felt a cold shock at his words. A silence fell over the dance floor. The other youth, his intended victim, lunged toward the knife, but his friends still held him, and Armand bent and picked up the weapon. It was a switch-blade, and he looked at its point before closing it and putting it into his pocket.

When he spoke, Armand's good-humored voice was loud enough for all to hear. "Hugh, that's what you used to say when I stopped you from fighting with your little coozanne after Mass.''

Light laughter of relief blew like a wind through the crowd. Their friends dragged Claire's two suitors away in different directions. Armand's father jumped up on the dais.

"Laisse les bon temps rouler!" he shouted. "We dance!"

He slipped his arms through his accordion's tapes and broke into what sounded like an old-time jig, and the other musicians joined in lustily. The dancers roared their approval and soon the floor was crowded again.

Armand looked for his sister, but Claire had disappeared. He saw Jessica then, standing with her arms crossed, looking pale, and realized she had witnessed everything. He touched her and exclaimed, "You're cold!"

Jessica glanced down at her arms and shivered. "I'm not used to seeing knives pulled on a dance floor." The realization had hit her that life was raw here, and emotions explosive. She had expected adventure, but not violence, and nothing in her tightly controlled upbringing had prepared her for that. It brought forcibly home to her how different this world of Armand's was from her own.

"We fin' Claire and take her home, anh? You don' min'? If she stays aroun', it's likely more trouble, an' she don' need more troubles, that one."

But when they found Claire, she was dancing with a third admirer and didn't want to leave the floor. "The evening's just begun," she objected. "I came with René. He'll take me home."

"Papa don' think you should let René take you home. There's bad blood already between him and Hugh."

She smiled at the young man, who still held her hand. "Then I'll let Henny take me home."

"Sure," Henny said, looking dazed with pleasure.

"You want Hugh or René coming after *you* with a knife, Henny?"

The young man looked at Claire and said bravely, "I can handle Hugh." But Jessica thought he appeared scared.

"But maybe not René, anh? Claire had better do as Papa advises," Armand said mildly.

"Okay, if Papa insists, I'll go home with him," Claire said, "but I'm stayin' for the dancin'."

"Papa thinks you should leave right now," Armand said, patient but inexorable. "You brought this down on your own head, Claire, carryin' on like you do with all those boys."

Henny was beginning to look uncomfortable.

"Oh, that Hugh!" Claire exclaimed, suddenly sounding furious. She broke into a torrent of angry Cajun French that Jessica didn't understand.

Armand replied in the patois, and Claire continued to hurl angry words at him, but she allowed him to take her as well as Jessica across the dance floor to the entrance and outside. Many eyes followed them.

The air had cooled, although it felt balmy after leaving the air-conditioning. A light mist hung over the bayou. Odors of decay rose in the miasma of the swamp. There was also the distinct smell of whiskey coming from the loiterers, all male, grouped around the entrance. Jessica looked anxiously for the tall youth who had pulled the knife, but didn't see him. Somewhere distant dogs were barking, sounding nearer when the doors closed on the blare of music from inside the hall.

Armand put Claire in the back seat by herself, but continued to argue with her in French as he drove away. Jessica sat beside him, arms wrapped around her body, feeling pretty much in the way.

"I'm sorry, Miss Jessica," Armand said at length. "I'm giving Claire a piece of advice. You see, Hugh was her steady, and now she flaunts all these boyfrien's in his face. It's enough to drive a man crazy, anh?"

"He's crazy if he thinks I'll go back to him," Claire snapped.

"A man who would pull a knife—" Jessica agreed.

But Claire interrupted her fiercely. "Hugh's *not* a man who would pull a knife!"

Thoroughly confused, Jessica remained silent, wondering why she had consented to come, anyway.

Armand and Claire continued to argue in French until Armand pulled up in front of his family home, a large unpretentious frame house surrounded by a screened-in veranda. She recognized the fishing boat tied up at the dock on the other side of the road.

Jessica realized then that Armand lived in Chauvin, and not far from her house.

"Excuse me," Armand said. He walked up the path with Claire and left her at the door, which was opened by a small woman holding a child in her arms. Jessica guessed she was Armand's mother, baby-sitting for her daughter. She was obviously surprised to see them, but the little Jessica could hear of their conversation at the door was in French.

Armand was back almost at once. He looked at Jessica's crossed arms and said, "Are you still cold? Come here." He extended his hand, inviting her to sit close to him and let him put his arm around her.

She shook her head, and stayed in her corner, wondering what had made Claire say Hugh was not violent after what had happened tonight.

Armand regarded her with concern. "I'm sorry about the fight," he said after a moment. "Did it spoil the *fais-do-do* for you?"

"No. Not really. I'm just . . . confused."

"It was my sister's fault, anh? Claire flirts with everyone. She doesn't know when to quit."

"Was that what it was all about? You were scolding her for flirting?"

He was silent for a moment, then said, "My baby sister is very unhappy. A man has disappoint' her, an' she reacts by flaunting herself, collecting admirers like bowling trophies. This offends my father. It's a hard time for Claire, so we all try to make her happy."

His words painted a picture for her of his affectionate family as a traditional unit. The father, a patriarchal chauvinist, playing in the band. His daughters, married and single, letting the good times roll, but under his supervision. His wife at home minding grandchildren. It was like stepping back in time, she thought.

And Armand, also watching over his younger sister. Like father, like son.

Armand started the car. "Shall we go back to the dance?"

"No, I think not."

He did not try to change her mind, but drove the short distance to her cottage and stopped at the side of the road, cutting his engine before he turned to her. "I wanted tonight to be special," he said, and waited.

There was an uninterrupted chorus of frogs from the bayou, mingling with the shrilling of the cicadas, a background noise that seemed to be part of every evening in this region of the country. Somehow it suggested calm and peace.

"Come," Armand said coaxingly. "Tell me w'at you think? The fight frightened you, no? Truly, Miss Jessica, we don' fight at every *fais-do-do*." He said it with laughter in his voice, and she felt greatly drawn to him.

"I enjoyed the dancing," she confessed.

She couldn't tell him that it wasn't the fight itself. It was that she had seen again the great gulf yawning between them. This man whom she liked so much was not only illiterate, but had a life-style so different from her own that, although she found it fascinating, she couldn't imagine him finding a permanent place among the friends who mattered to her.

She couldn't tell him that, so she smiled and said, "I never watch a fight on television. I've always hated violence. So when I saw how hard you were struggling to make him drop the knife, it was—"

"You were afraid I would be hurt? Me, I can take care of myself," he said with quiet conviction. "But I like it that you were frightened, anh?"

She could not bring herself to correct his interpretation of her reaction. After all, she *had* been concerned for him.

His arm slid along the seat back and encircled her shoulders, drawing her closer. He had a distinctive odor, his soap and shaving lotion mingling with the faint whiff of his perspiration on ironed cotton. And that smell of the marsh that she had always liked pervaded the air.

"You know w'at I think?" he said. "I t'ink I've found my woman."

The moment was electric. "That's insane," Jessica said unsteadily, just before he kissed her.

His lips were sweet as the local cane syrup she had come to love, and as dark with mysterious promise. A response vibrated deep in her body, and it surprised and terrified her.

She tore her mouth from his, and leaned away from him. "I'm a tourist in your world, Armand," she said hoarsely. "This evening was...fascinating, but we'll probably never see each other again."

He hugged her, laughing softly. "This is a small world, *chére*. You'll see me again."

She found the door latch and let herself out of the car. He followed her to her door and took her in his arms, but he didn't kiss her again. Gazing at her, he murmured something in patois, then said, "That means '*le bon Dieu* keep you safe.'"

"Good night, Armand," she said, stunned. She was embarrassed to hear how unsteady she sounded.

She reminded herself again that Armand could neither read nor write, and had no place in her life. She was going to marry Russ, after all. And Armand—there must be dozens of local girls who would love to be in her place right now. Nance Marie, for instance, who was obviously fond of him and so much at ease with his family.

She wondered what had been between those two. Something, she was sure. What was their relationship now? Armand's curious remark about love being a joke flashed into her mind. People, he said, were always falling in love with the wrong person. But he and Nance Marie seemed so right for each other!

She closed the door against him, standing for a moment in the darkness of her living room. She had wanted him to kiss her again, wanted it with an ardor that amazed her. Not even Russell, her sometime lover and the man she would one day marry, had so stirred her senses with one kiss.

Life had never before seemed hard to her, but tonight Jessica saw for the first time that it was mined with traps for the unwary heart.

CHAPTER FOUR

AFTER A NEAR-SLEEPLESS NIGHT, Jessica decided that it would only be common sense not to see Armand LeBlanc again. His kiss had left her fizzing with a sensual excitement. But it was what he had said that kept her from sleep. She had agreed to be friends. Hearing him say with that note of deep joy that he had "found his woman" was something else.

She told herself he couldn't have been serious! Yet her feminine instincts insisted that he was strongly attracted to her, and knowing that was like taking hold of a live wire.

She reminded herself that he was illiterate. She couldn't allow him to get romantic ideas about her—it wasn't fair to him. Besides, he was too attractive, too likable, too much of a temptation. Getting herself entangled in a relationship with no future could foolishly jeopardize her career as well as her emotional health. Best to remove the temptation.

It was a decision that her mother would consider wisely objective, but Jessica did not feel objective as she turned over at last, determined to nap at least until daybreak. She remembered how soft and coaxing Armand's lips were, and for an instant had total recall of the fragrances and night sounds that had accompanied the disturbing warmth of that kiss. It was a flash of memory that left her with a lingering sense of loss.

She ignored it, and when in the following days her thoughts strayed to the handsome fisherman, she set her mind to composing the little speech she would make when he again invited her to go dancing, or appeared at her door with a gift he had netted from the bayous.

But he did not appear.

After a few days she realized she was feeling lonely. She hadn't been in the community long enough to make friends outside of the lab. The local people were friendly, but they were involved with their church activities, their families and their own longtime relationships.

There were a few other single women working in the facility, most of them secretaries who were local girls. The majority of the scientists were married. Jessica had gone as a single to some of the spaghetti feeds and fish fries the wives of the younger scientists put together, but her date with Armand had been much more exciting.

When the weekend passed with no word from him, Jessica's resolve gradually weakened, and it was with an unexpected flush of pleasure that she looked up to see him standing at her screen door one evening after she had finished her solitary dinner.

"You are not busy?" he said with confidence.

"No. Come in, Armand."

"T'anks."

His difficulty with the *th* sound was slight, but her perception of it was hypersensitive. As he opened the door and stepped into her living room, she murmured, "Thanks."

"For w'at?" he asked, smiling.

Jessica opened her mouth, then shut it again, stifling embarrassed laughter. "Forgive me, Armand. I shouldn't have corrected you."

"Correct me?" His direct gaze demanded an explanation.

She hated herself, but she had begun it and she had to carry it through. "It was the way you said 'thanks.' Your—your accent."

"Yes?" he said encouragingly. "How do you say it?"

She repeated the word and explained, "You put your tongue against your upper teeth. Like this."

His gaze moved to the tip of her tongue, just visible between her parted lips, and stayed there with a rapt and speculative expression.

"Oh, skip it!" she said, becoming embarrassed. "What have you been doing with yourself, Armand?"

"You missed me," he said with a disarming grin.

"No," she lied. "I'm being polite."

"I'm sorry I couldn't come," he said gently. "I play' with my band in Lafayette las' weekend."

"And sang?" Why on earth had she asked?

"I always sing two, t'ree times."

"With Nance Marie?"

"You're jealous?" His smile was one of pure delight. He moved closer, so close that he was invading her space. Their bodies were only inches apart as he looked down into her eyes, and she felt threatened, a reaction that her mind told her was purely primitive. At the same time she felt a delicious trembling begin to weaken her knees.

"Of course not!" She stepped back, breaking the unbearable tension of his nearness. "Why have you come now?"

She was trying to remember the words she had planned to say that would keep him from coming back, but she had made such an awkward start that her mind was in a state of confusion.

"You will write a letter for me, anh?" He took a newspaper clipping from his shirt pocket, and began unfolding it. His sleeves were rolled up, and the cords of muscles in his tanned forearms fascinated her. She remembered the way they had bunched when he gripped the wrist of the knife-wielding young man. They were like those of a trained athlete—or a powerful workingman.

Which he was, of course. Working a shrimp trawler was hard labor. She thought of her first sight of him, standing on his boat with the sun gleaming on the curls of black hair on his golden chest, and how he had diminished the college students of her field group, some of whom she would have called "hunks" when she was in school. She had not realized before how very seductive male physical strength could be.

It occurred to her that she had been—up to now—one of those women who were vulnerable to seduction by words and ideas. Russell was a great talker. That was why he was successful at selling stocks and bonds. He and Armand were as different as apples and—and kiwis. Russell was a beautiful man, lean and fit, but his physical activity was limited to racquetball and tennis, at both of which he was fiercely competitive.

And why was she comparing Armand to Russell, the only man with whom she had been intimate? She was genuinely shocked by where her thoughts were leading her.

What had been unthinkable the first time she saw Armand—and even after that explosive kiss that had made the unthinkable clear to her—was straying into her mind too often and too distractingly.

He wanted her to write a letter? She moistened her lips and asked, "To whom?"

"I want to write a letter to the editor."

It was the last thing she had expected to hear. "The *editor*?"

"Of the newspaper. Many people read the paper, no? There's something I want to say to the crab fishermen, but I don't know how to say it. You'll know how."

"What's it about?"

"Those guys stealing crab traps."

"But you're not a crab fisherman, are you, Armand?" She had heard some talk about "the crab war" out at the lab. "Your boat is a shrimper, isn't it?"

"Me, I invested my money in a boat! It don't take much capital to fish for crab. A man can make his own traps for fifteen, twenty dollars a box. Or he can go out at night in a pirogue. He can set out stolen traps, and he's in business. Guys laid off from the offshore oil patch are doin' that. There's so many crab fishermen no one man can live off w'at he catch, and too damn many of 'em are usin' traps some poor bastard spent all winter makin'."

Jessica drew a deep breath "You want me to say *that*?"

"I want to say those thievin' bas—those thieves are takin' food out of the mouths of *bébés*. And I want to say every fisherman should come to the Elks' Hall when we talk how to stop crab fishermen from carryin' guns to protect their traps. We don't want violence in the parish."

Jessica gazed into his warm brown eyes, and liked what she saw. Some people would assume an illiterate man didn't know much, but Armand was far from stupid. She read in his steady gaze a hard strength born of experience, but there was also sanity and intelligence and caring in abundance. She thought of his quick action to control an ugly situation on the dance floor the week before, and his words, "we don' want violence" rang like a bell note in her mind.

"I want to say we fishermen must stick together, all of us. Our catch puts the food on our tables, but we don' kill over it. You see?"

"Yes," Jessica said. "I see." She went into her bedroom and Armand followed her there so naturally the protest that rose to her throat died unspoken. She took her portable typewriter from the closet, thrust it into his hands and pointed. "In the kitchen."

Quickly she put her dinner dishes in the sink, but left the checked cloth on the cypress trestle table. He sat opposite her while she opened the typewriter, looking so utterly at home with his strong forearms resting on the table that she felt quite undone.

"Bon!" he said, when she had rolled paper into the machine. "Now, here's the box number for the newspaper, an' this is w'at I want to say."

As she listened to his voice with its pleasant Cajun lilt, she marveled at the contrast between it and his incisive, well-organized thoughts. She put them into grammatical form and realized that it was a very good letter from a man who was obviously a born leader. It was tragic that he could neither read nor write. The tragedy of it preyed on her mind as she typed and retyped his sentences. It would be a lifelong handicap, one almost impossible to overcome.

Unless he could always persuade someone like her to write and read his letters for him. It wouldn't surprise her! He was a charmer, incredibly persuasive. A high school graduate—someone like Nance Marie—could easily be persuaded, she thought. Writing a letter for him was not a task that required a marine biologist, after all. She looked bleakly into the impassable gulf between them.

The letter took less time than she had expected, partly because he knew exactly what he wanted to say. She read her corrected copy back to him before she typed his name at the bottom of the letter: Armand LeBlanc.

"Can you sign your name? Of course you can! You have to sign checks, don't you?"

"I'll show you how I sign checks." He took a pen out of his shirt pocket and laboriously wrote his initials: AleB in a distinctive monogram below her typescript. His handsome face was serious, intent on his task.

"Aleb," she said playfully, to hide how heartsick she felt for him. "As in Caleb?"

He put his pen back in his pocket, and leaning across the table, kissed her startled mouth. She had not meant to let him kiss her again, but she hadn't seen this one coming. Nor did it seem possible to break the contact, although the table was between them and all she had to do was push back her chair. Their lips clung sweetly. Her heart was beating hard and the confusion in her mind deepened.

"You will teach me to write my own letters, anh?" he said, with his unshakable confidence. His eyes were warm with a tender glow.

She groaned. "You don't know what you're asking, Armand."

Armand looked at her with quiet joy, his gaze lingering on the incredible yellow-gold of her hair, which was as straight and silky-fine as *Mémère*'s embroidery floss. Her softly curved mouth trembled slightly, betraying her, he noted. Her eyes could remain that cool, grayish blue, rejecting him the way they had when she told him she was just passing in his world, but as they had then, her quivering lips belied the words they formed.

He knew exactly what he was asking of her, and he kissed her again to tell her that he knew she wanted it, too. Then he produced an envelope for her to address, and after examining the box number carefully—he knew his numbers, at any rate—went off to mail his letter.

Jessica put her typewriter in its case and carried it back to the bedroom closet, with her emotions in a hopeless muddle. She could have prevented him from repeating that outrageous kiss! Why on earth hadn't she?

THREE DAYS LATER Armand was waiting in his car, parked on the shoulder of the bayou road in front of her house, when Jessica drove home from the lab. She stopped in the driveway and he walked over to meet her as she stepped out of her car. He was carrying her daily newspaper and several letters, which he had taken from her mailbox on his way. He handed them to her, saying, "Mama is expecting you to eat *court-bouillon* tonight."

"What?" Jessica glanced down at her mail. The top letter was from Russell, and she slipped it into her purse. Now why had she done that? The name meant nothing to Armand, even if he could read it. The thought brought a now familiar churn of confusion to her mind.

When she looked up she saw that Armand's eyes were glowing with a secret knowledge. Panic gripped her, as she focused on the meaning of his words. Meet his *mother*?

"Why didn't you tell me sooner, Armand? I'm afraid I've brought home some work that I must finish."

"She's been cooking the sauce since ten this morning?" His rising inflection said that of course she couldn't disappoint Mama, and Jessica discovered to her dismay that, of course, she couldn't. She saw that he was bursting with something he wanted to tell her, and suddenly she knew what it was.

"They published your letter!"

His smile widened. She started to open up the newspaper, but he stopped her, taking it from her hands. "You read it at my house, anh?"

He was urging her toward his car, but she pulled back, protesting, "Armand! May I at least comb my hair?"

"Okay. But *Pépère* says, 'When a cat washes her face, look for rain.'"

He gave her an affectionate pat on the rump to send her on her way, a touch so slight she barely felt it, yet so possessive that it had the effect on her of an electric prod.

She whirled to face him, outraged by the familiarity. "Hands off, Armand!"

He gave her an abashed look, then gazed down at his offending hand. Slapping his wrist, he told it, "Take that back!"

Jessica leaped away from him. "Now, look, Armand—!"

He explained, "When you turn that sweet derriere on him, he lose all sense."

The amused affection in his eyes told her that he could read her feelings precisely. She pressed her lips together to hold in the laughter bubbling in her throat.

"Mama is waiting," he said. "She don' know about the letter yet."

What was she to do with this man?

A few minutes later she sat beside him, in a fresh blouse and skirt with her hair shining from a quick brushing. Her newspaper lay on the seat between them. He was driving across the bayou bridge toward his parents' house.

Seen by daylight, it was a square, one-story dwelling raised only a foot or so off the ground, since this village was on higher land than that of the fishing village that surrounded the lab. The roof of the LeBlanc house extended over an encircling veranda, screened and bordered by clumps of azalea. Armand drove up on the coarse grass and parked under a sweet gum tree.

Jessica picked up her newspaper and got out of the car. She paused to look at the hull of a boat under construction between the road and the bayou. It was cradled on four oil drums, and its skeleton resembled Armand's smaller boat in shape, wide-beamed but with a certain grace.

"My new boat," he said proudly. "It will be a Lafitte skiff, but bigger than my old one."

"I can't believe you're building your own boat," she exclaimed.

"Everyone does. *Pépère*—my *grandpère*—has built more boats than anyone on the bayou. But the whole family helps."

"Why do you call it a Lafitte skiff? It's much more than a skiff."

"See the wide beam? An' see how pretty she slope down on the sides? That's to make it easy to lay down the booms. The design came from Lafitte, the town that began as the pirate's camp. We're building it of cypress. Cypress never rots. This one will be big enough to trawl offshore." His enthusiasm told her he loved his work.

They walked up the crushed-oyster-shell walk to the veranda. A wonderful aroma of mixed herbs and spices greeted them as they climbed the steps. Armand touched her arm and guided her along the porch as if drawn by the spicy odors directly to the kitchen.

It was a spacious room, furnished not only with the usual appliances and a large round oak table set for a meal but also with a rattan sofa and several comfortable matching chairs. Armand's father was sitting at the table with a small coffee cup before him.

He got to his feet, shouting, "'*Allo, 'allo!* Mama, Armand has brought his Miss Jessica! Etienne!" he shouted. "Go to the trailer and tell *Pépère* and *Mémère* to come."

"My name is Steve," the boy muttered, unmoving.

Armand's mother turned from the stove where she was stirring something in an enormous soup pot. "*Va*, Steve," she said with authority.

Etienne obeyed, and Jessica began to revise her impression of a patriarchal family unit.

Mrs. LeBlanc smiled at her. She was so tiny that her smile seemed almost as big as she was. It lit her wonderful dark eyes, and Jessica knew intuitively that it came from a warm heart.

She spoke in French, and Armand said, "My mother says you mus' make this your home."

"*Café?*" Mrs. LeBlanc asked, and added in English, "Small black?"

"Yes, thank you," Jessica replied.

Mrs. LeBlanc responded with a curious mixture of French and English, which left Jessica with the sensation that she had communicated with her although she had understood scarcely a word. She felt strongly drawn to the energetic little woman with the eloquent eyes.

Her husband was already filling a demitasse with the rich dark Cajun coffee for which Jessica was developing a taste. "*Madame* can no leave her sauce," he said, "because it's nearly done, an' so thick it will stick to the bottom of the pot. She begs your pardon."

Mrs. LeBlanc nodded vigorously, smiling at Jessica. Her husband winked and said, "*Madame* is vain about her *court-bouillon, non?*" He refilled his own demitasse and tossed it off like a jigger of whiskey.

Etienne reappeared in the kitchen doorway, and said belatedly, "'*Allo*, Miss Jessica!"

"Did you tell *Pépère* we have company?" demanded his father.

"He's coming."

"How are things with you, Etienne, er, Steve?" Jessica asked, smiling at him.

He returned her smile, pleased. "Okay."

The door from the veranda opened again and a scrawny man with no teeth and little hair walked in, grinning shyly. Armand said to Jessica, "This is my grandfather." Then he asked the old man, "Where's *Mémère*?"

Pépère nodded at Jessica, his grin widening as he replied in French.

"My *grandpère* says I have good taste in women," Armand told Jessica. "My *grandmère* has gone shopping with a neighbor. I'm glad you're here, Etienne. You can translate something for *Pépère*."

"You translate it. You know I don' talk Cajun." Etienne gave Jessica a look that mixed defiance and embarrassment. "It's a lost language. It's pidgin French, anyway."

"Non!" Mr. LeBlanc's eyes sparked with anger. "It is the French of our ancestors. You will show respect for your *grandpère*, Etienne!"

"Steve!" the youth snapped.

Armand said, pleasant but firm, "Miss Jessica will read a letter and you will translate it. You will do this for me, Etienne." He picked up Jessica's newspaper and handed it to her.

"For you I will do it," Etienne said tautly.

"A letter?" his father inquired.

"To the editor," Armand told him. "Listen to Etienne, everybody!"

Jessica had to guess what he was telling them because they were speaking in French. She had found the editorial page. His letter was headlined, A Concerned Citizen, and that pleased her. When Armand nodded to her, she began reading it aloud.

The editor had printed every word she had typed. She was rather proud of that because she thought that while making Armand's message grammatical, she had kept its flavor as well as his intent.

She paused after each sentence for Etienne's reluctant translation, but in her mind she was hearing it in Armand's voice.

Dear Editor:

In our parish, crab fishermen say they can't keep their cages in the water forty-eight hours without thieves taking off with them. I am not a crabber, but I am a fisherman and these men are my brothers. Their families depend for a living on what they catch. It seems the water patrol of the sheriff's office can seldom catch these thieves, and when they do, nothing much is done. Check the records—the thief stands before the judge and gets a fifty-dollar fine and probation. He can make that up in a single night.

Is this fair? Many crab fishermen do not think so, and I hear them say they themselves will handle this. Some say they now carry guns. A single trigger pulled could make this bad situation much worse. I do not want to see this happen in our parish.

If you agree with me, come to discuss this problem at a special meeting of the Fishermen's Alliance at the Elks' Hall, Wednesday, April 2, at 8:00 p.m. This is a matter that should concern all fishermen. Bring your questions and your answers, but leave your guns in your *armoires*.

Armand LeBlanc.

"Exactly," Armand said with satisfaction.

Etienne had finished his translation with more enthusiasm than he had begun it. "Yo!" he exclaimed, in admiration.

Pépère was nodding his nearly bald head. Mr. LeBlanc had been listening intently and asked, "Did you write that letter, Armand?"

"I told it to Miss Jessica and she wrote it down."

They were speaking French again.

"She's a good girl," Mrs. LeBlanc told Armand. "It is good that you bring her to see me."

"I think I will marry her, Mama."

Everyone took care not to look at Jessica.

"Ha!" Etienne said in English. "Better ask her first!"

"It's time you find a wife," Mrs. LeBlanc said comfortably.

"It's a good letter," Armand's father said. "I'll go with you to the meeting."

Armand turned to Jessica, smiling happily. "They say it's a good letter," he told her. "Mama says you're a good girl, and Papa says he will go to the meeting."

"What did Etienne want you to ask your mother?"

"Oh, she never go to Fishermen's Alliance," Armand said, with laughter and affection shining in his eyes.

The front door slammed and light staccato steps approached the kitchen.

"Claire?" Mrs. LeBlanc called.

When there was no answer, a look passed between her and her husband. She turned off the gas under the soup pot and left the kitchen. *Pépère* raised his head and glanced at Armand.

From where she sat, Jessica had a limited view through the door into the hall. Claire came into her line of vision. Her beautiful eyes, so like her mother's, were brimming with tears.

"Ah, *bébé*," Mrs. LeBlanc murmured and held out her arms. Claire slipped into them and let them enfold her while she laid her cheek against her mother's. A quick exchange of French followed, words Jessica didn't understand but that were spoken in tones eloquent of sorrow and understanding.

Jessica felt a surprising rush of emotion that she instinctively concealed. She didn't know why the scene moved her so deeply, unless it was because she couldn't remember her own mother embracing her with such unabashed love.

But I must have been cuddled as a baby, she thought. A pity she couldn't remember those times. Such memories would be nice to have now that her own family seemed so far away, and not only in miles.

The two women came into the kitchen with their arms around each other. "Hello, Miss Mud Hen!" Claire said impertinently, and laughed with the tears still brightening her eyes.

Jessica laughed with her, thinking how very pretty she was and that her mother must have been just as pretty at her age. Claire kissed her father and gave both her grandfather and Armand an affectionate squeeze of the shoulder. The warm affection Jessica saw in the looks they exchanged made her ache with a mysterious longing. Then Armand turned to her, and the emotion in his eyes deepened and became so personal that Jessica felt as if she had been kissed. She looked quickly away, feeling the unfamiliar sting of tears in her eyes.

I must get away from here, she thought, yet knew she wanted to stay in this warm, spicy kitchen so filled with love.

Mrs. LeBlanc turned the gas on under the big pot, gave Claire an apron and a long wooden spoon and set her to stirring the sauce while she went to the refrigerator and took out several freshly cleaned fish. While she proceeded to cut them into chunks and put them into the sauce to cook, Papa LeBlanc, the little grandfather and Etienne teased and chided Claire, who easily held her own with the men.

Jessica laid her hand on Armand's arm, unable to resist any longer her desire to touch him. "What are they saying?"

"They want to cheer Claire. She was going to marry, had even made her wedding dress, but she broke up with her boyfriend. Now she wants him back, I t'ink."

"I'm sorry," Jessica said.

He shrugged. "They quarrel' all the time. Now she t'ink her mission in life is to break the heart of every man in the parish."

"Telling me I'm a tease is supposed to cheer me?" asked Claire, who had heard everything. She was cutting thick slabs of a French loaf. She put a platter of bread and squares of butter set in ice water on the table.

The door from the veranda opened, admitting a young couple, who went to the stove and kissed Mrs. LeBlanc and then Claire.

"You remember my sister Marie, and her husband, Jonquile?" Armand asked Jessica.

They greeted her warmly, and Marie kissed her father, and then with special tenderness, her grandfather. She was small like her mother, with dimples that bracketed her smile. Jonquile, short and sturdy, dropped into a chair at the table and Marie went to the stove, where Mrs. Le-Blanc was dishing up the *court-bouillon*. Marie began carrying the soup plates to the table.

"Jonquile sells fishing supplies. He's a razzle-dazzle salesman," Armand teased, and Jonquile smiled shyly at Jessica.

They all sat down to eat. Talk zigzagged across the table, mostly in French for *Pépère*'s benefit, but with both Armand and his sisters translating for Jessica. Rather defiantly, Etienne spoke only in English. The rich, spicy fish stew was delicious, red as tomatoes could make it, but surprisingly mellow in flavor.

Armand's eyes met Jessica's, asking her to share his obvious pleasure in the food.

"It's the long cooking that matures the sauce," Marie told Jessica. "It takes the acid out of the tomatoes." She then translated for her grandfather.

Mrs. LeBlanc said with her hands and expressive eyes and her accented English that any tomato sauce must be cooked "long, long," and that this was Armand's favorite.

Armand reached across his plate and with his finger wiped a bit of sauce from the corner of Jessica's mouth with a touch as sensual as a kiss, and then licked his finger, bringing a flush of embarrassment to her as everybody laughed, Armand's wizened old grandfather cackling loudly.

Marie said, "My mother will teach you to make it."

Jessica's eyes flew to Armand's and what she saw in them made her heart flutter in panic. She shouldn't have come—she must make it clear that she was only a friend, not a *special* friend. What on earth had Armand told them about her, anyway?

When they had eaten all they could of the fish and warm buttered bread, more dark coffee was prepared and served. Suddenly the kitchen was filled with new arrivals. The other sister, Danielle, carrying an infant, and her husband, Maurice, with a toddler, had arrived.

Etienne, his father and Claire rose from their chairs, a high chair was brought in for the toddler, and Mrs. Le-Blanc and Marie filled more plates. Jessica would have got up, too, to take her coffee cup into the living room with the others, but Armand said, "Stay and talk with Danielle, who wants to know you."

Danielle was the tallest of the three girls, and resembled Armand, especially in her warm brown eyes. Her husband was a tall, good-looking man who Jessica thought resembled Alain Delon, a popular French singer she had heard when she was in Paris. Maurice was an accountant and worked for an oil company, but his office was now in New Orleans. By this time Jessica's head was whirling with talk, most of which she scarcely understood, although Armand's sisters constantly turned to her with abbreviated explanations in English.

She was amazed at the intimacy of their talk. At one point, after an animated discussion in French, Armand's mother insisted, in her combination of French, meager English and body language, that Jessica be told that Marie could not produce a *bébé* and that this distressed both her and her husband and sometimes caused trouble between them, although they were very much in love.

In her own family, Jessica reflected, the subject would never have been mentioned. Even if it were Jessica herself who was barren and they were alone, her mother would have waited for Jessica to bring up the matter.

After the meal, when they joined the others in the living room, Armand asked Etienne to read his letter to his
sisters and their husbands and told them that Jessica had
written it for him. The men discussed the problems of the
fishermen, and asked Jessica's opinion, because she
worked at the marine lab. Then the whole family fondly
discussed Danielle's discontent because her husband's job
in New Orleans required such a long commute.

"He's never home," she complained.

"There aren't any jobs here since my company shut
down its oil rigs," he argued. "At least I still have a job!"

They were speaking English now, and someone had to
translate for *Pépère*.

"We need two paychecks," Danielle declared. Her husband retorted, "But if you worked, your paycheck would
go to the baby-sitter."

"Danielle, Mama has her own interests. You shouldn't
expect her to baby-sit for you while you work," Marie told
her sister, and explained to Jessica, "Mama enjoys her
Altar Society meetings and visiting with her friends. She
made a rule of baby-sitting no more than twice a week."

"Mama is right," Armand said. "They are Danielle's
bébés. It's a problem for Maury, anh, *mon ami*?"

"It's a problem for my banker," Maurice said, to sym-
pathetic laughter, and that had to be translated for the old
man who watched with lively eyes as they talked.

"Since the oil companies pull' out, our parish is the
most depressed in the state," Papa LeBlanc told Jessica.

"Here, we are used to being poor," Mama said, in firm
but heavily accented English. "We have always work'
hard, hard for w'at we have. Your family is rich, no?"

"Not rich," Jessica denied. "But they are not poor."

"W'at does that mean?" Papa LeBlanc demanded. "If
you're not poor, you're rich, anh?" He laughed hugely.

"He means if you have food on your table, and your
family and friends around you, you're rich," Jonquile explained.

"Do you agree?" Armand's father demanded of Jessica, and he looked satisfied when she said that she did.

When at last Jessica asked Armand to take her home
and said her goodbyes and her thanks for the delicious
meal, the impressions she carried away were mixed, but
vivid.

The LeBlancs were something new in her experience. She
was appalled by their lack of reserve, yet moved by the
deep family loyalty and genuine love that they had for one
another. Four generations had been present around the
table, and it was obvious that this was not unusual. They
were totally different from any family she had encountered in her own clan of relatives, and in a way she regretted that. Papa LeBlanc, she thought, was typical of the old
patriarchal head of the family. A patriarch who, sadly,
could no longer support his family. That was why Mrs.
LeBlanc sounded authoritative, and why Armand, the
eldest son, loomed so large in the group.

It had rained while they were eating and drinking coffee, but the rain had ceased when Armand stopped his car
in front of Jessica's cottage, and a pale lopsided moon was
visible. The chorus of frogs from the bayou sounded rau-
cously loud in the stillness after he turned off the motor.

"My family t'ink you wonderful! I told them!" he
bragged, as Jessica laughed helplessly.

"I t'ink they wonderful, too," she said, teasing him.

"Okay," he said with a grin. "And w'at you *thh*ink?"
he asked, showing the tip of his tongue.

She said recklessly, "I think you have the most loving,
caring family I've ever known—including my own."

His arm lay along the car seat behind her. He let it drop to her shoulder and looked down at her with concern. "Your family isn't loving?"

"Oh, sure," she said. "We just don't show it like you do. And sometimes, like tonight, I wish we did."

"In w'at way is your family different?" he asked curiously.

She thought of her busy professional parents and their social life in Manhattan and was suddenly oppressed by the great chasm between Manhattan and Cajun Louisiana. How to make him understand?

"My friends would call your father a male chauvinist."

"Why?"

"Because he rules as head of the family, like a—a little tin god—telling everyone what to do."

Armand laughed. "You wrong, Professor. Mama, she rule the family."

Jessica looked at him in disbelief.

"Cajun women have always worked beside their men. *Mémère* used to skin the 'rats *Pépère* trapped. And she always speaks her mind, jus' as Mama and my sisters do. So how is your family different?"

Jessica thought for a moment. "What made your mother want to tell me that Marie is unhappy because she can't have a child?" she finally asked.

Armand said in surprise, "It's true."

"But it's a very personal problem, isn't it? Didn't Marie resent her telling me, a total stranger?"

Armand looked faintly embarrassed. "You're not a stranger. You met Marie."

"Once. On a crowded dance floor. We exchanged greetings. That's all."

"I've talked about you," he admitted. "That's why they treat you like family."

"My mother would never—" She closed her mouth abruptly. Treated her like *family*? She turned wide accusing eyes on him.

He touched her cheek. The skin of his hands felt rough, but their touch was infinitely tender. "How can your family not love you? How can anyone not love you?"

Her pulse quickened in panic. She cast around in her head for the words that she had planned would prevent a conversation like this, but her mind refused to summon them. Her heart was certainly working all right. It was going like a motor out of control, fueled by his nearness to her in the front seat of his car, pumping the hot blood through her body. And her traitorous body was crying with a dozen silent mouths, *Touch me again, here, and here....*

But her controlled voice said, "We do care about one another. My parents are coming to visit, Armand. You'll see."

"*Bon*. I want to meet them."

Guilt was mixed with the panic that was growing stronger in her breast. Why couldn't she tell him she could see no future that included him? Now he was expecting to meet her parents! She must put an end to this.

But the shine of moonlight coming through the windshield was on his mouth and the curve of his jaw, and although his eyes were in shadow, the shape of his lips took on a magic that held her rapt attention. She knew she had been anticipating this moment all evening, longing to be close to him, to be in his arms. It had been growing all through the intimacy of shared food with him in the circle of his doting family.

When they kissed, the sweetness of their coming together was all that mattered. But on another level, it was as if something deep in each of them, a thing over which they had no control, leaped up to meet and obliterate the vast distance between them. Holding her close with one arm, he laid his hand on her throat, as if to feel the pulse beating there. Then his fingers moved upward, exploring the texture of her hair while with his tongue he lightly traced the shape of her lips. Her desire, banked but glowing all evening, erupted in flames.

She put her hand inside his shirt, and as she laid it over his thundering heart, her fingers brushed wiry hair and the bump of a nipple. He groaned in his throat and thrust his tongue deep into her mouth in a symbol of possession that caused a spasm deep within her.

She whispered, "No!" against his lips, and pushed him away with her hand still on his bare chest. She had to stop this thing that was happening. It was not fair to him. It would be disastrous if they followed where their senses were leading them. Her lips quivered but were silent, and he kissed her again. And that was what she really wanted.

His hand moved lovingly down from her scalp, across her ear and over her shoulder, down to the curve of her breast. She gasped at the sweet urgency of her response as he caressed it. She wanted his fingers on her bare breast. In another moment, her control would be gone and she would unbutton her blouse.

"No, Armand, no!" Her heartbeat was so loud in her ears that she did not immediately hear what he said when he released her and straightened, with a sigh that expressed both his pleasure and regret.

"I better go, then, *chére*—while I still can."

She heard her involuntary sound of regret, and he said tenderly, "Our time will come, my pretty mud hen."

"No, Armand, I'm afraid not." But for the first time she envied those women who followed their impulses without stopping to count the cost.

"You are afraid to love?"

"Love?" She shook her head helplessly. "Oh, Armand, we are too different!"

"Are we?" he asked. "In ways that really matter?"

"You don't know—" she began, and was unable to go on. How could she tell him how she felt, when he did not even guess how very different their backgrounds were? He would think she was telling him he was inferior, and she liked his sense of self-worth because she knew that in his own world it was well deserved.

She stumbled from the car and walked swiftly away from him, as he leaped out to accompany her. She didn't wait for him to catch up with her, but shut the door quickly, almost in panic, and listened as he walked slowly away.

The chorus of the frogs shrilled in the night until the sound of his departing car drowned them out.

CHAPTER FIVE

THE NEXT MORNING Jessica met Dr. Chris in the hallway just outside his office. "Good morning, Jessica," he said. "Did you see that letter in last night's daily about crab pot thievery in the bayous?"

Jessica's heart gave a startled leap. "Yes, I saw it."

"Armand surprised me."

She felt a curious discomfort in hearing Armand's name. Here in the Marine Biological facility, sitting high on its foundation pilings with its scientific laboratories and orderly classrooms, she seemed to be on a different planet from the private world inhabited by Armand and his voluble, demonstrative family. Somehow she hadn't been expecting the two worlds to overlap.

But she didn't wonder that Armand's letter had caught Chris's attention. The work the marine biologists were doing was important to the fishing industry, and relations between the scientists and the Fishermen's Alliance were friendly.

"Why were you surprised?"

"Don't get me wrong. It was a good letter. The crabbers have a serious problem, and Armand addressed it thoughtfully. I've always found him to be a solid, responsible sort of guy," Chris said, "but I'd heard he was practically illiterate."

Solid. Responsible. The swelling warmth in Jessica's breast blossomed into a fondness for Dr. Chris. "Someone wrote it for him?" she suggested.

"I suppose so," Chris said, not picking up on her clue. "His kid brother's in school. When he's not on Armand's boat. But a kid didn't write that letter."

"His sisters must have gone to school." The notion had just occurred to Jessica. Why hadn't Armand asked one of those pretty dark-haired women to help him with his letter? Or their husbands? She'd bet that Jonquile and Maurice could read and write English at some level.

The suspicion that Armand had been seeking an excuse to see her again stole into her mind. Was he that attracted to her? A smile curved her mouth.

Dr. Chris was looking at her curiously, and she realized she had just told him that she had been seeing Armand. She felt heat flow to her face.

But Chris said only, "I wonder what Armand means to propose the crabbers do?"

Jessica wondered, too. Her feelings were ambiguous, hovering between a secret pride in Armand and humiliation at his limitations. And why was she so sensitive to what other people thought of him? Armand apparently felt no humiliation. He simply went after what he wanted, undaunted by the obstacles in his path. She admired him for that.

"It'll be interesting to find out what happens at that meeting," she said. "See you later, Chris." She walked on to the lecture room, where a new group of students awaited her, college majors with some graduate students in marine biology who had been oriented by the faculty director and were now ready for field study.

Twelve young faces regarded her with expressions ranging from shy interest to bold appraisal. The group changed every three weeks during the season, and yet remained essentially the same, except that this time there were two young women, who looked both excited and wary. Jessica wondered how they would have reacted to the encounter with bottomless marsh mud the day her last field group had gone out with Armand LeBlanc. They couldn't have been more panicked than that young man she had had to almost push into the mud!

How would they have reacted to Armand?

From the back of the room came a whistle, subdued, but definitely sexy, and a ripple of tentative laughter spread through the class.

"Thank you, I think," Jessica said. She allowed herself a small grin, then tossed her gold ponytail over her shoulder and began her lecture in a brisk voice.

It was not until noon when she opened her purse in the cafeteria to pay for her shrimp gumbo that Jessica remembered the letter she had tucked in it the evening before. She couldn't believe she had let a letter from Russ remain unopened for almost twenty-four hours. She ripped open the envelope, thinking that he had probably written to tell her he was coming to Louisiana with her parents.

Several of her new crop of students were behind her, filling their trays, but they passed her with diffident nods and she didn't ask them to join her. Dr. Chris and the director entered the cafeteria, and Jessica quickly scanned her letter, knowing they would probably eventually arrive at her table.

As usual, Russell had typed the letter on his office stationery. She skipped quickly through paragraphs describing his recent activities and came to the one that read, "I regret that I can't make the trip to Louisiana with your folks, but I'll try to get away later in the spring. I'd rather come by myself, anyway. Time we had some privacy, agreed?''

Once that last question would have triggered erotic memories of other private moments and an overwhelming desire to see him, but today it was nothing but words on the page—and that was frightening. What was happening to her?

"Mind if we join you?" Director Tarbell asked, setting down his tray.

"Please do."

"My wife has written to invite your parents to be our houseguests," he said. "We're looking forward to their visit."

"So am I. It's very kind of you to put them up."

"It's not kind, at all. I suggested it so I can monopolize your father's time, and pick his brain. He's tops in his field, as you know. You're fortunate to have been trained by him."

"I know." Smiling, Jessica tucked Russ's letter back in her purse and resolutely put him out of her mind as she moved her tray to make room for Dr. Chris.

But that night, when she was alone in her little house on the bayou, Russ stole back into her thoughts. They had known each other since childhood, because their parents were friends and had established a custom of spending holidays together before their children were born. Skiing in Vermont at Christmastime. Summers on Fire Island. They'd even driven across the continent together one year to Yellowstone National Park.

She and Russ could have hated each other, but they had grown up best friends. Norm, Jessica's brother, was younger. He and Russ had never hit it off. Although Jessica and Russ had gone to different prep schools and eventually to different colleges, they had kept in close touch.

It occurred to her that sharing memories going all the way back to their first Christmases was not necessarily a reason to marry. But something else had compelled Jessica.

On one of those holidays, when they were in college, she and Russ had engaged in some sexual experimentation. Looking back on how it all began, Jessica thought that both of them had been rather embarrassed by their virginity, and there had been no one they trusted more to change that situation than each other.

Whatever the reason, they had begun a love affair that had lasted through several Christmas and summer vacations. The assumption of everyone, including their families, was that it eventually would progress to marriage.

Jessica, who loathed the idea of promiscuity, wondered if her promise to marry Russ was not largely a result of the fact that they had become lovers. Less naive now, she was willing to concede that a woman's first lover was not necessarily Mr. Right, although she still thought that would be ideal.

On the other hand, the absorbing interest she was developing in a certain sexy fisherman was completely unrealistic. Even if she eventually discovered that her scruples were guiding her into the wrong marriage, she told herself, a gorgeous but illiterate fisherman was not the man to take Russell's place.

She resolved that she would not see Armand or his exuberantly affectionate family again.

RESOLUTIONS WERE MADE to be broken, Jessica admitted, as she stood beside Armand at the wheel of his fishing boat and watched the stars fade as the *Cajun Pride* moved down the bayou toward Terrebonne Bay.

It was six o'clock on Saturday morning. The windows were lowered in the small half-circular wheelhouse, letting in the fresh morning air. The light over the wetlands was a pearly gray; under it the cordgrass was almost black. The boat's engine was the only sound in a vast silent world, and even it seemed muted by the empty desolation of the marsh.

Jessica knew the appearance of emptiness was completely misleading. Beneath the blackened bent grass, the marsh teemed with life, much of it just beginning, because the marsh served as a nursery for the creatures of the sea.

The aroma of fresh coffee drifted up from the engine housing where Etienne was brewing it on a hot plate. It mingled with the harsh odor of engine fuel and salty smells of sea grass and mud, as well as the faint aroma of wet fur and feathers and decaying grasses that was the complex fragrance of the marsh. It was a distinctive odor that always recalled for her the happy explorations with her father when she was still a teenager. Jessica inhaled it with intense pleasure.

The solid presence beside her of Armand's body in a white cotton T-shirt and tight chino pants, not quite touching her but sending signals of awareness that bounced off her body like sonar, added to her extraordinary feeling of well-being.

She had not been able to say no to his invitation to go out with him on his boat. "Fishing?" she'd queried. "The season isn't open on shrimps, is it?"

"*Non.* First comes the blessing of the fleet," he told her, "an' we can't fish the inshore waters until May."

"Then why are you going out?"

"Etienne and me, we go scouting, so we know where are the shrimps, and how big, anh? And a scientist should know somet'ing about the industry, no?"

"A scientist should," she'd agreed, capitulating to the warm appeal she saw in his lively brown eyes. After all, Etienne would be with them, she reasoned, to excuse her failure of resolution. And it was important for her to learn more about what marine biology could do for the fishing industry. She was sure Director Tarbell and Dr. Chris would both agree with her, although she had failed to mention the weekend invitation at the lab.

The sun's rays shot above the eastern horizon in a golden fan and the dark cord grass was immediately given texture and line.

"There's a haze of green this morning," Jessica said in wonder. "It wasn't there two days ago."

"New growth at the roots," Armand said. "See?" He pointed.

It was true. Tender shoots of a light fresh green were springing up between the decaying blades of grass.

"It's spring," Armand said. "See that marsh wren? She's carrying a blade of grass in her beak—"

"*He's* carrying it," Jessica said. "It's the male wren who starts the nest. He may build a half-dozen sloppy versions before he finds a female who will take over and finish one for him. Nobody knows why he does that."

"Nobody?" The corners of Armand's mouth turned upward. "I know."

"Then tell me so I can inform the scientific world," she said dryly.

"It's simple. He's saying, 'Look, *ma'am'selle*, it's nesting time and I'm here if you want a few *bébés*."

She laughed. "You may be right."

"But, yes, I'm right!"

A faint honking in the sky drew their gazes. High above them, barely discernible in the yellow sky, was the V of a flock of geese winging their way toward Canada.

"Beautiful, anh?" Armand said. His arm swept the horizon. "A sea of grass."

A sea of grass. She recalled the day she and her students had gone out on his *Cajun Pride* and her impression then that the marsh was like a dark sea. It pleased her that Armand, who could neither read poetry nor write it, had come up with the same beautifully apt simile. He, too, had seen that the bent and broken blades of six-foot *Spartina* had formed ridges in the endless marsh that imitated the swells of the ocean.

Winding through the grass were bayous and little lakes that were as smooth as mirrors, reflecting the bright sky. Jessica lifted her face to the warm sun and expelled her breath in a long sigh. She realized that she was completely happy.

"I have t'ings to show you, anh?" Armand seemed to know what she was feeling. His face was alight with eager interest and his enthusiasm moved her like a physical touch. She had never felt this sharing of her interest in the peculiar landscape that was a salt marsh with anyone except her father.

"My father is going to enjoy this," she told Armand.

"We'll take him out, anh? They call us 'swamp rats,' you know," he said, "people who live off the marsh? *Pépère*—my *grandpère*—says we had to grow webbed feet to survive."

"He was a fisherman, too, you told me."

"Yes, before he get too old. An' in the winter—before fishing season open—he trap' the muskrat and the mink for the hides? He maybe trap the fur coat your *grandmère* wore, anh?" He touched her arm and she wondered how two fingers on her bare skin could carry a sensual current that she felt flow through her whole body.

Jessica moved just beyond his reach. Armand was a wonderful friend, but she reminded herself that he could never be more than that.

The change in his face was subtle, but she had the impression he knew exactly why she had moved.

Etienne came up with three mugs of coffee. He gave them each a mug, then took his own to the stern, where he had Armand's shrimp net spread out on the deck, checking it for broken strands.

"How did you tear your net?" Jessica asked Armand, after a few swallows of hot coffee. "Did you catch a big finfish in it?"

"A turtle."

"That would tear it! Do you catch many sea turtles?"

"Not many, me, because I fish inshore. But a few. If she's heavy, she tears up my net. If she's not heavy enough, she can drown."

"Like the porpoises."

"Exactly. I caught one on the last day of the season, and she dumped a fine catch of shrimps for me."

For some reason the eager pleasure had drained from her face, leaving her looking rather pale. Was she that distressed about the drowned sea creatures? he wondered. Or was it something else? He yearned to understand her. He said, "My boat, she's small. When I get a bigger one, I'll have to use a TED."

"A turtle excluder device?"

"You know about those, anh?"

"Of course. The turtle's weight opens a trapdoor. It saves her life."

"And those door boards let half my catch out, too. It'll be worse when my big boat, she's finished. But I'll stay out longer and my catch will be bigger."

She pushed aside a wisp of pale hair that had fallen across her face, and studied him. "That's your dream, isn't it?"

His look was quizzical. She had asked him before if he wanted to be a fisherman all his life. "It's no dream. It's w'at I am. Does it bother you that I fish for a living?" he asked her.

Her eyes slid away from his. "The men at the lab are saying that there are too many shrimp boats out there. That if there were fewer boats going out in season, you'd each make more money."

He shrugged. "That's true. The men going out—they're not all fishermen. But LeBlanc men have done nothing else. I'll always catch shrimps."

He was steering the boat in close to a bank where a narrow strip of mud shore separated the bayou from last year's broken grass. "We check the *bébé* crabs, anh?"

They could see them from the deck of the *Cajun Pride*, a platoon of tiny fiddlers scurrying over the mud bank to hide themselves among the black stalks and fresh green soots of grass. Armand had set his controls to keep the boat idling in position just off the bank. Etienne left his net and joined them at the side of the boat to watch.

In seconds the mud bank was bare of any living thing except a grasshopper that dropped from the stalk of grass to which it had been clinging. A lone egret rose with a baby crab's legs protruding from his beak and flapped graceful wings over their heads.

Armand's hand dropped on Jessica's shoulder and pressed it lightly. She leaned toward him, sharing the moment.

"Have you seen the male fiddlers do their mating dance?" she asked him.

"Anh! That one! He's a sight in summer, no? When he stands up and waves his fiddle an' pokes his big eyes up on stalks?"

"I could watch them for hours."

"We come back this summer, anh?"

The sun was still short of the meridian when Etienne demanded, "Hey, when do we eat?" Armand sent him back to the wheelhouse for the plastic cooler containing the picnic Mrs. LeBlanc had prepared for them. They sat crosslegged on the deck to eat crisp fried chicken, crusty homemade rolls and thin slices of pecan pie.

Etienne mumbled, his mouth full of pie, "I like it better before the mosquitoes come. You tell us, Professor. Where do they come from? One day there's none, and the next day the water's full of little wigglies, hatching like lice."

"The eggs stay buried in the cool mud until the spring floods wash them out. Then they turn into the swimming larvae you see, and when it warms up, they hatch."

"You've studied the little devils, anh?" Armand said. "But Etienne and me, we know them from sad experience."

"They bite scientists, too," Jessica said, laughing.

Armand listened to the sound of her laughter with a deep pleasure. When she was happy like this, her eyes were a warm blue that spread a blanket of contentment around her. He would like to keep her happy always, if he could.

THEY DROPPED OFF Etienne at the LeBlanc house before going to have dinner at a Cajun family restaurant up the bayou. While Armand showered, Jessica sat in the kitchen visiting, mostly by means of smiles and nods, with Armand's mother, who insisted on brewing coffee for her.

When he came out, freshly shaved and dressed in a clean shirt and chinos, he looked wonderful. His curling black hair was still damp and his skin glowed. Jessica knew she couldn't keep her pleasure out of her eyes. They sat at the kitchen table and drank coffee with Mrs. LeBlanc before they left to drive across the bayou to Jessica's house.

She told Armand to entertain himself while she showered and dressed. "There's some wine in the refrigerator, and a *National Geographic* there—" she began, before she thought.

Embarrassed, she escaped into the bathroom. Well, he could look at the pictures, couldn't he?

While she stood under a stream of tepid water—she had found that shower temperature the most comfortable in this climate because it didn't leave her overheated—her thoughts dwelt on the day she had just spent with Armand.

There had been a rapport between them deeper than she had found with any of her fellow scientists. Not since she had explored the marshes with her father had she enjoyed a day more. Armand's study of the environment had been self-directed, but his devotion to it matched hers. And there was that added excitement of sharing an activity she loved with a person she—

Oh, no! She was not falling in love with Armand. She couldn't love a man who could neither read nor write! Desperately she called up Russell's image.

WHEN JESSICA ENTERED the room, the sweet fragrance of flowers came with her. Armand looked up from the pictures of colorfully dressed African natives that had caught his interest. He wondered if his friend, Jocko, the black musician, had seen them. Wooee! Wilder than the Mardi Gras!

Jessica was wearing a sleeveless dress of a pale color that reminded him of violets and that made her skin and her flowing hair glow with golden lights. He dropped the magazine and got to his feet.

"You're beautiful, *chère*," he breathed. A look came into her eyes that squeezed his heart. He took a long step and put his arms around her. She melted into them.

When he felt the softness of her breasts against his chest, all caution fled. He dug his fingers into her hair to tilt her head, and kissed her lips. They were soft and warm. She made a sound in her throat, and her arms slid around his waist, holding him tight.

His thumbs moved over her cheeks, caressing them. Her hands slipped under his knit shirt and she pressed her palms hard against his bare back, where he felt their imprint like a burning brand.

He raised his head long enough to take in a great gulp of air, and intoxicated by the fragrance of her hair and her skin, kissed her again. Still kissing her, he put one arm under her knees and with the other around her shoulders, carried her to the sofa and sat down with her on his lap.

Jessica gasped as she felt his hard arousal. But he gave her no chance to escape. His mouth still on hers, he curled the fingers of one hand around her breast with great tenderness. When he brushed her nipple through the fabric of her dress, her excitement was intense.

Her hands moved up his back, exploring its muscles and hollows. His shirt was riding up on her arms, and he wore nothing under it. Suddenly her breasts were crushed against his bare chest. She pulled away from his kiss to see what she had exposed, and followed an impulse to lay her cheek against the dark wedge of curly hair and flick her tongue over the nipple buried there.

"Ah, chère, J' t'aime, j' t'aime," he said in his throat, softly caressing her knee, then moving his hand up her thigh.

Oh, God, she thought, *I can't let this happen. I'll hurt him.*

But she wanted to be close to him, wanted to be swallowed up in his arms and his kisses...she was losing all sense...and if something, somebody didn't stop her...

The phone rang.

She did not have to understand French to know Armand was cursing fervently. "Don' answer, *chère.*"

She held him tighter, unwilling to return to the real world. But a thought nagged at her, penetrating her dazed mind. "It could be my mother," she said.

"She can call again."

Jessica sat up, pulling away from him. "She said she would call tonight to give me their flight number. I have to answer it."

Reluctantly he let her go; reluctantly she got up.

She picked up the telephone. "Hello?"

"You're home," her mother said crisply. "I've called several times."

"I'm sorry, Mother. I just got in. I've been out in the marsh all day." She glanced over at Armand, still feeling out of herself. His lips looked flushed and his eyes had a faraway expression.

"Working? Today?"

"No, not working. Out with a—a friend who has a boat."

"Oh?" Her mother's antennae had picked up something revealing in her voice. When she spoke again, she sounded studiedly casual. "One of the biologists?"

"No." Jessica looked again at Armand, who was smiling broadly at her. This time she heard the surge of warmth that colored her voice, as she said, "You'll meet him when you come down." She regretted that her mother was hearing it, too, but she had been unable to repress it.

After a tiny pause, her mother said, "He's not from the lab? What does he do?"

"He's a fisherman."

"A—fisherman?" There was another slight pause, a little longer this time. Just as Jessica was about to break the silence, which was growing uncomfortable, her mother said, "I haven't heard from Russ lately."

"I have," Jessica said quickly. "He isn't coming with you."

"Oh, too bad."

"He wants to come later."

"That's all right, then. Have you a pencil, dear? Here's our flight number."

Jessica wrote down the information. "I'll meet you at the New Orleans airport and take you to the Tarbells'. They're expecting you."

"I know. I've had a nice note from Louise. I can't wait, darling," her mother said, without changing tone.

"Give my love to Daddy, and Norm. I'm glad you're coming," Jessica replied, and hung up.

She turned back to Armand. He patted the sofa beside him, but she shook her head. "No more kisses, Armand."

"W'y not? You enjoyed them, no?"

"Too much," she said, wrinkling her nose at him, and he laughed. She looked at Armand's smiling lips, at his firm jaw and chin with a hint of a cleft, at the shapely dark brows above his brown eyes, and hoped her intimate—very intimate—thoughts did not show in her face.

"Who's Norm?"

"My brother."

"Is he a scientist, too?"

"Yes. A research physicist."

"He's the one who isn't coming?"

"No," she said, then quickly added, "Norm's not coming."

Armand felt the distance that had opened between them during the conversation with her mother and wondered about it. He knew her answer had been evasive. He wondered, not for the first time, whether there was another man. He had not been able to forget her saying that she was a tourist in his world.

With Nance Marie and other Cajun girls he had grown up with, he had little difficulty in figuring out what they were thinking. With Jessica it was impossible, she was so cool and self-possessed. What was she thinking now? Why was he so sure she was his woman, when she was a mystery to him?

Her head was lowered and her hair hid most of her face. He was on the point of asking her directly who was coming later, when she said, in a tentative voice, "Did you say you wanted to learn to read and write?"

"I'm s'pose' to be goin' to a class in Houma two nights a week."

" 'Supposed to'?"

He shrugged. "It's a half-hour drive—not so much, anh? But t'ings always come up." Like coming here, he thought, but did not say.

"Maybe . . ." She hesitated. "Could I help you?"

Surprised, he asked, "You mean you'd teach me?"

She nodded.

"Here?"

"Yes."

Her face was very serious. He sensed that her concern was for him, and he was filled with such joy that he thought he could not contain it. For a moment he could not speak.

She said, "It's more important than you realize, Armand. If you can read and write, you can achieve anything you want. You can get an equivalency high school diploma that will let you enroll in a college of your choice—"

"Hey!" he said. "W'at do I want with college? They don' give a degree in fishin', do they?"

Her expression froze. "Sorry," she said, in a clipped voice. "I guess I was carried away."

Somehow he had said the wrong thing. But *college*?

He stood up and walked toward her. "But I'll take you up on those lessons, Professor," he said warmly. "With you teachin' me, I guarantee I can learn to read and write. When do we start?"

Jessica saw the eager light in his eyes, and her heart turned over. "Soon," she promised. "Very soon."

Her parents were coming, and it was suddenly important to her that Armand not make a bad impression when they met.

"I t'ink I promised you dinner, Professor," he said.

CHAPTER SIX

WHILE SHE ATE her breakfast, Jessica looked over the materials she had picked up at the parish library the evening before. The literacy program seemed quite elementary to her, and she wondered how far along Armand had gone with the lessons. Perhaps she should just start at the beginning, although she hoped that would not be necessary. Surely he must have some knowledge of the written word!

It was depressing to remember that he could not write his name, but encouraging that he signed his checks with a distinctive monogram instead of simply with an X. She looked up the telephone number listed for the LeBlancs and dialed it, hoping Claire or Armand himself would answer.

"'*Allo?*" It was Mrs. LeBlanc.

"Mrs. LeBlanc, this is Jessica Owens. Is Armand there?"

A flood of mingled Cajun French and incomprehensible English answered her, its tone warm and welcoming.

Helplessly she listened, then said, "I'm sorry. Claire?"

"Ah, Claire! *Oui!*"

Presently Claire said, "Hello, Jessica."

"I did make myself understood, then?"

"Mama understands English much better than she speaks it," Claire said, and giggled.

That was an understatement, Jessica thought.

"Armand left early this mornin' for N'Orl'ns. Do you want him to call you when he gets back?"

"Yes, please. Tell him I have the literacy workbooks. Did he tell you I offered to teach him to read?"

"That's great!" Claire said. "If anyone can get learnin' through that hard head, you can."

"It won't be difficult if he's serious about wanting to learn."

"Oh, he's serious, all right. And when he decides he wants something, he finds a way to get it." She giggled again. "You could take that as a warnin', *chére.*"

"How's *your* love life?" Jessica asked in a cool voice.

"Messed up, as usual," Claire admitted cheerfully. "I'll tell lover boy you called."

Now that she had committed herself, Jessica was having doubts. Was Armand's enthusiasm for the lessons inspired by the excuse they gave him to see her? Claire's teasing suggested that possibility. And how could she stay out of his arms if he came almost every night to study with her? She would have to make it very plain—no kissing the teacher.

Armand didn't call before he showed up on her porch that very evening. Her heart leaped when she saw his tall silhouette and his white smile through the dusk at her screen door. She had meant to keep her distance, but as soon as she let him in she found herself enveloped in a loving hug. Their lips just naturally met, and she marveled that with all the time he had occupied her thoughts she could have forgotten how sweet and seductive his kisses were. She must *not* kiss him!

She made herself break away and say, "Students don't kiss their teacher, Armand. You'll have to remember that we're just friends, and you are here to work."

"But after work?" he suggested, his gaze moving admiringly over her.

She had just showered and was wearing a pink tank top and white shorts. It was an outfit she wore to the lab when she was going on one of the boats, but his rapt expression made her feel she had too little on.

She said tartly, "You mean after you've learned to read and write?"

He groaned.

"I can't help you, otherwise. Do you understand, Armand?"

"I'm moving too fast?"

She could control her expression, but she could not prevent the heat she felt rising to her face. "*No* moves, Armand! You're here to work."

"I'll give you all the time you need, *chére*," he said softly, "but it's not easy."

It would not be easy for her, either, with him looking at her in that tender rueful way, pretending to misunderstand her, while she longed to brush back the dark curl that tumbled over his forehead.

She turned and led him to the kitchen where she had laid out the beginner's workbook for him on the table. "Can you read at all?" she asked him. "You must recognize highway and navigation signs?"

"On my boat, I don' need signs. I've got my radio. I can talk to anybody out there any time I want."

"Do you talk to other fishermen in French or English?"

"Mostly French." He grinned. "We keep our secrets, anh?"

She opened the workbook and checked his knowledge of the alphabet and its English pronunciations, emphasizing the *th* sound. She discovered that although he knew both French and English names for each object pictured, he had no idea how either was spelled. She put Vivaldi's *The Four Seasons* on the stereo, and set him to copying the alphabet in print, and then pronouncing the sound of each letter.

"I've done this before," he commented, "in kindergarten."

"Then it will go faster."

"Yes, ma'am." The glint in his eyes mocked her teacherish tone.

It went very fast. They covered several lessons, and over ice cream and a slice of the coconut cake she had bought for an after-lesson treat, they decided, encouraged, that he would come three times a week.

"How did the meeting of the Fishermen's Alliance go?" she asked him, when that was settled.

"Fine. We talked of many things."

"What did you suggest as an improvement over shooting the thieves?"

He loved her when she slyly teased him in her crisp but soft Northern voice. She made her point, but was never sarcastic. "I said the crab fishermen must every one put his mark on his cages in a bright color, and every one must use a different color. Like branding cattle, anh? Some do that now."

"Yes," she said doubtfully, "I suppose that would make it easier to catch the thieves."

"But yes! Then I said we must find more money for the sheriff so he can put a bigger water patrol on the bayous. For that we may have go to Baton Rouge. To our legislators," he explained.

"I suppose you'll want more letters written for you," she said resignedly.

"And who can do that better than my teacher, anh?"

He had offered no information about why he had driven to the city. "Claire said you went to New Orleans today."

"Yes. I went with Nance Marie to see a man about playing his club."

She felt a constriction in her throat. "You and Nance Marie?" How close were they, really? She wanted to ask, but couldn't bring herself to utter the words.

"And all the band," he said, confusing her. Had they *all* gone to New Orleans? Or was he talking about playing in the club?

"Did he hire you?"

He was spooning the last of his ice cream and didn't seem to notice her stiffness. "We don't know if we'll get the job. But I t'ink yes. He likes zydeco."

"If you go to New Orleans—" Her throat closed, and she began again. "What about your lessons?"

"They'll wait 'til we come back. I need money to equip my boat. I need a new CB radio—"

"I see," Jessica said, "that learning to read isn't as important to you as fishing."

"Fishing is my livelihood," he reminded her gently.

She felt reproached, and she was immediately remorseful. "Of course it is. I'm sorry!" But didn't he realize how important learning was to his future?

"Sorry for w'at? I'll miss you, too."

Again she felt heat rise to her cheeks. "I didn't mean—"

Armand grinned, and she closed her mouth abruptly. She thought that it was a pity Russ was not coming with her parents—and then with a feeling of panic realized she was glad he was not. She wasn't ready to see Russ when her feelings about the Cajun fisherman were so confused.

She said abruptly, "Armand, your sisters can read and write, can't they? And Marie and Danielle's husbands? Didn't they all learn to read?"

"They went to school, yes."

"Why didn't you ask one of them to help you write to the editor?"

"When I can put my hands on a real professor?" he asked, with a grin.

She was not sure whether his double meaning was deliberate or not, but his wording was far too apt. She was tempted to pick up on it and begin his lessons in grammar by pointing out his questionable use of a figure of speech, but she hastily reconsidered the idea. The less they talked about his putting his hands on her, the better!

"They can write a letter, yes," Armand said. "But it wouldn't have been a good letter, and maybe not so many important fishermen come, anh?" He tapped his temple. "I t'ink about dat."

"*Thh*ink about *thh*at," she said, in her most teacherish voice.

His smile was indulgent. "*Thh*ink about *thh*at," he repeated, and leaned forward so quickly to kiss her that their noses bumped.

She jerked away. "Armand!"

"I won't do it again," he promised, but he looked very pleased with himself.

"I hope you mean that." Jessica closed the workbook between them with a little slap, and stood up, signaling the end of the lesson.

Armand's *au revoir* was perfectly circumspect, but the glint was back in his eyes, making her suspect he was secretly laughing at her. She had decided more than once to put him out of her life—and here she was committed to teach him to read and write! What was she to do about him?

ON SATURDAY Jessica lunched in Houma with Louise Tarbell, who wanted to talk with her about how best to entertain her mother and what foods she and Jessica's father preferred.

"No problem," Jessica told her. "They both love seafood, and what they've tasted of Cajun cooking. They're looking forward to some fabulous eating experiences down here."

"Of course, they've been in New Orleans before," Louise said.

"Yes, and loved it. But they're not expecting to find gourmet food down here in bayou country. They're in for a pleasant surprise."

They discussed the quality of various restaurants they knew and the restored plantation mansions in the area open to tours. Louise asked about Patricia Owen's hobby.

"It's early in the year for butterflies...I don't know much about it, but I imagine the swamps are difficult hunting grounds."

"Mother's practice doesn't allow her to go out with a net much anymore. She just enjoys her mounted butterflies and seeing other great collections. Or talking to other collectors."

"I'll see what I can find here for her."

When they parted after lunch, Jessica decided to spend an hour shopping while she was in town. In the department store where she purchased three pairs of panty hose, she heard her name called and turned to see Armand's sister Marie smiling widely at her. She was the married sister who had no children, Jessica remembered.

Marie was buying a dress length of silky blue cotton. "Do you like the color?" she asked. "I'm going to make it up for Claire."

"It's a beautiful shade. How lucky she is to have a sister who can sew. Is it for her birthday?"

"Oh, no, I'm just trying to cheer her up. She's so miserable."

"Claire is miserable?" Jessica exclaimed. "With all the admirers she has?"

"She's trying to forget the one she sent away. But I don't think she's succeeding. A pity, anh?"

The one she sent away... Jessica was suddenly intensely curious to know what had happened, and if it had anything to do with that fight on the dance floor at the *fais-do-do*. But her innate reserve kept her from asking questions. She said, "Claire certainly won't be unhappy about the new dress."

Marie looked pleased. "Mama is so glad that you are teaching English to Armand. We all are."

"He's a good pupil," Jessica said.

She left Marie waiting for her material to be wrapped, and walked to where she'd left her car. The encounter had left her feeling warmed and happy. There was something about the LeBlancs that enabled them to do that.

The days before her parents' arrival went by in a blur of activity. Jessica welcomed another group of students. By the time they were ready for field trips, her father would be there to accompany them, and she was looking forward to that. But she had butterflies in her stomach about introducing Armand to her parents. She wanted more than she would admit for him to make a good impression on them.

Would they see the man she knew and admired, a man who passionately loved life and his small piece of the earth, a man with a song on his lips and a sense of humor, who respected his parents and worried about his young brother and his sisters, and who cared about his fellow fishermen?

Or would they simply see a man who in thirty years had learned neither to read nor to write?

She worried, too, that Armand was becoming bored with his lessons, and she was not surprised when one night he threw down his pen and said, "I'm tired of these stories that don' tell me anything I don' know!"

"I'm sorry about that," Jessica said. "I realize that your own life has more excitement than these little stories. But they were written to tell refugees from Vietnam and other places things they need to know about America. I promise you more excitement when you've mastered the basic tools."

"The Viet don' need teaching," he said, throwing down his pen. "He knows plenty about fishin'!"

"But you know so much that they don't know about American ways."

"Then w'y must I read these hafass stories?"

"The value of the lessons to you is in helping you fix the meaning of combinations of letters in your memory."

He didn't respond to that. Instead, he followed his own thought. "Some fishermen think the Viet should stay out of our fishing grounds."

"The Vietnamese are very hard workers, I've heard."

"I guarantee! An' he's building his own boats with the help of his kin, like us. He talks his own language. Nobody but his kin can understand him on the CB."

"Keeping his secrets. Just as you and your kin have been doing for two hundred years."

"An' he's catching my shrimps, ahn?"

"Forget him. Write!" she commanded. "You must practice."

He slapped the table. "But I want to learn to *write*, not print, okay?"

"Okay," Jessica replied, meeting his gaze levelly. "Draw me a circle, moving your pen from left to right."

With a quizzical glance at her, he obeyed.

"Now draw a circle going in the other direction."

This wasn't as easy for him, but he did it.

"Now draw two half circles, one from left to right and the other from right to left." When he had done that, she said, "Practice those movements and you'll be able to do everything necessary to write script."

"Is that all there is to it?"

"It takes practice." She had not realized how difficult learning to read and write were. Once learned and the early lessons forgotten, the skills were taken for granted.

"What about readin'?" he asked. "Is there a shortcut for that?"

She had an inspiration. "Buy a newspaper. Try to read the ads. Look for ads about fishing supplies. After a while the combination of letters will begin to suggest sounds to you—"

"Like *t-h*," he said with a grin.

"And then they will make sense."

"Thh," he said, showing the red tip of his tongue, "will never make sense to me."

THEY WORKED HARD, but they couldn't make up for Armand's lost years before the arrival of Jessica's parents. The appointed day came, and she took off early from the lab to drive to New Orleans, an hour and a half away, to meet the plane from New York.

She met her parents in the VIP lounge, since they traveled first-class. Her mother entered first, a tall slender woman with cropped gray hair wearing a lightweight business suit. Jessica saw her with a familiar clutch of painful pleasure. She had always admired her mother's patrician good looks and her natural grace.

Perhaps it was her mother's habits, developed in her medical practice, that often made Jessica feel as if she were being inspected like a butterfly specimen on a pin.

Now was one of those times. Patricia Owen came toward Jessica, smiling with her lips but with a familiar appraising look in her eyes. It must be, Jessica thought, much like the one she turned on her patients.

"Mother." They embraced lightly, barely touching cheeks. "How was your flight?"

"Fine, dear. You're looking a little thin, Jess."

"That's Dr. Owen talking. I'm fine."

Jessica's father gave her a real hug, and she felt a rush of affection for him. When he let her go, she stood back and studied him. His hair was a little grayer, perhaps, but his scholarly face was still youthful and his eyes behind their rimless glasses were fond.

She took them to the baggage retrieval area, then went for her car. "I thought we'd have dinner here in the French Quarter," she told them when she picked them up. "After that, I'll drive you to the Tarbells'."

"Where in the Quarter?" her mother asked. She had attended medical conventions in New Orleans. Her father had been here, too, but this was their first trip to Louisiana together.

"The Court of Two Sisters?" Jessica suggested.

"Wonderful!"

The ambience of the patio restaurant was uniquely New Orleans, bounded by the surrounding building, its atrium filled with flowering trees and plants, with overhanging eaves to protect the tables lining the walls when tropical rains fell. There was a trio of musicians performing against one wall. Unobtrusive waiters walked about, and a bright-feathered parrot called out raucous greetings from its cage by the kitchen door.

"Oysters, of course," said Jessica's mother. "I adore Louisiana oysters."

"Pompano *en papillotes*," said her father. "That's worth the flight. Norm sent his love, Jess."

"How's he doing?"

"He's reading a paper in Italy next month on his most recent research project."

"Norm's pretty young for that kind of recognition, isn't he?" Jessica asked, impressed.

"He's an Owen," her father said complacently.

As if they were all a cut above mortal, Jessica thought, with amused affection.

"Russ was absolutely crushed that he couldn't come," her mother put in. "He's involved in a big leveraged buy-out his firm is handling."

The waiter came and for a few minutes the talk was all of food and wines. Then her father began asking questions about her work at the lab, and the shoptalk lasted through the meal and most of the drive out of the city.

It was nine o'clock when Jessica drove her parents to the large Victorian house in Houma where the Tarbells lived. They were greeted warmly, their luggage transferred upstairs to a suite of rooms, and Jessica was invited to share an after-dinner drink while they discussed the agenda of the Owens' visit.

"I'll bring your father in to the lab with me in the morning," Herb Tarbell said. "Louise has something planned for your mother."

"I'm going to take her for a drive. Perhaps to Bayou Teche, Evangeline country." Louise Tarbell was a small vivacious woman with prematurely white hair.

"You know the story of Evangeline and her lover, who were separated when the French were moved out of Nova Scotia, of course. But did you know that St. Martinville on the Teche was the 'Petit Paris' established by the French nobility who fled the revolution? And that they continued their extravagant nightly balls there? Or so the legend says. Even today the town keeps a two-hundred-year-old flavor! That is, we'll go if you're not too tired, Patricia," Louise Tarbell finished.

Jessica's mother made a sound of pleasure. "No, indeed."

"I'd like to invite you to watch the blessing of the shrimp fleet from my place on Sunday," Jessica said. "The parade of boats will go right by my house, and we can take our chairs and a picnic out under the big oak tree on the bank."

"Perfect!" Louise Tarbell exclaimed. "They mustn't miss that! We'll plan on that, then."

"Will we meet your fisherman friend?" Jessica's mother asked.

Her mother would remember that! "His boat will be in the procession, I'm sure."

The Tarbells were both looking at Jessica questioningly.

"You haven't met Jessica's friend?" her mother asked them.

Jessica felt all her muscles tautening. "You know him," she told Dr. Tarbell. "You hired his trawler when the shallow-draft boat was being overhauled."

"Armand LeBlanc?" Herb Tarbell looked faintly surprised.

"LeBlance?" Jessica's father echoed. "Isn't that a French name?"

"He's a Cajun fisherman." Herb turned to his wife. "He took Jessica and her students out on his trawler one day last month."

Louise glanced at Jessica's mother, then said brightly, "He'll know people at the lab, then, won't he, Herb? I'm thinking we could invite him to the dinner I'm giving for Phil and Patricia later in the week."

"Oh, yes, everybody knows Armand! Charming fellow. Plays the accordion, I believe."

"Marvelous!" Louise said in the same bright tone. "The accordion's a popular instrument down here," she told Jessica's mother. "Typically Cajun, although I believe German immigrants introduced it. I want your folks to get some local color while they're here, Jessica."

"Armand can supply that," her husband observed.

Jessica was furious, though she kept her temper under control. She suspected her mother had written Louise Tarbell asking about her "fisherman friend."

"I think Armand wants to take them out for a special gumbo dinner—" she began. She wanted to be in control when Armand and her parents met, and the plan Louise and her mother had maneuvered her into was going to throw a public spotlight on their meeting.

"He can do that another night," her mother said.

"He will be an addition to our party." Louise rushed on. "There are so many places I want to show your mother! You can spend Saturday with us, can't you?"

Jessica could cheerfully have throttled her mother. "Yes, of course." She had promised Armand he would meet her parents, Jessica reminded herself. It was inevitable, however it turned out.

"I'll walk out to your car with you," her mother said, giving her father a meaningful look.

"I'll see you tomorrow at the lab, then," he said dutifully. "I'm very anxious to see the results of the work you've been doing down here."

"She's a fine instructor," Herb Tarbell said.

"She's much more than that," her father said so pointedly that Jessica had to laugh.

"My fond parent," she told the director, embarrassed. She had forgotten just how proud her father was of his family's reputation in scientific fields and how much he expected of her and Norm. "I'll probably have to put up with more of this kind of stuff tomorrow."

Herb Tarbell laughed. "Don't worry. We know the real you."

Outside in the warm humid night, her mother said casually, "Apparently you haven't told Dr. Tarbell that you're only temporarily in Louisiana?"

Jessica's head jerked around to stare at her. "What on earth do you mean, mother? My job here is permanent."

"You and Russell are still planning to marry, aren't you?"

Of course they were, weren't they? But Jessica didn't immediately answer her mother's question.

"Russell is making a name for himself in a very fine Wall Street firm," Patricia continued. "He told me the senior partners are very pleased with his work."

"That's wonderful," Jessica said. "But Russ can just as well sell stocks and bonds in New Orleans, can't he?"

Her mother turned a calm speculative look on her. "Undoubtedly. But I'm sure you'll admit he has more opportunities in New York. And I'm sure you can find as challenging a job nearer Wall Street. After all, your father finds plenty to study in the New Jersey salt marshes."

"Oh, mother, how old-fashioned can you be? Why should I be the one to move? Because I'm a woman? After all," Jessica said, with a touch of irritation, "I've embarked on a study of an organism that's native here. It's important to me to continue. Russ understands that."

They reached Jessica's car in silence.

"You really like it down here, don't you?" her mother observed calmly.

"Love it!"

"I've been looking forward to these next few days. Good night, Jessica," she murmured, and offered her cheek.

Jessica was seething. It was so like Patricia Owen to calmly drop the argument as if it were resolved, without giving an inch.

It was nearly midnight but still pleasantly warm when Jessica arrived at her cottage. She felt as if she had been away for a long, long time. It was almost as if she had been to New York and back, so completely had the atmosphere of her old life enveloped her. She felt tense and nervous, her muscles all knotted. Had she always felt like this at home?

Or was it the talk about her marriage and the possibility that Russ would demand that they live in New York? She thought about how very different life was on the bayous of Louisiana—complex and fascinating, but less pretentious and filled with an enjoyment of good living. Why couldn't he adapt to this life?

She looked with pleasure at her cozy living room with its well-used thrift-shop furniture and the few personal things she had added—her stereo and an Indian rug and a few bright pillows—and listened gratefully to the familiar monotony of the unceasing song of the night creatures pouring in through her screened windows.

Yes, she thought, relaxing gratefully, *I love it here*. It would do her parents good to let the good times roll, now and then, she thought, with warm recollections of her evening with Armand LeBlanc's family.

But when she tried to imagine the two families together, she couldn't quite get the picture clear.

CHAPTER SEVEN

ARMAND STOOD BACK and regarded his *Cajun Pride Too* with pure delight. All day he and Etienne and his sisters had been engaged in decorating the new boat for the procession of the blessing of the fleet. She was not equipped yet for the season, but her engine had been installed and the booms mounted. The women had cut strips of white and yellow plastic and Etienne had shinnied up the mast to tack the long streamers to its top. Down on the deck, Armand had twisted the streamers into spirals and attached them inside the rail.

Papa LeBlanc stood on the bank and directed the placing of the strips. "A little to the left, Armand! Now right...just a leetle!" he said, squeezing together his thumb and forefinger to indicate just how far. The effect, when they finished, would be that of a sort of floating striped tent.

In the kitchen, Mama made coffee and fried twisted strips of dough in deep fat to make *beignets*, which she dipped in powdered sugar. When Papa called for coffee, she carried a tray of the delicious warm bread out to the dock, and they all sat and admired their work and discussed the best way to continue.

The sun was sinking. Armand went into the house to telephone Jessica, but there was no answer at her place. He hadn't seen her since her parents arrived. He and all his male relatives had been working sixteen hours a day to get the boat finished for this weekend. He couldn't wait for Jessica to see *Cajun Pride Too*. He wanted to see her surprise, see that warm glow change the depth of color in her eyes. Besides, he had a growing hunger to hear her voice.

But she wasn't home.

They worked until dark, then went inside and sat down to a supper of Mama's gumbo filé just as the telephone rang. Claire rose immediately to answer it, but this time it was not one of her admirers. "It's for you, Armand. A woman." She returned to her seat at the table, and reported, "It's not Jessica."

"Nance Marie?"

She shook her head.

Armand got up and went to the telephone.

"Mr. Armand LeBlanc?" a strange voice said. "This is Louise Tarbell. I believe you know my husband, Dr. Tarbell."

"Yes, *'Allo*, Miz Tarbell," Armand said warmly.

"We're giving a small dinner party to welcome Jessica Owen's parents to Louisiana next Tuesday evening. We would like you to come. Jessica will be here, of course, and some others from the lab I believe you know. Can you come?"

"I'd like to, ma'am."

"Good. Tuesday evening at seven. Informal."

"Yes, thank you, ma'am." *What the hell?* he thought. *Weren't they always informal on the bayou?* He took a chance and asked, "Does Jessica happen to be there, Miz Tarbell?"

"Why, yes, she's here with her mother, Mr. LeBlanc. Hold on, please."

Over the telephone, Jessica's voice sounded much more Northern. "Hello, Armand. Can you come to the dinner party?"

"I guarantee, if it's the only way I can see you," he said warmly. In the kitchen the voices behind him fell silent, and he lowered his own voice. "I've been calling your house—"

"I haven't been home." Jessica was gripping the phone. She was uneasy about Louise Tarbell's plan to include Armand with the scientists she was inviting Tuesday evening, and was sure it was her mother's suggestion. She knew her mother had sensed her personal interest in the Cajun fisherman and was curious about him, but why not meet him privately as Jessica had suggested? Why did she want him at the Tarbells'?

"I've been spending all my time at the lab or here with my parents."

"I wish I could take y'all out on my boat tomorrow, but we'll be putting the fine touch to her for the blessing of the fleet." He paused. "I thought you might like to help."

"I'm sorry. Mrs. Tarbell is taking my mother and me to Lafayette to see some old mansions there tomorrow, and Dr. Tarbell is taking my father out."

He had been going to ask her to help plan what flowers they should use, and had pictured her surprise when she saw it was the new boat they were decorating. But if she could not come tomorrow, he would save it all for a grand surprise on Sunday. So he didn't tell her about the flowers, which had to be picked early Sunday morning, so they would be dewy fresh.

Neither did he tell her about the silk pennants Danielle was sewing to be flown from the booms and the mast, nor the new name Etienne was painting on the bow—it had been Etienne's suggestion—large enough to be read from the banks in the widest part of the bayou; nor the enormous poster of a painting of Christ that Marie and Claire were mounting on plywood and he would affix to the mast between the booms. It was going to be his most elaborate entry yet in the annual religious rite, and a lucky launch for his new boat.

"Well, we'll be finishing up Sunday morning, anyway. You'll ride with us, anh? You and your folks?"

"Oh, Armand! I've invited the Tarbells and my mother and father to view the parade from my house."

He was disappointed, and he didn't try to hide it. "We'll all be aboard," he coaxed, "and the band will play."

"On your boat?"

"Yes!"

Then Nance Marie would be on the *Cajun Pride* with them, Jessica realized, and felt an intense longing to be with him and his lively family on that day.

"Everybody's coming with us." Without covering the receiver, he called, "Claire an' her boyfriend, Henny— anybody else, Claire?"

Jessica heard a giggle. "Maybe René will come."

"You crazy? Not on my boat, *chére*!" To Jessica, he said, "I can make room for all your guests, anh?"

Jessica wondered how he could accommodate so many. She was very conscious of her mother and Louise Tarbell standing at the kitchen sink preparing vegetables for their dinner and listening to her conversation. She said somewhat coolly, "I think my parents would enjoy seeing the whole fleet pass by, Armand . . . thanks, anyway."

She could feel his disappointment traveling across the wires to merge with her own, but he agreed, "It's something they must see, no?"

"We'll be watching for your boat," she told him.

"She'll be the sweetheart of the fleet, I guarantee!" he bragged.

"Yo!" Etienne called from the table.

He lowered his voice. "No lessons this week, anh? When do I see you?"

She hesitated.

Armand waited, hearing his heart beat in the still kitchen. Everyone at the big round table was listening. When her voice came, it sounded very reserved. "I'll see you Tuesday night."

"Not until Tuesday?" The cooler she sounded, the more he wanted to break through that reserve to the warm loving woman he had glimpsed beneath it. He had a sudden sharp longing to hold her soft body in his arms, feel her breasts crushed against him.

"I'm afraid not."

"Okay," he said. "Tuesday, then."

He hung up thoughtfully. The visit of her parents was changing her, and for the first time his confidence was dented as he saw that his pursuit of the lovely professor could run into more problems than he had imagined. There was much he didn't know about her. Perhaps it wasn't her brother who was coming later, after all?

Had he found his woman, only to discover that he was too late?

No, he couldn't be mistaken about her response to him. And would she have taken on the almost impossible task of making a reader of him if she didn't care?

Her face came vividly before him as it looked sometimes across her kitchen table, intent on him and deeply concerned, as she pronounced for him the sounds of the letters he was learning to recognize more easily. A deep yearning that was more than desire was causing him an embarrassing erotic arousal. Etienne would spot that in a minute, the little cabbage! Probably Claire would, too.

He delayed returning to the table to finish his supper until he could control his passionate response to Jessica's cool voice. *Mon Dieu,* but he had it bad!

Jessica's neighbors had marked the boundaries of their share of the bayou bank with ribbons that stretched from stakes driven in on the bayou side of the road that ran in front of their houses to stakes at the bayou's edge. Since the families on each side of her had done this, Jessica's own viewing space was marked off, also. She carried her kitchen chairs out and grouped them under the great oak that spread shade on the bank.

The water was still and dark, with a dusty-looking surface that reflected the oak tree, the small pier and the lush growth of vine-tangled trees and shrubs on the opposite bank.

Next door, her landlord's guests had already arrived and were gathered around a table spread with newspapers to receive the crayfish from the iron pot that was coming to a boil over firewood in his front yard.

At about ten-thirty, Director Tarbell's car rolled to a stop in the driveway behind Jessica's Rabbit. Her father got out and opened the car doors for Mrs. Tarbell and her mother. Patricia Owen looked up and down the street with a keen appraising glance at the row of small houses, each with its dock fingering out into the bayou across the road.

"Darling, how quaint! It's charming."

Jessica took them into her house, which she had spent some time scrubbing up for their arrival. The furniture, scarred by years of use, still shone with the polish she had given it. Over the nondescript sofa, she had hung a painting by a New Mexico artist that matched her Indian rug, and she had arranged a bowl of huge magnolia blossoms on the table beside her stereo.

"The whole house is about the size of your room at home," her father observed, looking around with a bemused smile.

"I'm not here much of the time," Jessica told them, "and I can clean the whole house in an hour."

"Well, that's an advantage," Louise Tarbell said cheerfully.

"It's adequate, I suppose," said Jessica's mother, adding, "for temporary quarters."

"It's right for me," Jessica said firmly. "And not necessarily temporary."

"I hope not," Dr. Tarbell said. "She's an important addition to our team."

She poured some coffee in mugs and they took them outside and across the road to the chairs under the oak. Jessica introduced everybody to her landlord and his wife.

Mrs. Thibault greeted them hospitably from across the ribbon that separated them and began asking with warm interest about their families and their homes. Jessica saw her mother stiffen at the flood of personal questions, and was reminded of herself at the *fais-do-do*, when Armand's sisters had embraced her. Was she that much like her mother? She didn't want to be!

Mr. Thibault and one of his guests came carrying a washtub of boiled crayfish between them and dumped it on the newspapers covering his wife's table. The guests crowded around the hot boiled delicacy and began eating, tossing the shells into the lined garbage cans he had provided. The Owens and the Tarbells watched curiously.

Mrs. Thibault, still standing just beyond the ribbon, called one of her children to her and sent him to the house for a large bowl. When he returned she filled the bowl and offered it to Jessica.

"Here! Enjoy!"

The Tarbells had been in Louisiana for previous crayfish seasons, and thanked her handsomely, but Jessica's
mother shuddered. "Not with their legs on!" she said under her breath, watching Mr. Thibault enthusiastically
sucking juices from the head of a crayfish. He looked as
if he were kissing it.

"Oh, Mother, try one. They're delicious."

"I'll take your word for it, dear."

"Do as the natives do, and let the good times roll!"
Jessica advised.

"Mais, oui!" cried Mrs. Thibault, from her side of the
ribbon. *"Laisse les bons temps rouler!"*

Laughing, Louise Tarbell explained to Jessica's parents
at some length that the oft-heard phrase represented a sig-
nificant part of the philosophy of the bayou region.

A child cried, "They're coming! The boats are coming!"

A large shrimp boat decorated with scarlet streamers was
coming around a bend in the bayou. Dr. Tarbell had told
them that a ritual Mass, with prayers for a good harvest of
fish, had taken place in the Catholic church in the small
community where the shrimp boats had gathered to form
the procession. "It's a good-sized boat!" Jessica's father
said.

"A two-master!" Patricia exclaimed.

"Those are booms," Dr. Tarbell corrected her. "See
how they're placed? At the rails, on each side? They're laid
down to pick up a net full of fish after the net has been
winched in."

Twisted blue ribbons of wide plastic ran from the deck
on each side to ascending spots on the booms. Between the
two openwork curtains this created, a banner was
stretched, and below it hung a large cross. On the boat's
upper deck, directly below the cross, stood the priest in

robes of white and gold, sprinkling holy water as the boat moved in stately fashion down the center of the bayou.

Cheers and greetings rose from the watchers on the banks. Other boats came into view behind the leader. Some were strung with blue and white streamers, others with a multitude of colors that gave them a circus look. One gleaming white boat had no decoration except for its net hanging in brown tentlike folds from its winch.

"Jessica, it's Armand!" Mrs. Thibault screamed from her place at the crayfish feast next door. "It's his new boat!"

Jessica turned quickly to look, but did not miss her mother's raised eyebrows. She saw the beautifully decorated boat, twice as long as the *Cajun Pride*, and wouldn't have recognized it as Armand's but for the name on its bow: *Cajun Pride Too*. It was pristine with fresh paint and garlanded with flowers and pennants.

Through the lacy tent of yellow and white streamers that completely enveloped the boat, she saw several couples dancing to the lively accordion and fiddle music that floated across the water from its deck. She made out the figures of the orchestra grouped on the covered hatch: the young black drummer, another man with a fiddle, Armand playing guitar and his father the small Cajun accordion. And there was Nance Marie, dancing and snapping her fingers! Jessica couldn't see who was at the wheel, which was apparently in the spacious cabin, rounded at the front to match the curve of the bow.

The music was that combination of rock and jazz that had the fast new rhythm Armand had called zydeco, sounding just now like a syncopated square dance or a very fast jig.

A great roar of admiration greeted the music and the dancers. As the *Cajun Pride Too* came closer, its beautiful silken banners fluttering in the breeze, Jessica saw the bouquets of flowers tied to the rail at intervals with bright green ribbons. "Ohs" and "ahs" rose from the crowd when the painted Christ against a background of fleecy clouds became visible between the booms.

The boat came slowly opposite Jessica. She saw Claire and Marie among the dancers. They were having too much fun to see her, but Mama LeBlanc, sitting aft on her rocker, waved.

"*Jolie*, anh?" Mrs. Thibault called.

Jessica surprised her mother and herself by yelling back "*Jolie!*" and clapping with her hands held high, so that Armand would look over his accordion and see her. When he smiled at her, she recognized the pride in his face and felt a little flutter of her heart. She was filled with regret that she was not with him on his boat for its maiden voyage.

Only, of course, because it would have been such an interesting experience to remember.

BY TUESDAY EVENING Jessica was in a state of nervous excitement, wondering what Armand would think of her parents and how they would react to him. The private dinner she had hoped for had not materialized. Nor had there been an opportunity for Armand to take her father on an excursion into the marsh. Instead her father had gone out with her and her students on a facility vessel, a most rewarding day for her students.

She tried to calm her nerves by telling herself it didn't matter that much. Why was she so edgy about their meeting, when Armand could never be more than a special friend whom she was helping learn to read?

She knew that it was having her parents there that made her so nervous. She loved them dearly, but spending so much time with them was like reverting to her childhood when she was still dependent on them, and feeling stifled by the easy living they provided. After being on her own and choosing her own very different life-style, she was uncomfortable with them. She had changed, and they had not. It had nothing to do with Armand LeBlanc.

All of Louise Tarbell's guests except Armand had arrived. Jessica was talking with Dr. Chris and his wife, Andrea, when she heard the familiar voice with its distinctive lilt. For a few seconds she resisted looking toward the entrance. When she did, she gave a little gasp of astonished pleasure.

Armand in a white linen suit was not only the best-dressed man in the room—everyone else was wearing a sport shirt and slacks—but easily the handsomest. The white suit displayed his broad shoulders and narrow hips, and against it the dark beauty of his deep tan and his unruly black hair was remarkable. When he smiled, it was heart-stopping.

"A coat and tie, Armand?" Dr. Tarbell teased good-naturedly.

Jessica felt hot with embarrassment. Armand looked wonderful, but as Dr. Tarbell had pointed out, he was overdressed in this crowd, and she felt it more keenly for him than if she herself had made a social blunder. She glanced at her mother, her nerves tightening.

"'*Allo!*'" Dr. Chris called, imitating Armand's accent. "Look at you, man! Are you trying to make us all feel sloppy?"

Armand said, "If the shoe fits, Dr. Chris, anh?" Apparently undisturbed, he continued, "I jus' got back fron N'Orl'ns an' I don' have the time to change."

There were teasing quips from some of the other young men, and much laughter in which Jessica had to admit she detected warm liking. Armand was obviously at home with the young scientists, or else unaware of any undercurrents, but Jessica was tense, listening for signs of condescension in their greetings.

"Well, shed your coat," Dr. Tarbell said, "and take off that tie and be comfortable with the rest of us. We're not all used to your climate, you know."

"What took you to New Orleans, Mr. LeBlanc?" Louise asked curiously, as she took his coat.

"I went to sign a contract for my band. We'll play for two weeks this summer at a Bourbon Street club."

To sign a contract? Who had gone with him to read it? Probably Nance Marie. "In white suits?" Jessica blurted.

"Ahh, *non,* Miss Jessica. They want that low-down bayou flavor. *Frottoir,* an' all. But a man don' negotiate over lunch at the Roosevelt Hotel in his workin' clothes, anh?"

He grinned so infectiously that everyone, Jessica noticed, was smiling with him.

"What's a *frottoir*?" her father asked her.

"A percussion instrument developed from the old washboard. Actually, it's worn like a vest and is called a rubboard."

Dr. Tarbell was making the rounds with Armand. He stopped to shake hands with Dr. Chris and other men he knew, who introduced him to their wives. All the women, Jessica observed, waited with an expectant expression on their faces. Armand had brought a subtle change into the room, an electric interest that had been missing before. Louise Tarbell looked very pleased.

"This man knows the marsh better than anyone I've met," Dr. Tarbell told Jessica's father. "His boat is shallow-draft so he fishes mostly inshore, and he knows the lakes and bayous better than you know the back roads of

New Jersey. I don't think you could lose him out there in the wetlands. He's a valuable man to know."

From then on, Jessica's father plied Armand with questions about the salt marsh, probing for differences between it and the estuary marshes of the Atlantic coast where he did his research. The other men joined in, answering questions as well as asking them.

"What do you do during the off-season, Armand? Do you trap?"

"When I was a boy I trapped the 'rats with *mon pépère*."

"Muskrats or nutria?"

"No nutra. Nutras like the freshwater bayous. The muskrats live in the marsh, an' their fur is prettier. Not so soft, but shinier, anh?" He turned to Jessica's mother, and asked disarmingly, "Don' you like muskrats better?"

"I don't wear furs," Patricia said.

"I don' trap no more," he assured her. "I trawl for shrimps. This winter I build my new boat. She's big, big! Now I can trawl offshore."

Every grammatical error he made, Jessica heard with the painful certainty that her mother was filing it away in a private list.

"Didn't you trap one of those alligators we have at the lab?" Dr. Chris asked him.

"*Non!* I don' trap 'gators, me. Now, *mon pépère*, he trap lotta 'gators when he younger. You gotta use a fifty-foot line to trap a 'gator, he say, and bury the hook deep, deep in your bait. If the 'gator don' swallow the hook, he can spit it out, that one."

The lively talk went from the wildlife found in the bayous to the erosion of the coastline due, some said, to the changes wrought by the introduction of canals into the marsh.

Armand explained to Jessica's father in his inimitable way, "Every time the tide come in, it brings saltwater up the bayou, no? But the bayou winds like a snake through the grass and the tide came up slow and easy. Then the oil companies dig a canal straight as the heron flies, so their motor launches can bring the workers out to the rigs fast, fast every morning. An' w'at happen? Now nothing stops the salt tide! It come in twice as fast, twice as far, and kill all the cypress trees in the swamp, anh?"

"He's right," Dr. Tarbell told Jessica's father. "That's just one of the problems we're addressing now."

The guests continued to encourage Armand's stories of his experiences growing up in the wetlands, and to ask about the traditions of his Cajun ancestors. His talk was sprinkled with local expressions; even his accent charmed them.

Jessica listened with a mixture of pain and pleased surprise, realizing that she was not the only one to fall under his spell. Then she noticed that her mother had risen to help Louise put dinner on the table, and went to join them.

She opened the kitchen door in time to hear her mother say, "I'm not surprised that there's so much interest in this Cajun country. It's been isolated for so long that it has a flavor all its own." She heard Jessica and, turning, said, "Your fisherman friend is a wonderful source of local color. I can understand why you've been spending time with him."

"Isn't he fascinating?" Louise exclaimed happily. "I'm so glad you suggested inviting him, Patricia!"

Aha! thought Jessica.

"He's making my party go," Louise burbled, unaware that she had given away Patricia's machinations. "And the remarkable thing, Herb has just told me something I find incredible—he said that Armand is actually illiterate!"

"What?" Patricia Owen exclaimed.

Louise nodded. "Herb says that he is able to conceal the fact that he can't read or write because he's very clever and gets along so well. Herb knows about it because the lab has hired his boat. He says LeBlanc endorses his checks with an X."

Jessica felt a familiar cramping in her stomach. "It's a monogram."

Her mother looked at her. "You *knew* that about him?"

"Yes, Mother. I'm teaching Armand to read and write."

The look of incredulous shock on her mother's face was one Jessica knew she would not forget.

For her, the rest of the dinner was a nightmare. The focus of interest changed from local issues to the guests of honor, and her parents were plied with questions. Jessica sat and listened as Dr. Tarbell recited a list of her father's awards in his field and some of the distinguished scientists he worked with. And then her mother made matters worse by telling everyone about Norm's remarkable invitation to read a research paper on his project in physics at a meeting of European scientists in Italy, and bragging about how quickly Jessica achieved her doctorate, besides answering questions about her own practice in pediatrics.

Across the table from her Armand sat in silence, until the Tarbells told their guests about Patricia's collection of butterflies. He responded with a story of some of the beautiful large moths he had seen in the swamps...and for a few moments captured her mother's interest.

But a little later, while Jessica squirmed, her mother began talking about "Jessica's friend, Russell," and how his *hobby* was difficult mathematical equations. "His ability in mathematics has brought him remarkable success on Wall Street," she said, and the young scientists fell silent, as if aware that Wall Street put their academic salaries to shame.

Then, as if that were not enough, Patricia Owen began asking questions about the fishing industry.

"It's hurting right now," Dr. Tarbell answered her, "because there are too many fishing boats going out now that many of the offshore oil rigs have been shut down. How about that, Armand?" Dr. Tarbell asked. "Are you going to stick with fishing? It's not an easy life."

"I'm a fisherman," Armand said simply. "How else would I make a living? I have my music, *oui*, but I'll still fish. That's w'y I built a bigger boat."

"Adding to the competition that divides the profits," Dr. Chris commented.

"Money isn't everything, anh? I could make a pile of money, me, if I wanted to let my boat be used for smuggling." There was a tinge of color under his tan that told Jessica her mother had got under his skin.

"Smuggling!" Patricia exclaimed.

"The bayous have always been home to smugglers, ma'am," Armand told her, "because a man, he can lose himself so easy in our marshes. First it was slaves, anh? Then during prohibition, it was the whiskey and rum that came in from Cuba by boat and got trucked up by night to Chicago and New York. Now it's drugs."

"I thought the drugs came in by plane?" Jessica's father said.

Armand shrugged. "On boats, too, I guarantee. Me, I don' need money that bad. I'll stick wit' shrimp."

Jessica looked at her parents' fascinated faces, and knew that Armand hadn't helped himself with them by these revelations. It hadn't gratified the Owens to hear him say he wasn't tempted by the fabulous profits in drug-running. They saw only that he was not of their world. Fascinating local color, but alien. Not only was he outside the world of scientific discovery, but in his milieu he rubbed against ugly realities that her parents were isolated from by their own life-style.

When the party broke up, Armand left with the other guests, not trying to speak privately with Jessica, but giving her a wink when he said his goodbyes.

Jessica stayed behind and helped Louise and her mother clean up the kitchen. Louise was driving her parents to New Orleans early the next morning to catch their plane home. When her mother asked her to come upstairs for a few minutes while she did some last-minute packing, Jessica followed her glumly.

In the guest bedroom, her mother said, with the detachment she nurtured so carefully, "This fisherman friend of yours is a very attractive man with a great deal of natural charm."

"So you felt it, too," Jessica said deliberately.

Her mother immediately withdrew, as she always did from any expression of emotions.

"You know I wouldn't think of interfering in your personal life, Jessica," she continued. "After all, you're a grown woman. But if you look at what you're doing objectively, do you think it's wise to—to expose yourself to his charm when he is so obviously impossible? For you, I mean."

It was exactly what Jessica had been telling herself, but she didn't want to hear it from her mother. "You mean, can I resist going to bed with him?"

Patricia sighed. "I suppose that's exactly what I do mean, dear."

"I've resisted," Jessica assured her. "So far. After all—"

"There's Russell," her mother finished for her. "It's not that I question your motives in helping the man learn to read—"

"It's just that he's such a hunk?"

Patricia smiled. "Something like that."

Jessica was silent for a moment, disarmed by her mother's smile. This was a rare moment of intimacy between them, and she couldn't let it pass unacknowledged. She said slowly, "I adore his family, Mother."

Her mother said in genuine surprise, "You've met his parents?"

"Yes, and his grandparents, and his brother and his sisters. It's a large family. There's something about their closeness and the way they express their affection for one another that—"

Her mother's slight sound of distaste stopped her, but she finished. "Well, it appeals to me."

Patricia was silent.

"Mother, I've often wondered.... Did you ever hug Norm when he was little? I never saw it, if you did. I don't suppose you hugged me, either, when I was too small to remember?"

Her mother's expression had subtly changed. "I don't know. I was always so busy...."

"But ... but you have to touch your young patients?"

"That's different."

"Why?"

There was such a baffled look in her mother's eyes that Jessica said no more, and Patricia never answered her.

A half hour later, Jessica kissed her parents goodbye and drove alone to her little house, feeling very depressed. She had sensed the liking the men from the lab had for Armand. They knew and respected him for his expertise in his own field. But he hadn't been good enough for the Owens. The meeting between Armand and her parents had been a total disaster.

CHAPTER EIGHT

TEN DAYS AFTER her parents left for New York, Jessica received a telephone call from Russell.

It was not particularly welcome at the time it came, because Armand was working on a writing assignment in the kitchen just on the other side of the open door, and obviously could not help hearing her side of the conversation.

"Darling," Russell said, and his familiar voice came over the wire to her laden with associations that pulled her back into the world they shared. It was a world inhabited by her family and a few close friends and Russell, who was almost family. Yet at this moment it was an intrusion.

"I hated not being able to fly down with Patricia and Philip," Russell said. "Patricia called to tell me how happy you are in your work and what a wonderful time they had."

And I'll bet that's not all she told you! Jessica thought. She glanced at Armand, sitting hunched over the kitchen table in a blue work shirt, with his pen held too tightly in his strong brown hand. An image flashed through her mind—Armand as he had looked when he walked into the Tarbells' living room in that spectacular white suit. It was a memory that recurred to her at odd times, causing little ripples of delight. Even her mother, who thought wearing it was a social blunder, had been bemused.

Jessica moved away from the door so she couldn't see Armand, and lowered her voice. "They really enjoyed the ceremony of the blessing of the fleet," she told Russell. "I'm sorry you missed it."

"So am I. I thought about you all week. I desperately need to see you, darling."

Her vague feelings of guilt crystallized. Russell was her oldest and dearest friend—more than a friend—and lately he had been seldom in her thoughts.

"I can't get away before July, dammit," he said. "The weekend of the Fourth. If it's a convenient time for you, I can fly down Friday morning and come back Monday. That will give us three days together. Sound good?"

"Wonderful." Of course she wanted to see him! But she felt relieved that it was not next week. July was far enough away to give her time to prepare herself for his visit. The thought startled her. Why should she have to prepare to meet Russell?

"I have a lot of things to tell you, Jessie, and something very important I'd like to talk about."

She swallowed. "I want to talk to you, too."

His voice lowered. "I guess you know it's more than talk I want. I dream about it all the time, Jessie, how when we're together I'll nibble on you, taste you all over—"

She cleared her throat loudly, covering the rest of his sentence. She could not possibly listen to Russell's love talk with Armand LeBlanc in the next room!

He finished, "I love you, Jess."

She had replied, "Love you, too, darling," so many times! But always in privacy. She was very conscious of Armand's presence, and could not bring herself to say the intimate words.

She moved again and stole a glance at the man sitting at her kitchen table. His dark curly head was bent over the literacy workbook, apparently intent on it.

"Me, too," she finally said.

"Is someone with you?" Russell asked quickly.

"Yes."

He laughed. "I get it. Patricia described your doll-house for me. 'Very close quarters,' she said. How far are you from New Orleans? Can you meet me there?"

"Yes, of course. It's only an hour and a half. I can probably get that Friday off, too, because it will end a student session."

"Great! I'll make a hotel reservation for us in New Orleans."

Jessica drew in her breath. "No, don't do that!"

She was looking forward to Russell's arrival with pleasure—she had so much to tell him! But for some reason his suggestion of a shared hotel room in New Orleans sent her thoughts skittering. It had been too long. And she was too aware of Armand, listening to her side of the conversation.

Russell did not speak at once, and she realized the sharpness of her tone had surprised him. "I'll get something for you here." She glanced at Armand. His dark head was still lowered, and he was laboriously copying the exercise she had placed before him.

"New Orleans is a hundred miles away," she explained. "I want you to see where I live and work."

"Of course. I want that, too. I'll call again when I get my flight. 'Bye, love."

"'Bye."

She turned back into the kitchen, feeling oddly tentative. She wondered what Armand was thinking about what he had overheard.

"That was an old friend," she explained. "A very good friend from college days." She felt unreal when she heard herself. Why was she volunteering information about her personal life? Why couldn't she think of Armand as another student?

Armand laid down his pen and stretched his legs under the table, placing his hands behind his head. The movement pulled his knit shirt tight and made her very conscious of the beautifully proportioned torso beneath it. "How good a friend?" he asked.

Her heart skipped a beat.

His warm brown eyes were direct. "Or is he a lover?"

They might as well have it out in the open, she thought. She should have told Armand about Russell long ago. "He has been, yes."

"An' now?"

"I may decide to marry him, Armand. He's a terrific guy."

A hint of a smile relaxed his lips. "You haven't decide' yet?"

"Perhaps I will when he comes."

Armand said, "I t'ink—*thh*ink you will not marry this college friend."

"What makes you say that?"

"Mama says you love me."

She felt a tightening of her nerves. "Your mother knows nothing about me."

"She says you can't get your eyes off me."

"Mothers are notoriously prejudiced in favor of their sons."

"An' w'y not?" he said, grinning.

"She should have named you Narcissus."

"W'at does that mean?"

"It means you're in love with yourself."

He laughed. "But it's *your* love that puts up with me, anh? W'y else would you give so many nights to teach me w'at I don't know?"

"Because I've had so many more advantages than—" She stopped herself from saying, "than you," and finished, "than many people. It's the humane thing to do— you know—brotherly love."

"Anh! But do you kiss your brother like you kiss me?"

"I don't kiss you at all!"

He pushed back his chair and stood up. "Shall we test that?" He moved toward her, brown and strong and deliciously threatening.

She backed away. "Armand! We agreed—"

"*Non, chére!* You made up that rule about not kissin' teacher. Was that the humane t'ing—*thh*ing to do?"

She was backed against the kitchen counter and could put no more distance between them. He put his hands on her shoulders and his gaze demanded honesty from her. "You asked me once w'at I want from life. W'at do you want, Jessica?"

"I want to do my work," she said evenly. "My career is important to me."

His hands were burning through her thin shirt. Her breasts tingled, begging to be touched.

"Don' you want love? And chil'ren?"

He was standing so close that she was aware of his presence in every cell of her body, and those cells were trembling with need. Right now she wanted nothing more than for him to stop talking, pull her close against his muscular body and kiss her until she was beyond resisting him. She closed her eyes so he could not read the hunger in them, and whispered, "Someday."

"Open your eyes, *chére.*"

She forced them open, feeling drugged, and saw his lips coming to meet hers. He stopped just inches away and she gazed into his eyes. She saw tiny sparkles of amber light in their brown irises. His lashes were full and long, curling slightly like his hair. His skin was an even tan with a faint shadow of a beard showing on his cheeks.

He kissed her lips lightly and a shock of delight made her tremble. His tongue traced the shape of her mouth, leaving a quiver of response wherever it flicked.

She moved her hands up his shirt, feeling the taut muscles beneath it. She touched his neck and immediately felt his arousal against her. Then their mouths were seeking and tasting with such ardor that their passion blotted out the kitchen with the workbooks lying open on the table and the coffeepot burbling on the counter and the night songs from the bayou sounding outside the windows of the little house. Everything was blocked from her consciousness but the magic of feeling.

Armand broke away to demand, "Does *he* kiss you like that? Do you want *his* chil'ren?"

Dazed, Jessica twisted out of his embrace. "You can't ask me that!"

"Or is it the money he makes on Wall Street? If I'd gone to work offshore, I'd have plenty, plenty money now. But I'll make enough with *Cajun Pride Too*."

"This is a ridiculous conversation. I only promised to teach you to read. Do you know how many *thousands* of books I've read? And you're just learning the alphabet! What do you imagine we could have to talk about?"

Armand's tense mouth relaxed in a little grin that told her she had said something ridiculous. "When does this man come?"

"In July." Suddenly she felt like crying, and it angered her.

"I'll be in N'Orl'ns then, playin' wit' my band."

"And Nance Marie," she heard herself say with horror.

"Yes."

"Are you lovers?" she asked, and was appalled at herself because she didn't ask personal questions.

"Once we were in love. Now we're good friends." He reached behind her for a tissue from the box on the counter and handed it to her.

She blew her nose. "What happened?"

"Nothing happened. Nance Marie is too much like my sisters, anh? Now she's another *chére* sister. One of the family."

"Right, one of your family," Jessica said. "She still loves you, Armand, and she's from your world. You're good together."

"We *sing* good together." He took her chin in his fingers. "I'll never meet another woman like you. And you'll never meet another man like me, my little mud hen. Remember that when this college friend comes."

He stepped away, releasing her, and closed the workbook on the table. "I'll be rehearsin' wit' the band most nights for a while, because we can't get together when the shrimp season opens. I'll take the book and do the exercises when I can, anh?"

"What about your fishing when you go to New Orleans, Armand?"

"We play two, t'ree weeks, an' that's between the brown shrimps and the white shrimps. I have to do this, to earn money for the 'lectronic equipment I need. But I won't miss the fall season. Papa and Etienne, they count on me."

She blew her nose again, and said indignantly, "You're doing the same thing to Etienne that your father did to you—keeping him out of school!"

"But Etienne, he can read and write," Armand pointed out. "Right now he needs to learn how to handle a trawl. And he's worked as hard as I have on my new boat."

He was impossible! She was glad he was going away, and that Russell was coming.

"But t'anks—" he corrected himself, smiling, "—*thh*anks for worrying about Etienne." With the book under one arm, he tilted her chin and kissed her. She was powerless to prevent it. *"Bonsoir, chére."*

He left her feeling as if her insides were jelly, and she hated it.

JESSICA'S DAYS WERE BUSY with a new group of students starting field studies, and she refused to admit that she missed Armand's evening visits for his lessons.

Five days went slowly by before she heard from him, then he telephoned her late one night. In the background she could hear a guitar being plucked in a minor key.

"Where are you?" she asked.

"At Nance Marie's. We've been rehearsing here every night. You like that melody?" he asked her.

"It's pretty. What is it?"

"A love song we're learnin'."

"What's it called?"

He sang in his rich baritone voice to the syncopated rhythm of the guitar, "'W'y does love got to be so sad?'"

Someone in the background yelled, "Hey, Armand, c'mon!"

"Who's playing the guitar?" Jessica asked.

"I am."

She'd forgotten he played that instrument, too. "Will you be playing a guitar in New Orleans?"

"Sometimes. Gotta go, *chére*, the band's waitin' on me. Just wanted to tell you I read two stories in the book."

Before she could respond, he hung up.

It was not enough to satisfy her; it left her edgy and wanting to hear his voice again. "You're behaving like an idiot," she told herself.

The local paper was full of speculation about the size of the shrimp harvest, which would begin late in May, according to the Louisiana Wildlife and Fisheries Commission. The commission fixed the date of the season each year, based on the size of the shrimp. The marine biologists at the lab were talking about it, too, saying their tests forecast a meager harvest, but with a greater percentage of large shrimps than the year before.

On the night before the season's opening, Jessica was awakened at midnight by a knock on her door. She shrugged into a cotton robe and padded in bare feet to see what the emergency was. Claire LeBlanc stood beyond the screen door, in cutoff jeans and a rosy shirt.

"Get some shorts on, *chére*, and come with me if you want to wish Armand luck."

"Luck?" Jessica repeated, still blank with sleep.

"On his first trawl in the new boat," Claire said, her voice impatient with excitement. "It'll tell us whether the harvest's any good this year. A good first day can mean two, t'ree t'ousand dollar." It was the first time Jessica had noticed Claire's Southern drawl had traces of a Cajun accent, too. She was obviously greatly excited.

Jessica threw on some warm weather clothes, and slipped her feet into casual flats.

"We're getting the *Cajun Pride Too* ready so Armand and Etienne can take her down the bayou to where the fleet's gatherin'. They'll start trawlin' at six sharp. That's when the season opens. Papa and *Pépère* are going out with 'em this first trip."

She kept talking while Jessica was grabbing her purse and locking the door. "You've never seen such excitement at our house! But it's this way every openin'. We all go nuts!" Claire gave her infectious giggle. "But we don't have a new boat every year! Hurry up, *chère*! This is something you gotta see."

They climbed into Armand's battered car and Claire drove Jessica across the bridge to the LeBlancs' dock. In the warm midnight, the bayou was alive with lights. Kerosene lanterns were carried back and forth between the boats that lined the bank and the house, as ice chests were filled and engines fine-tuned. Yellow mosquito lights gleamed on the docks where children ran about, revved up by the tension and anxiety betrayed by the adults' bragging jokes and loud laughter.

All of Armand's family were there, with friends and more relatives whom Jessica hadn't met. Everybody seemed to have something to do. She didn't see Armand immediately, but he soon appeared at her side. His eyes were glowing with excitement. Taking her arm, he swept her with his superior strength over the side of the dock and onto the deck of the *Cajun Pride Too*.

"We're gonna soon find out if the shrimps are good this year," he said, as he propelled her through the galley, past the two bunks and into the compact wheelroom of the cabin where his captain's chair stood behind the wheel.

"See?" He switched on the sonar gadget and a grayish scene came on the tiny screen. "I can turn this *chu chut* on—"

"Chew what?"

"This hay-ya-call-it. I can turn it on and see the shrimps on the bottom right where I'm trawling. This other little box here is my navigator. It computes my exac' position in seconds." His enthusiasm was endearing.

The new CB radio, high on a shelf to his right, was cracking with conversation in both French and English, as boat captains all over the bayous and bays checked with one another on their plans for the day.

"Zydeco, Zydeco, you there?" the radio demanded.

Unexpectedly Armand flipped a switch and said, "Zydeco here." He grinned at Jessica's surprise. "That's the radio name they give me 'cause I play wit' the blacks."

"This is Pelican," a scratchy voice said in English. "Where you trawlin' today, Zydeco?"

"Down Terrebonne Bay."

"I hear the test trawl showed big, big shrimps in Vermillion."

"You wait. I'm goin' get me some pretty ones. I got my own special place."

Armand's arm had fallen around Jessica's shoulders in the crowded space and he pulled her gently against his body. "I shouldn't a said that. Now Terrebonne Bay'll be chockablock wit' boats, anh?" She could feel his elation in the quick beat of his heart. Her own body quivered with the intimate contact.

"Wish me luck, my little mud hen?"

"The best of luck, Armand."

Etienne came into the cabin and behind him she saw Armand's father and his shy grandfather. "All ashore that's goin' ashore," Etienne said, grinning. He waved his elders back on deck, so Armand could escort Jessica through the cabin between the bunks and through the small galley and out on deck, where Armand's brothers-in-law gave her a hand as she climbed over the rail to the dock.

She stood with Armand's sisters and Mama and Mémère LeBlanc while the boats' motors began purring, and one by one, they pulled out into the bayou to begin their voyage down to the bay and the Gulf where they would compete for their share of the harvest. The women stood on the docks, watching as long as their men were visible, then following the long line of lights moving down the waterway. They watched until the lights were no more than twinkling stars fading into the blackness.

"Now you can go back to bed," Jessica told Armand's mother.

The tiny woman shook her head. "Me, I wait for sun."

Jessica misunderstood at first. "For Armand?"

Claire explained, "She means daybreak. If the catch is small, they'll be back in a few hours, predicting a bad year. It costs too much to trawl for a few shrimp. But if the first trawl brings in forty pounds, they'll stay out there and trawl as long as they can. And they'll come in singing."

She slanted a teasing glance at Jessica. "A fisherman's wife prays for a good year so she can buy a new dress."

Jessica ignored Claire's implication. "Are you saying that in a few short hours, the success or failure of a whole year of a fisherman's life may be decided?" she exclaimed. Jessica hadn't thought of that angle of the short shrimp season before. How had women like Mama and Mémère LeBlanc lived all their years with the uncertainty?

Claire shrugged. "The shrimps were always plentiful before." But she put the question to the older women in French. Her pretty face suddenly looking drawn, she translated the answer for Jessica. "They loved their men, and *Mémère* says it was all she knew."

Jessica wondered if the young man Claire had "sent away" was a fisherman. "Are you going to marry a shrimper?" she asked her.

In the yellow glare from the mosquito light, Claire's young face seemed older. "This crazy Cajun land's half water, and fishin's about all there is to do here, since so many oil companies pulled out." She laughed, and the sound hurt Jessica. "Maybe I won't marry. Maybe I'll just be Tante Claire to Danielle's children."

"That's nonsense," Jessica said.

Claire was no longer laughing. "Come on, I'll take you home. You don' want to stay up all night, *chére*?"

"No. I have to get some sleep before I go to the lab in the morning."

"Let's go, then." Claire's expression had briefly reflected her private hurt, but it had passed like the ethereal moth drifting to its death in the mosquito lamp. She said lightly, "Anyway, I'm having too much fun to marry!"

CHAPTER NINE

ARMAND CALLED JESSICA that evening.

"How was your catch?" she asked him.

"Good, but not good enough. *Cajun Pride Too*, she's an expensive lady. But she's a fisherman's dream, *chére*."

He was obviously enjoying himself. He was in his element and still high on the excitement of owning a new and larger boat. "I'm gonna take her out in the Gulf and trawl along the coast. Offshore, that's where to fin' the big, big shrimps."

"How long will you stay out?"

"As long as the shrimps last! But I'll be bringing my shrimps in to Dulac and taking on fuel and ice. I'll call you then. I miss you, Professor."

"Did you take your workbook with you?"

He laughed. "When I have time to study, anh? Not while the shrimps are running."

Well, she thought, it had seemed a worthwhile endeavor, but his enthusiasm hadn't lasted. It just reinforced her judgment that he was wrong, wrong for her. Perhaps now she could forget him.

At the lab the biologists who studied them said that the brown shrimps were more numerous than the year before, but the season would be a short one. As soon as the cost of trawling exceeded the catch, fishermen would be returning to other jobs to await the season of the white shrimp, which began coming up into their marsh nursery in early July and matured in late summer and fall when they started to migrate back to the Gulf.

It was more than two weeks later that Armand appeared at Jessica's door one evening with his workbook under one arm and carrying a basket exuding the odor of fresh fish. He walked into her kitchen and put the container of iced shrimps on the table.

"Did you catch these?" Jessica exclaimed. "They're huge!"

"I brought you the pick of my catch, *chére*."

"They're beautiful. Thank you, Armand."

"Boil them, and put them in your chester-freeze," he advised, grinning. "But eat some fresh, anh?"

The hot Gulf sun had darkened his skin, and the smoothly working muscles in his bare arms testified to the hard physical labor involved in trawling. He looked scrubbed clean, as if he had just stepped out of a shower, but after she put the shrimps in the refrigerator she could detect the faint odor of the sea that still clung to him. The physical attraction, still strong between them, was making her nervous.

He threw his workbook on the table, but didn't open it. Instead he began talking to her of his days and nights on the boat. He told her of seeing the beds of shrimp ahead of his trawler in the tiny video of his finder, and described his best trawls. She listened, fascinated, not only because trawling for shrimp meant so much to him, but because it gave her a new slant on her study of marsh life.

They didn't accomplish much in the literacy workbook. The battle against the physical attraction between them that Jessica insisted on waging took all their energy. Armand left early because he was taking his boat out before daylight, and Jessica was extremely busy now with her summer schedule of student field instruction.

Toward the end of June, Armand called to tell her that he and his band were going to New Orleans to fill their summer engagement. "Not many shrimps now, and it's too early for the whites. You'll come in to hear us play, anh?"

"If I can." Russell's visit was imminent, and Jessica's edginess was extreme.

"You can," Armand said. "W'y not?"

As always, his confidence was unsettling.

Jessica's emotions, as she drove to the airport to meet Russell, were both nostalgic and apprehensive. While she waited in the terminal for his plane, her thoughts went back to the summer their two families had driven across the continent to visit Yellowstone National Park. On the five-day trip, she and Russ and Norm had shared the back seat of one of the two cars. Russ was a bright, rather serious eleven-year-old, she was a shy girl of ten and Norm an active eight-year-old who had trouble sitting still longer than thirty seconds. For Norm, Russ had been the big brother he didn't have. For her, he had become her closest confidant during that summer.

Each car had pulled a tent trailer for the use of the parents. The children shared an unfloored canvas tent that was erected each night to shelter their sleeping bags. They spent the long daytime hours of driving singing songs, arguing or playing word games using the license plates of other cars on the highways. Sometimes Russ and Jessica wrestled with Norm, whom they considered a pest.

The Owens and the Brants camped in Yellowstone for a week, eating and sight-seeing together, completely awed at Old Faithful and the Mammoth Paint Pots, proof of the inner liquidity of what Jessica had always thought was solid earth.

The nights belonged to Jessica and Russ. Norm fell asleep as soon as he was zipped into his sleeping bag, but Jessica and Russ held long conversations, lying in their separate sleeping bags with the pest unconscious between them.

They discussed their school life and the things they were seeing on the cross-country trip, but the isolation of the dark night encouraged intimate talk of other things, too, things like God and the universe and their fears and uncertainties, their dreams and hopes. One night Jessica remembered vividly, they had pushed their heads outside the tent under the rear canvas wall so they could look up at the stars, so mysteriously bright away from the lights of the city, and so inspiring of large thoughts.

We might have ended up hating each other, Jessica thought, as she had before. Instead, during those weeks they had entered a state of innocent intimacy that had endured even through the wild emotional upheavals of puberty.

Arriving passengers now began entering the waiting area. She spotted Russell, walking briskly up the ramp with his carry-on flight bag. He was wearing the kind of suit that quietly announced "affluent young executive," but he looked overheated.

She waved and he came toward her. He put down his carryon to take her in his arms. She caught a whiff of his cologne as they kissed, swirling nostalgia around her.

"You look wonderful, Jess."

She felt a confusion in his embrace because he was at once familiar and a stranger. "And you've put on a little weight," she teased him.

Since they didn't have to wait for any luggage, they walked out of the terminal together and headed for her car.

"Gad, it's like walking into a steam room," he said. "How do you stand it?"

"It's no hotter than New York, is it?" she said, laughing.

"Well, it feels hotter," he said, with his lopsided grin.

"I thought we'd have dinner in New Orleans, and then drive down to bayou country," she told him.

"I hoped you'd enjoy spending the weekend with me in New Orleans."

"Oh, Russ, I'm sorry! But I especially want you to see the parish where I live, and we don't have much time."

"From what Patricia said, you're practically out in the Gulf, aren't you? Do you really like being so far from the city?"

"Love it! But life's very different down here. You'll have to see it to believe."

The strangeness was still between them. Had he changed, or had she? Or was it just that her life in Louisiana was so different from his in New York?

"How abut Antoine's, then?" Russ asked.

"It's the tourists' mecca. There are many other fine restaurants."

"Don't go native on me," he begged. "I've been looking forward to a dinner at Antoine's ever since you came down here."

"Then that's where we'll go."

She got into the car and started it immediately to prevent him from pulling her close for a more intimate kiss. There was a question in his fine, intelligent eyes, but she avoided them, backing out of her slot. She wasn't ready for more intimacies. She began talking.

"Russ, I've got a dream job here. I'll take you out to see where I work tomorrow. The facility won't be open, unfortunately, but it's a fantastic building you've got to see."

"I can think of better things to do," he said softly, laying a hand on her knee. "In fact, I'm damned hungry, or I'd take you to bed right now."

"You always talked a good loving," she teased him.

"What are you saying—that it wasn't that good?"

"Is your confidence slipping?"

"Hell, no." He laughed and squeezed her knee.

The little exchange had eased the tension between them. His intimate hand on her knee had not aroused her, but there was an unnerving familiarity in his sitting beside her and she was slipping back into it like a comfortable old coat. She thought about the wild passionate response that Armand LeBlanc's kisses had aroused in her with a kind of disbelief. Of course she loved Russell! But she felt the same tautening of her nerves that being with her parents had brought. What was the matter with her?

Across cocktails and a leisurely dinner at the famous old restaurant, Jessica studied her friend, seeing not the sophisticated stockbroker who dealt suavely with the maître d' and the sommelier, but the young college freshman with the soft tentative face who had come to her room at the ski lodge where the Owens and the Brants were spending that Christmas vacation. She had complained that she was the only girl in her crowd who was still a virgin. So was he a virgin, Russell had confessed, and proposed that they discover together what apparently everyone else knew.

She could remember how cold her bed was—there was fresh snow lying on the windowsills outside the panes—and how thin his young body was. But it had been warm and comforting to have him slide in beside her and take her, naked and shivering, in his arms.

There hadn't been much pleasure in that first encounter, but it got better. And since they had talked about marrying some day ever since their childhood, they had simply assumed their sexual experiments were a prelude to their wedding.

Russell was the only man she had known intimately, and her dearest friend. She had told him all her secrets, and he had understood. But how could she tell him about the confusion Armand LeBlanc had brought into her life? She gazed across the silver and the crystal wineglasses on the napery between them and saw a man whose face had filled out and firmed and whose eyes looked around him without illusions. She felt again that she did not know him. But wasn't she the one who had changed?

Although they had been apart far more time than they had spent together, a certain fastidiousness had prevented her from experimenting with another lover. What had Russ done during those long frustrating separations? She wondered why she hadn't asked that question before.

She didn't ask it now. She listened as he talked about his work and his parents, who were wintering in Spain.

He was a good-looking man, with his open countenance and alert blue-gray eyes and his impeccable grooming. Not handsome, but attractive enough so that women noticed him. He was good company and he was perceptive. Certainly he had picked up on her feelings of unease with him.

He proved it when, after dinner, they walked through the French Quarter to where they had left her car. The strains of jazz poured out the doorways of the clubs they passed. Russ said, "Shall we stop in one of these places and listen to some music while we have an after-dinner liqueur?"

Jessica made a quick decision. "Yes. There's a band I want you to hear."

Ten minutes later they were being shown to a table in the Bourbon Street club where Armand's band was playing.

While Russ ordered two King Alphonses, Jessica looked to the stage, and immediately met Armand's welcoming smile. The band had just finished a number, but he lifted his guitar and strummed a little riff, winking at her. He stepped up to the mike, bending slightly to speak into it, and said, "This next song is for Dr. Jessica Owen and her frien' from New York. Welcome to Cajun country!"

The audience applauded and Russell raised his head, a look of surprise on his face.

Armand added, "It's called 'W'y Does Love Got to Be So Sad?'" Tapping his foot, he led the band into the love melody he had played over the telephone for Jessica.

"Gad, what is that drummer wearing? I thought they only used washboards in Oklahoma."

"It's a *frottoir* or 'rubboard.' Listen!"

"What kind of music is this? I expected New Orleans Dixieland."

"What you're hearing is Cajun music with a new beat. It's called zydeco."

"I call it Louisiana country rock. Friends of yours, I suppose?"

"Yes. Armand lives near me."

Just then Nance Marie rose and came to the microphone. Her luxuriant black hair tumbled in large curls over her shoulders. She was wearing an off-the-shoulder peasant-style blouse that showed the creamy swell of her breasts, and her flouncy flowered skirt emphasized her slender ankles and pretty bare feet. As she poured out the lyrics of "Why Does Love Got to Be So Sad?" in a thrilling contralto voice, Russ watched with obvious appreciation.

Then Armand joined her in harmony, and Jessica's heart swelled. She looked around the club. It was early, yet the room was two-thirds filled, and the two had the audience in their palms. No one was talking.

At the end of their duet, Russ clapped. "Hey, she's pretty good. And it's refreshing to see a singer in something simple and becoming."

"He plays the accordion, too," Jessica said, lost in her own enjoyment.

To resounding applause, the band put down their instruments to take a break. Armand gave Nance Marie a hand as she jumped down from the stage, and brought her with him to the table where Jessica was sitting with Russ.

Jessica introduced Russell, who stood and shook hands with Armand, and told Nance Marie, "You were great!"

Nance Marie sat down beside Jessica and gave her an affectionate hug. "You're the first of our friends from home to come to hear us!"

"How's it going?" Jessica asked.

Armand dropped casually into a chair opposite her. He had let his hair grow a bit longer, Jessica noticed, and his shirt was open almost all the way to his waist, exposing tanned skin and a curly mat of hair. He looked as vibrant and confident in the crowded club as he had on the deck of his boat. She felt vibrations of tension in the smoky air, and her breath came unevenly.

"We made a video this morning!" Nance Marie told Jessica, excitement coloring her voice. "The man who filmed us said it would get us some more dates."

"Can I buy you drinks?" Russell asked.

Nance Marie shook her head. "We don't drink when we're playing."

"No, but thanks," Armand said with his infectious grin. "When you get in?"

"Just before dinner."

"Where the professor take you to eat?"

Russell shot Jessica a look of amusement at the title he had given her.

"He insisted on Antoine's," she said.

"Not bad, not bad," Armand said. "But he must eat gumbo in the bayous, anh?"

"You're a professional musician?" Russ asked him.

"No, I'm a fisherman."

The comprehension that leaped to Russell's eyes told Jessica that her mother had informed him about her fisherman friend.

"I'm trying to convince him he's a musician," Nance Marie said, smiling at Russell. "Terrebonne parish is full of fishermen, but musicians don't grow like moss on our trees."

"But musicians don't make much money, as a rule, do they?" Russell observed sympathetically. Jessica knew the remark was aimed at her. "Unless, of course, they're the Rolling Stones or Bruce Springsteen."

"Nance Marie is dreaming about being discovered," Armand said, with a gentle teasing glance at her that triggered a mysterious ache in Jessica's throat. "That's w'y she's excited about the video. She'll be disappointed if nothing comes of it."

"And you won't?" Russell asked him.

"*Non.* I just want to get home before the shrimp boats go out again. That's w'at I want."

"But fishing isn't very profitable, either, is it?" Russell probed.

"Money is your line of business?" Armand asked politely.

Russell laughed. "You might say that."

"Some of our fishermen are as well educated as you are and very successful," Jessica began defensively. "They take their boats all over the world—"

It was not until Russell raised his eyebrows that she realized she had said "*our* fishermen."

Nance Marie steered the conversation back to the topic of the band's prospects, asking Russ, "Would they like our kind of music in New York?"

"Zydeco is still a novelty there," Russ told her, "but New Yorkers go wild over something new."

The other musicians were returning to the stage, and Armand stood up. "Gotta go," he said. His eyes met Jessica's, but she could read nothing except pleasure in their expression. "*Thh*anks for comin'."

Russell lifted his drink to Nance Marie, and took a long sip of it.

"So that's your fisherman," he remarked as the band swung into a lively number with no lyrics except occasional shouts from Armand and the black drummer.

It was a rhythm that whipped up the emotions. Jessica felt it go rocketing through her nervous system.

"The one you're teaching to read and write?" he continued.

"Mother's filled you in, I see."

"She told me I'd better get down here and help you shake the bayou water out of your eyes. My God, Jess, he talks like one of those Brooklyn comics with the old 'dese, dose and dem' routine!"

Jessica's face flamed with sudden anger. "Why don't you shut up and listen to his music?"

"Why don't we get out of here so we can talk?" Russell retorted. "I came down here to talk about us, dammit, not zydeco or fishing!" He signaled the waiter.

Jessica didn't try to finish her drink. She was ashamed of her outburst, and realized that Russell had been patient with her coolness since he had stepped off the plane. Although he'd accepted her suggestion that they drive back to Terrebonne parish when she made it over the telephone, he must have been still hoping she would spend the weekend with him in the city.

They walked out while the band was still playing. Jessica refrained from turning around, but she knew Armand's gaze was following her out of the club. Outside, they could still hear the drummer shouting, "Ya, ya!" to a syncopated rhythm that Jessica found incredibly sexy.

In silence they returned to Jessica's car, and she got behind the wheel. Russell reached out and put his hand on hers holding the ignition key. "I didn't come to New Orleans to quarrel with you, Jess," he said. "Actually, I came down to propose to you."

Jessica slowly turned her head toward him. The ornamental streetlight on the corner threw a slanting beam on his handsome face.

"Shall we go back to the airport and start over?" he asked, with his familiar rueful grin.

"I'm sorry, Russ." She relaxed against the seat, returning his smile. "I'm edgy, too. We've been apart so long."

"True, and I regret it. What I planned to lead up to telling you is that since my last promotion, I'm making enough money to marry. My prospects for the future are very good. At last we can talk about setting a date."

He put his hands on her arms, keeping her from starting the car, and turned her to face him. "I didn't expect to propose marriage in a parked car on a New Orleans street. But that's what I came down for, and what do I find? You're more interested in my meeting some ignorant folksinger you've made your charitable project. Can you blame me for getting upset?"

"You're such a snob, Russ," she said tautly. "My parents were snobs about Armand, too. He's far from ignorant! He knows how to enjoy life—I've seen him break into song out of sheer joy at being alive! He can survive and save other lives in a world that would defeat you and me in hours. He has a great sense of humor and a natural courtesy."

"He's a charming fellow," Russ admitted dryly. "But he's still illiterate, and I always thought illiterate meant ignorant."

"Armand's an original. He talks the way he does because French was his first language. It's not Brooklynese. It's a French accent, for heaven's sake! And it's not that obvious, unless you're looking for something to criticize!"

Russell regarded her in silence for a moment. At last he spread his hands, palms up, in a helpless sort of way that tugged at her heart. "I come down to propose marriage, but instead of talking wedding bells, you tell me what a great guy you've met. You may as well let me have it, Jess. Have you gone to bed with this great guy?"

"Of course not!" she cried. "That's simply impossible!"

"And *I'm* the snob?" he said pointedly.

She drew in a deep breath. "Is it snobbery to recognize there are important differences between people?" She stopped. She had never felt so confused and unsure of herself. "I've seen snobbery in myself, too," she admitted after a moment, "and I hate it, Russ. Does everyone have to be the same?"

After that they were both silent. Jessica started the car and maneuvered through the streets to the highway that crossed the Mississippi River and headed west. It was too dark to see much of the scenery she was driving Russell through, but the light from a waning moon illuminated some of the large bodies of water that appeared first on one side of the highway and then on the other.

"Crayfish farms," Jessica explained. "This is the old highway that was built across swamps. That's why the road is always bumpy. It's built on a foundation of peat. A heavy rain can make it spongy, and it gives. There's a newer road, but I—"

"You wanted to take the long way home?" His dry tone did not suggest pleasure, and she knew he was accusing her of putting off the moment as long as she could when she would refuse to spend the night with him. He knew her too well, she thought unhappily. She was not sure why, but she knew that whatever she had done in the past, she simply could not go to bed with him tonight.

When she pulled up in the porte cochere of the hotel in Houma, she said quickly, "I'll pick you up early in the morning. Suppose I meet you here for breakfast?"

"Just tell me this, Jess. You needn't spare my feelings. If you're not sleeping with LeBlanc, what are you talking? What kind of relationship is it, anyway?"

"We're not talking anything but friendship—a teacher-student relationship." But she knew she was not being entirely honest. She knew Russ was hurting, and there was such a bewildering churn of pain and confusion in her head that she wondered if she were coming down with something.

"I'm sorry, Russ," she said miserably. "I don't know why, but I seem to have changed. Please try to understand—"

"Understand?" He drew her firmly into his arms, and with a no-nonsense air kissed her thoroughly and at length, but even with his expertise and his deep knowledge of her it was a kiss that failed to ignite, and they both knew it.

He let go and reached into the back seat for his carry-on bag. "See you tomorrow," he said tightly, and let himself out of the car.

Jessica drove away from the lights of the town, fighting panic. Armand LeBlanc had come between them. She knew it, and Russ suspected it. But it was a physical thing with Armand, wasn't it? That and his charming novelty. It was the strongest physical attraction she had ever experienced, and it could lead nowhere.

It was a dead-end street she would be foolish to enter.

CHAPTER TEN

JESSICA SPENT a thoroughly miserable night, remembering what a good friend Russell was and how close they were during their high school and college years, and feeling guilty because although she had been delighted to see him, she felt no passion for him. Surely it would return.

She rose early, made coffee and dressed for the day, then drove the thirty miles up the bayou to the hotel where she had left Russell. Already there was traffic on the bayou, a few outboards towing water-skiers and small fishing craft returning with an early-morning catch. The sun sparkled on the wake thrown up by the skiers. Gulls swooped over the fishing boats, screaming their excitement.

Houma's streets were already busy with shoppers. When she called Russell's room from the hotel lobby, he said cheerfully, "Good morning, darling. Come on up. I've ordered your favorite breakfast from room service."

She bit her lip. He knew exactly what to order for her, and how she liked her eggs. He was deliberately choosing to remind her of mornings they had wakened together. She squared her shoulders and went up to his room.

He opened the door wearing a light silk travel robe over his trousers. His feet in scuff slippers were bare. He smelled of soap and cologne, and the odors mingled with the rich aroma of coffee.

He was smiling. "Come in. Our tray was just delivered. Coffee's strong and hot."

She walked in and dropped her purse on his bed. He put his arms around her, and she found the familiarity of his embrace unexciting, but comforting.

"Can we forget last night?" he murmured against her hair. "I was angry."

"Yes," she said. "I don't want to fight with you, Russ. You're too dear a friend."

"Ouch!" he said, with an exaggerated flinch. "Maybe I should have offered you some coffee first. I might have rated more than friendship."

She laughed uncomfortably.

"Never mind," he said, and kissed her lightly. "I won't pressure you, Jess. You know how I feel about you."

He seated her at the table by the window, poured her a cup of coffee and set a glass of orange juice before her. He lifted the lid of a silver dish, exposing a delicate omelet with a creamy seafood sauce ladled across it.

"This looks quite edible," he said.

"You'll be pleasantly surprised at the food down here in—what was it you called it?—'alligator heaven'?"

"You know I didn't say anything like that," he protested, laughing. "Anyway, this is a new day, and I'm not going to insult anyone, if I can help it."

They ate the omelets, and drank their dark roast coffee. Russell did not refer again to their conversation of the night before, but talked only of the success he was having in his brokerage firm. She listened with interest, feeling a glowing pride in him.

When they had finished breakfast, he put his hand over hers and stood up, pulling her to her feet. His robe fell open, exposing his smooth muscled chest. Intimately he drew her into his arms with one hand on the curve of her buttock in a way that had always aroused her.

She parted her lips and waited for the pleasure his kisses had once given her to work its magic again. But her nerves were jumping—was it because she hadn't slept?—and she was stiff in the circle of his arms.

After a moment she pulled away from him and picked up her purse. "Now it's my turn to tell you about my job," she said brightly. "I'll bring my car around while you finish dressing. You're going to get the grand tour today."

"Whether I like it or not?" he asked her ruefully.

"Right," she said, her smile and her eyes asking his forgiveness. "I thought you'd be interested in seeing where I'm living and what I'm doing."

"Oh, I am!" he said with a humorous twist of his lips. "But that's not as high on my priority list as what I'd like to be doing at the moment."

"Please, Russ." For just a second she let her confusion show, and he sobered.

"Give me five minutes."

She waited for him in the lobby. The misery she had wakened with was growing into an ache in her breast. When he joined her, she took him to her little car. "There are at least five waterways leading out of Houma," she told him. "The bayou we'll be following goes all the way to the Gulf."

On the outskirts of Houma, the bayou road was lined with beautiful modern homes surrounded by acres of grass. Russell observed them with pleasure. "Life as a Southern gentleman still has its attractions, doesn't it?"

"Oil built those houses," Jessica said. "In the days of prosperity a roustabout on an oil rig probably made more money than you do."

"No kidding!"

"Now that most oil companies have moved out of the Gulf, some of the people may commute to jobs in New Orleans."

"A pretty long commute," Russell commented.

As she drove farther south and closer to the marsh, he was silent, and she found she was looking at her surroundings imagining how they must seem to Russell, fresh from New York. The bayou grew wider, and the houses smaller and closer together. Boats began appearing tied up to small docks. Before long, the boats were bow-to-stern along the banks. They were fishing boats of all sizes and colors, with that functionally beautiful wide-beamed bow and graceful curve down the sides that Armand had told her made pulling up the loaded nets easier. Some were equipped with booms and a winch, and all had small cabins where the crew could get out of the weather.

"No luxury yachts?" Russ finally commented.

"This is fishermen's territory."

He was silent again.

She kept driving. The oak trees, draped with moss, and the willows, sweet gum and sycamores along the banks disappeared. The marsh, looking flat from this distance, became visible behind the small houses, which were now all raised off the ground. A few miles farther they came to the houses built on twelve-foot stilts that marked the last solid ground, only a few feet above sea level. They were approaching the end of the road.

Beyond the little community of Cocodrie stretched the marsh, its tall grasses undulating in the breeze off the Gulf, broken by lakes and winding bayous, and spotted with white where snowy egrets were feeding.

To the right of the road sprawled the laboratory. To Jessica it always looked surprisingly airy for its size, elevated on its eighteen-foot pilings, with lacy metal stairways ascending from its concrete pad.

She gestured toward it with a hint of drama. "That's the laboratory, Russ. There's a dry lab and a wet lab with saltwater piped in."

"My God," Russell said, glancing around them. "You're really at the far end of nowhere, aren't you? Are the tides that high?"

"They could be, in a hurricane." She found his reaction disappointing, but she kept her voice cheerful. "That's where my work is. If we marry," she added deliberately, "you could work in New Orleans, Russ, and we could both commute from, say, one of those pretty ranch houses outside Houma?"

He looked at her as if she had lost her mind. "My firm doesn't have an office in New Orleans."

"You could open one, couldn't you?"

"Be reasonable, Jess. I've always assumed we'd live in Manhattan. That's my turf."

"And this is mine," Jessica said quietly.

They looked at each other with sober expressions.

"The New Jersey marsh was good enough for you at one time," he finally said. "It's good enough for your father."

"This is a new and exciting facility. I'm lucky to be part of it, Russ. And to tell you the truth, I've fallen in love with these bayou marshes."

His face was reddening. "Or with your Cajun fisherman?"

She was silent. Was that really why Russell's kisses had left her cold? The thought was like an open pit yawning before her. She closed her mind to the panic that started to rush in.

"Your mother was right to be concerned," he said. "You're out of your element here, Jess. You'd better come back home."

"But I love my job, Russ! There are endless possibilities here for more research. And I love the food and the people and their way of life."

"You're letting this get to you, aren't you? It's the novelty of everything, isn't it? This country's something different, all right. But as a steady diet? This is *not* your turf, darling. It's not right for you. Come back where you belong."

"Russ, my work is here! I thought you of all people would understand."

"Understand! What am I supposed to understand? Your notion about my working out of New Orleans is ludicrous! You can forget it!"

She hesitated for a few seconds, then said sadly, "I don't want to quarrel with you, Russ. But haven't you always known how important my work is to me?"

"I'm not asking you to give it up. I'm asking you to carry on with it from New York."

"I can't do that."

"Are you saying you no longer want to marry me?" Russ said stiffly. "Are you trying to tell me it's over, Jessie?"

"I—I don't know." Her voice choked up. Was it over? "I'm sorry, Russ."

"Are you really thinking of marrying an illiterate fisherman? Have you gone that far out of your mind?"

"I'm not planning marriage, Russ!"

"Your mother will be relieved to hear that," he snapped.

"I'm fully aware of the folly of making a long-term commitment to someone who doesn't share my interests."

"As I *do*?"

"Do you?" she challenged. "If you do, you know how important—"

"Of course I do! Jessie, this is *me*!"

"Oh, Russ," she cried. "I'm so mixed up I can't think straight. We've shared so much! No one else knows me so well. Can you tell me why this is happening?"

"You tell me."

She drew in a deep breath and let it out in a long sigh. "There's a restaurant down at the end of the landing that serves wonderful seafood. Shall we have a beer there and stay for lunch? It's high up on pilings, too, and there's a good view of the marsh from its deck."

Russell's face was looking pinched. "I'd just as soon go back to the hotel, Jess. If this is an indication of what kind of weekend we're going to have, I'm not going to stick around."

She looked at him, stunned with remorse.

"Maybe you need a little time," he said. "I don't want either one of us to—say things we'll regret."

Tears came to her eyes. "Oh, Russ, I'm sorry."

"Actually, it wasn't a particularly good time for me to leave. I can probably get back to New York tonight. That is, if you'll drive me to the airport."

"Of course. Russ—"

He looked at her, his expression hurt and angry.

"Whatever happens, you know you'll always be my dearest friend."

"Dammit, will you stop talking about friendship? I didn't say I was giving up, Jess. I think you'll come to your senses. But I think it's best that we have our reunion in New York. You're not yourself here." He said again, urgently this time, "Come home with me, Jess. Now!"

Not herself? She knew then. Nothing was the same. Everything had changed. "You know I can't do that, Russ."

They had little to say to each other after that. At his hotel, she went upstairs with him while he changed his plane reservation and packed his small bag.

"Look," he said after he had checked out, "why don't I just take a cab to the airport?"

But she wouldn't hear of that, insisting that she would drive him herself.

It was a silent, miserable ride. She must have been punishing herself, she decided long before they reached New Orleans, and was sorry because she saw that she was punishing Russell, also. When she pulled up in front of his departure terminal, he grabbed his carry-on bag and opened the car door as soon as she stepped on the brake.

He looked back at her and hesitated when he saw the tears that were suddenly filling her eyes. "Goodbye, Jessie," he said. "When you get over this obsession, call me. Because that's what it is, a temporary madness. Remember that I love you." He slammed the car door, then was gone, striding through the opening as the glass entrance to the terminal parted and swallowed him.

Jessica drove on with tears streaming down her face. She had bypassed the city, coming directly to the airport down the River Road from the Luling-Destrehan bridge across the Mississippi. Now she headed into the city, unable to face another drive over the highway leading back to Houma.

Before long she was in the French Quarter. She parked the car and walked through the narrow cobbled streets to the Bourbon Street club.

It was midafternoon. Heat lay in a humid blanket over the nearly deserted streets. A man was languidly hosing down the sidewalk in front of the club. The door stood open and she could see the chairs upended on the tables inside. The big fans that hung from the ceiling were turning, stirring the heavy, only slightly cooled air. Out of her sight, somewhere inside, Armand's band was playing.

"The club's not open yet, ma'am," said the man who was washing the sidewalk. "That's a rehearsal you're hearin'."

"I know," she said. "I'm a friend of the band." She walked past him into the dusky interior of the club.

Armand and Nance Marie and the others were on the stage. Armand had his back to the room and didn't see her take a seat at a back table. They were playing "W'y Does Love Got to Be So Sad?"

Jessica sat and looked at Armand while they played the song through. His back was turned to her, but she couldn't have mistaken him for anyone else in the world, and that was astonishing to her. Every line of his posture as he shifted his weight, strumming his guitar, or threw back his head to shout an answering response to Nance Marie's lyric, was imprinted on her consciousness as uniquely his.

She had no doubt at all that it was Armand who had somehow broken the connection between her and Russell and changed the direction of her life. Armand was all wrong for her, and yet for some reason he was special. What had happened between her and Russell today had been inevitable from the time Armand had pulled her out of the mud, put his hands on his hips and laughed at her.

"BON!" ARMAND SAID. He slipped off his guitar strap, turning to face the empty room, and stopped dead, seeing Jessica.

"W'at you doin' here, Professor?" he called.

She didn't answer him, just shook her head. Even in the dusk of the unlit room her yellow hair gleamed. He jumped down from the stage and strode back to where she sat. When he got close, he saw the single tear that rolled down beside her nose, and something inside him twisted painfully.

"Where's 'New York'?"

"Over Mississippi by now, I should think." She licked the lone salty tear from her lips.

His heart was suddenly pounding. "He's gone?"

"I left him at the airport." She looked up at him. Her eyes were a bruised blue. She was hurting, but she had come to him.

Nance Marie called, "Hey, Jessica. You two gonna eat with us?"

"You go on," Armand said in a distracted tone.

"We'll be down the street," the black drummer said.

When the three musicians had left the building, Armand asked Jessica, "When you eat last?"

She thought for a moment, remembering breakfast with Russell in his room and felt ill. "I'm not hungry. But I—I just can't drive that highway again."

He could see that she was exhausted. "You drove home last night?" he asked carefully.

"All the way to Chauvin. I've been driving forever." She pushed her hair behind her ears. "I picked up Russell in Houma early this morning, and drove him down to Cocodrie—and then I—I brought him back to the airport."

It had been a short visit, he thought, elated. "I'll take you over to the hotel where we got our rooms, anh? You can stay there, an' tomorrow I'll drive you home."

"But I've got my car—"

"No problem, Professor. I'll jus' ride the bus back from Houma. We don' play on Sunday. Right now I t'ink you need a 'tee nap? After that, we eat, anh?"

A *petit* nap, Jessica thought, a little nap. She smiled. "I didn't sleep well last night," she admitted.

They walked the short distance to the small hotel in the Vieux Carré where Armand's band was staying, and the walk seemed to revive her. The hotel was in a restored residence of Colonial style, built around a central patio. A room was available and she registered. Armand went with her as she followed a porter into a flower-filled garden and up a single flight of steps to the room, which opened off a gallery.

Over the bed a large ceiling fan whirled lazily. The light slipped in through shuttered windows. Armand tipped the porter and asked him about parking for Jessica's car. "Give me your key and I'll bring it around while you're restin'," he said.

She opened her purse, and brought out her car keys. The door closed behind the porter. Armand reached for the keys, but Jessica dropped them on the bed beside her. Her face was mysteriously beautiful; the look in her eyes stole his breath away. She took his hand and gently guided it to her breast.

Instantly he hardened. His pulse was racing. His hand instinctively fitted itself to the exquisite round of flesh that he'd dreamed over and over again of cupping in just that way. Questions awhirl in his head were battling his strong desire for her. What had happened between her and her college friend? Why was she offering herself to him now, when she had always been so controlled in spite of her body's response to his overtures?

He'd be a *byok* to take her now, wouldn't he? She was vulnerable, suffering from some hurt that he sensed and wasn't sure he could heal. But ah, *Dieu*, how he wanted her!

Her hands slid inside his open shirt, and his bare flesh shuddered under their delicate touch. He couldn't stop himself. He put his fingers into her silky hair and held her head while he kissed her. And then he was lost in the passion of her response. It was a kiss that begged, demanded his love. It fused them together. With a groan he pulled her hard against his aroused body.

She moaned.

Hearing the pain in the sound, he made a valiant effort to break away from the exquisite torture of her breasts, but she held him tightly and said, "Don't go, Armand."

He could hardly speak. "Are you sure, *chére*?"

Her voice was little more than a whisper, so sensual that it inflamed him unbearably. "I want you to stay with me. Please, oh, please—"

He could no longer control himself. He picked her up and laid her gently on the bed. The fan turned slowly above them, stirring the fine hairs at her temples. Her eyes, looking up at him, were drugged with passion, their color deepened to a warm blue.

He unbuttoned her blouse and ran his hands over her breasts, reaching under her to unfasten the lacy bra that encased them. When they were exposed, he knelt beside the bed and began teasing the pebble-hard nipples, at the same time caressing her stomach. She arched herself toward him, repeating urgently, "Please, Armand, please..."

It was more than he could stand. He eased her skirt and panty hose off her. His lips moved down her body until they were buried in the soft golden hair of her mound, and she cried out. Then in a burst of speed he finished undressing himself. She was ready for him, opening herself to him, taking his face in caressing hands as he positioned himself above her. Seconds later he was plunging into her, taking her sweetness and giving himself in wild ecstasy, while a refrain in his head sang over and over, *My professor, my little mud hen.*

Afterward, relaxed but not sated, still in the warm glow of shared ecstasy, they explored each other's bodies. Armand stroked her long legs and caressed her smooth knees and her narrow feet.

"Your skin is soft, soft," he murmured, "an' my fingers are rough from the guitar strings. I t'ink I only play accordion from now."

Laughing, Jessica took his hand in hers and kissed his fingers. "Don't say that, Armand. I love the sound these fingers make on your guitar."

"But they scratch, anh?"

"Deliciously."

He kissed her. "You're some woman, Professor. That's w'at I say to myself the first time I see you. I knew you were my woman."

He kissed her again, a slow exploratory kiss that was like drinking nectar. The taste and feel of him was still exciting. She closed her eyes, feeling desire stir again, not as desperately but just as urgent. She thought she could never have enough of him.

He didn't hurry this time, but moved his hands over all her body, finding the places that teased and excited her, learning how to please her. When at last he took her again and brought her to a stunning climax, she thought she had never been so completely loved before and felt the warm flood of tears pour from the corners of her eyes.

"W'y do you cry?" Armand, collapsed against her, asked anxiously. "Because he hurt you? Or because you're happy?"

She touched his cheek. "*He* could never hurt me. He's made me understand myself."

"I'm in heaven, me," Armand said, caressing her. She suddenly realized that he was tracing circles on her stomach, a half circle to the left, a half circle to the right.

With amused surprise, she asked, "What on earth are you doing?"

"Me, I'm practicing writing, Professor."

Jessica laughed shakily. And then they were laughing together, a laughter that was close to tears and that expressed the joy and wonder of finding each other.

AFTER A WHILE Armand stirred and said, "We must eat. It's soon time to go to the club. You want to come with me?"

"Yes," she said without hesitation.

They showered and dressed and walked to a small restaurant where Armand said he'd found the best gumbo— she was going to have to learn to make gumbo—in New Orleans. At the Bourbon Street club, Nance Marie and the two men were already setting up.

"You still here, Jessica?" Nance Marie looked searchingly at Jessica and Armand. Jessica knew immediately that the other woman sensed what had happened. She felt a compassion for the singer. Her own happiness must be a shining aura around her. Armand was looking very content—and Nance Marie knew him so well.

"Jessica's staying over," he said easily. "I'm drivin' her car back for her tomorrow."

"I thought we were rehearsing that new song tomorrow," Nance Marie said. She told Jessica, "Monday's not a holiday for the band. The club expects a full house."

"That's why we're leavin' at dawn," Armand explained. "Anybody wants to come along's welcome."

"How you gettin' back, man?" asked the drummer.

"On the bus."

Jocko laughed. "I'll stay in town."

Armand put Jessica at a table just to the left of the stage where he could join her during breaks. In a state of euphoria she listened to the music the band made. She couldn't take her eyes from Armand. The Saturday evening crowd was enthusiastic about the band's zydeco style, and she cherished every round of applause.

The evening went by in a blur of pleasure. Jessica was not in the least weary and went happily with the band for their customary snack before calling it a night. They were all high on the positive reaction of the audience. Nance Marie had spotted two record company executives among the listeners.

"I don' know how she fin' out," Armand said admiringly. "She can *smell* a big shot in the music business, that one."

"I'm going to get us recorded," Nance Marie said confidently. "You wait."

Her friendly attitude had not changed. So it surprised Jessica when, while Armand was paying the bill, Nance Marie said casually, "You won't keep him, you know. You'll never fit in our world."

Jocko, the drummer, looked uncomfortable. "Hey, Nance, it's Armand's life, right?"

Armand joined them, and Nance said no more. They all walked back to the hotel together. Jessica sensed the curiosity of the others and was conscious of their gazes as she picked up her key at the desk. They parted on the gallery, each with a separate key.

Jessica was brushing her hair when Armand knocked softly on her door. She put down her brush and let him in, her eyes devouring his strong frame, from the lean hips in jeans up the white shirt he had left partly unbuttoned, exposing the brown body she now knew intimately. Her gaze stopped when she met his eyes. They glowed with warmth. Quietly he closed the door behind him, shutting them in their own private world. He opened his arms.

She went into them as eagerly as if it had been days instead of hours since she had left them. For what remained of the night, they made love, and Jessica thought there could be no two happier people on earth.

CHAPTER ELEVEN

WHEN ARMAND DOUBLE-PARKED Jessica's car at the bus station in Houma, he looked over at her and said, "You'll go see Mama when you get to Chauvin, anh? Me, I don' have time to phone." His bus was loading, almost ready to leave. "You can tell them w'at we do?"

"I'll tell them you're the toast of New Orleans!"

He laughed, pleased. "*Non, chére.* Just tell Papa he must bring Mama to hear us play. And take her to the convent. Tell her Nance Marie went with me to the convent to see Sister Catherine. Catherine was glad to hear news of the family, but would like to see Mama. Will you do that?"

"Of course," Jessica said, absorbing this evidence of how close Nance Marie was to the LeBlanc family.

"And ask Claire w'y none of her cabbage-head boy-friends don' bring her to hear a good band play? And Marie and Danielle! W'y those husbands of theirs don't bring them? W'at's wrong wit' those guys?"

"I'm to scold them all?"

His laugh was a happy confident sound, beautiful to hear. He leaned over and kissed her. "No," he said tenderly. "Just tell Mama everything's going fine, and I'll be home next weekend."

Jessica promised she would. Armand held her as if she were something precious, and kissed her again. His kiss started an ache deep inside her that she knew wouldn't go away until she could be with him again.

He got out of the car, then leaned back in. "It's never goin' to be easy to leave you, *chére*," he said soberly. *"Au revoir."* A car behind them honked. He moved out of the traffic lane and eased his narrow hips between two cars to reach the sidewalk.

He had left the engine running. Jessica slid behind the wheel and waved to him before she drove on. She stopped at the service station where she frequently took her car to fill it with gas, relieved to find it was open on a Sunday morning. While the attendant scoured the bugs—plentiful in this season—from her windshield, she began reflecting on the extraordinary changes she had made in her life in the past two days.

Now that she and Armand had become lovers, she wondered why she had fought so long against her natural response to him. No other outcome had been possible, she thought now, her lips still tingling from his goodbye kiss. She didn't understand it, but she didn't regret it. The tensions that had been with her for months while she fought giving in to her desire for him were gone, and she felt deeply happy.

The service station attendant asked, "Are you headin' for Chauvin now, Miss Owen?"

"Yes, Rufe. Why?"

"Got a fella here needs a lift. I'm fixin' his car and it's gonna take a couple days. Think you can give him a ride home?"

"Where is he?"

"Over there in the shade. He's okay, Miss Owen. I know the family."

Jessica glanced at the young man leaning against the building. He looked to be about twenty-two, with the recognizably French heritage of the Cajun in his straight dark brows and even features. Rather attractive, she thought.

"Well..." She didn't really need company. She wanted to relive the past amazing twenty-four hours that had turned her world upside down.

"He'd sure appreciate it, ma'am."

There was something familiar about his looks, but she was sure she hadn't met him. A family resemblance to someone she knew? There had been intermarriages between some of the Cajun families in the parish for generations, Armand had told her, so there were pronounced resemblances.

"Sure, I'll take him to Chauvin," she said.

When the attendant beckoned him, he came over with alacrity, and opened the passenger door. "Thanks," he said shyly. "I was about to go over to the bayou and see if I could hitch a ride on a boat."

Jessica smiled at him. "I'll be glad of your company."

He did not offer conversation as she took the car through various stoplights on her way out of town. She thought his expression was rather sad.

It was not until they were on the bayou road heading south and a shaft of sunlight struck his profile that it came to her where she had seen him before. He was the young man who had pulled a knife in the fight she had witnessed at the *fais-do-do*!

She examined his expression again in a furtive glance, and this time it struck her as sullen. She could not stop the little gasp of breath she took.

He turned and looked at her questioningly.

"I've just realized where I've seen you before," she said.

"Yes?" he said, unsmiling.

"You're a friend of Claire LeBlanc's, aren't you?"

His eyes darkened. "One of her many friends," he said, a bitter edge to his unexpectedly soft voice. "My name is Hugh. You were at that *fais-do-do*?"

She nodded apprehensively. What should she do? Had she been foolish to tell him she recognized him? In the next instant she knew she would keep driving, and try not to upset him in any way.

"Claire makes me crazy," he said. Hugh was obviously educated to some degree. "She nearly got me in bad trouble that night." Although he had hardly a trace of the Cajun accent, there was still that little questioning note that often ended a sentence. "I'm not normally a guy who pulls a knife, but it's just more than I can take sometimes, havin' to watch her battin' her eyelashes at every Tom, Dick and Harry in the parish. She's been actin' like some little tart in the movies, all because I wanted to take her away from here?"

Jessica drew in her breath again, not so audibly. "You wanted to marry her?"

"If it weren't for her stubbornness, ma'am, I'd be a married man right now, making a pile of money in Saudi Arabia. But Claire wouldn't go so far from her family, so I'm still here, not getting rich? Out of a job, in fact. And I tell you, it's more than I can take sometimes."

"Saudi Arabia," Jessica mused. "That's a long way from Louisiana. And Claire is very attached to her family."

"Yes'm. She backed out on me. And my job on the rig had been filled? I haven't worked since. Jobs are not so easy to find since most of the offshore rigs shut down."

"No, I don't suppose so." Jessica had gradually relaxed, and instead of being apprehensive, she was feeling sympathy for the young man, who was obviously miserable. On this day when she was so incredibly relaxed and happy, she wanted no one to be so depressed.

"I'm going to get out of this backwater," he said, his voice still soft, but furious. "I'm not going to spend my life being a laid-back Cajun, letting the good times roll."

Jessica looked at him, startled. "But I think that's charming."

"Charmin'!" he repeated angrily. "It's giving up. It's laughing at ourselves to make others laugh, like the blacks, doing it to get along. But some, like my father, hate our French heritage and try to erase it. After all, we've been Americans since before the United States existed! My father wouldn't let us speak what he called '*boogally* French.' My father said, 'Take French in school if you want to, but you'll speak good French, or not at all!' "

"But now there's great interest in the Cajun traditions. Your people are proud of your heritage," Jessica protested.

Hugh couldn't seem to stop talking once he'd begun. "My father said, 'They've isolated us and made us poor for generations because we couldn't speak English and we keep doing things in the same old way.' My father said, 'Tradition's all right, if you don't let it trap you? But you'll never get anywhere if you cling to a language and traditions that nobody else understands.'

"And he's right. That's why I jumped at the chance to work offshore. It's dangerous work, ma'am, but oil brought us prosperity and the good life enjoyed by other Americans. Our grandfathers never made that kind of money trappin' 'rats."

He was silent for a moment, then he said, "That's why I wanted to go to Saudi Arabia. I wanted to get out of the marsh and see the world?"

"You could have gone alone," Jessica reminded him.

"And leave Claire? She's acting like a woman on a motorcycle, riding around in circles, not knowing how to turn the damn thing off. Excuse my language, ma'am."

She smiled. Hugh might have a short temper and carry a knife, but he was still traditional enough to be mannerly in the appealing way most Cajuns she had met were. She remembered how Claire had fiercely rejected her remark about "a man who would pull a knife," and understood it now. Hugh didn't seem to be the type.

"I wish she'd settle down," he muttered. "I guess I'll always worry about her."

Jessica wondered if she could find a job for him at the lab. When he indicated the corner where he wanted to be let off in Chauvin, she fished in her purse for her card case, and gave him a card. "Sometimes there's an opening for a helper at the lab where I work," she said. "Call me in a few days after I've had a chance to talk to some people."

He looked stunned, and then a wide smile broke across his face. "Golly, thanks!"

She glanced in her rearview mirror as she drove off. He was standing beside the road, looking after her car, clutching her card.

When she came to the bridge, she crossed it and followed the few turns to the LeBlanc house, large and comfortable looking, squatting on its raised foundation blocks. The yard appeared empty with no vehicle parked on the lawn under the oak tree. Where was everyone?

It was nearly noon. The family could be gathered at one of the married daughters' homes. Or they could all be at church. She started to drive away, but then decided to check, just in case.

She smelled corn bread baking when she reached the veranda, and she continued on around to the kitchen door. "Come in," Mrs. LeBlanc called when she knocked.

"Ah, Jesseeca! *Entre, entre!*" she exclaimed, beaming. "I'm bakeeng."

"I can smell it, my mouth's watering," Jessica said. "Where is everybody?"

"At Mass. *Moi*—" she gestured toward herself, smiling, "—go seex o'clock." With animated gestures and her limited English, she told Jessica that she was fixing Sunday dinner for her family. "You stay, *non*?"

"Thank you," Jessica told her, "but I have work to do at home. I've just come from New Orleans. I was with Armand."

"Ah!" his mother said, with such understanding in her beautiful deep brown eyes that Jessica felt as if she had told her all that had happened in that hotel room in the Vieux Carré. Her dark eyes searched Jessica's face, which Jessica realized was flushing and confirming everything the older woman was probably imagining.

"You love," she said with quiet conviction. "*Moi*, I know long time you both love."

"I didn't know," Jessica confessed.

"You go see Père Naquin, anh?"

The priest? Jessica felt all her nerves tighten. She said hesitantly, "No...not yet." Honesty compelled her to add, "Maybe never."

She received another searching look from Armand's mother, but there was no shock or anger in it. Only sorrow.

"Armand, he's strong an' he's a good man, like his *père*. My man was a strong young man, too, but now his heart—" She fluttered her hands. "A fisherman's life is hard, hard."

Jessica felt a rush of love for the older woman. She said unhappily, "I'm not the right wife for Armand. We're too different. I told him he should marry Nance Marie—"

"Non."

"—but he said she was too much like his sisters."

Mrs. LeBlanc shook her head vigorously. *"Non, non!* Nance Marie is *non* like! She—"

She fumbled for words but Jessica was beginning to understand her talk with her hands and her flashing eyes and a mix of French and sometimes oddly pronounced English. "Nance Marie has ambitions. She will not stay in the bayous, that one. *Mes filles, comme moi*, we have swamp water for blood. We can never go! Claire, it make her ill to t'ink about! But Nance Marie, she go. An' try to take Armand."

Mrs. LeBlanc put her hand over Jessica's, her dark eyes suddenly warm. "But Armand, he stay. His heart is here."

"I know," Jessica said. "I love the marshes, too."

"Anh," his mother said, the curious Cajun syllable that seemed to say everything, or nothing. Just now it seemed to be saying, "It's your choice, *chére*." and Jessica could feel the tension flowing out of her and a quiet peace taking its place.

"Armand visited his sister in the convent. He asked me to tell you she would like to see you, too."

"Ah, Soeur Catherine," Mrs. LeBlanc said with pride. "She is my first *fille*—the first to live. After Armand, two *bébés* die. I promise the Virgin I give my next *bébé* to God. And then come Danielle and Marie and Claire and Etienne!" She laughed and threw up her hands. "I had to keep my promise, me."

Remembering Claire had said her mother understood more English than she could speak, Jessica stayed for fifteen minutes, telling her about the band's activities and its success in the New Orleans club. When she rose to leave, Mrs. LeBlanc put her arms around her and said, "I t'ink Armand ver' happy now."

Quick tears of emotion flooded Jessica's eyes, and she surprised herself by hugging the tiny woman fiercely.

ARMAND CALLED JESSICA every evening as soon as she arrived home from the lab, telling her what had happened at the club the night before, and what the crowd had been like and the way Nance Marie and Jocko had cut up. Then he would listen to her account of her day with a new class of students.

"Twenty-five this time! It's like a circus every day, we're so busy."

"It's good I don't have to pull all twenty-five out of the mud, anh?"

"Thank heaven we haven't encountered that problem again!"

The lilt of his voice was as exciting as his touch, and the genuine interest with which he listened to her account of her activities in the marsh was intoxicating. Her days were too busy to think of what had happened between them in New Orleans, but nights she relived the hours in his arms and counted those remaining until they could be together again.

Armand's lovemaking had awakened sensual desires, ignored and denied for so long, and her body was fiercely demanding satisfaction. Her desire for him was a torment and a source of amazement to her. It was so strong, she began to think of herself as almost virginal before she had made love with Armand. Certainly, in her on-again-off-again relationship with Russell, she had never known such depths of passion.

The week seemed endless, but at last Armand told her that Friday was the band's last evening at the club. A new group was starting on the weekend.

Saturday morning Claire called to tell her all the family would be gathered at the LeBlanc's to welcome Armand and the band home from their engagement in New Orleans. Mama was going to prepare her famous shrimp *rémoulade*. "You want to be here, don't you, *chére*?"

"Yes, indeed, I do."

"Come over a little before six, then."

When Jessica approached the house that evening, several cars were parked in the yard. She looked quickly for Armand's aging Chevy. It wasn't there yet. Dusk was falling and light streamed from all the windows. The sounds of excited talk and laughter coming from the house were familiar and warming. Someone heard her heels on the wooden veranda and threw open the front door.

"'*Allo, 'allo*, Jessica!" shouted Papa LeBlanc, and she was drawn into the room with warm greetings and affectionate hugs. She was filled with emotion. It was like a fulfillment of a childhood dream to be with Armand's big loving family and made to feel at home. His two married sisters were there, and Danielle's children were running from one beloved *oncle* or *tante* to the other, lapping up affection. With all her heart Jessica envied them the happy childhood she had missed.

Claire came up to her. "Armand was very mysterious about why they wouldn't arrive before dinner tonight. It's something about an appointment. I can't wait until he comes."

"Neither can I," Jessica confessed. She hadn't seen Claire since her weekend in New Orleans, and she was reminded now of Claire's ex-fiancé, whom she had given a lift to Chauvin.

"I met a friend of yours last Sunday, Claire. He said he was looking for a job, and I asked about one at the lab for him."

Claire's dark eyes sparkled. "Was it Henny Dupré? He's dying to get on the crew of one of those beautiful boats at the lab. I told him he could wait forever for that job."

"He said his name was Hugh."

Claire paled visibly. Though she kept her smile, it was obviously forced. "Wherever did you meet him?"

"He was hitching a ride—" Jessica began. But she was interrupted by a clattering as of a herd of horses on the veranda, and the unmistakable tones of Nance Marie's voice raised in excited talk.

"It's the band!" Etienne yelled.

The children, catching his excitement, ran to the door, screaming, "Nonc Armand!"

Jessica turned back to Claire, but she had slipped away.

The band entered in a conga line with Nance Marie leading, carrying a small square object she held up before them. Armand's hands were on her shoulders and Jocko, the drummer, followed him. Last came Picou, the fiddler, so thin he had to wear suspenders to hold up his trousers. His drooping sandy mustache framed a wide smile, and he was still wearing his straw hat.

"It's a cassette!" Nance Marie cried, waving it. "We taped it this afternoon. Etienne, where's your tape player?"

Armand saw Jessica, and his wide wonderful grin split his face. He broke out, shattering the conga line to grab her in his arms. His exuberant kiss sent prickles of delight cascading through her. Her hands could not let go of him, it was so wonderful to touch him. Then she became aware again of all the other persons in the room, and he laughed at her as the heat of embarrassment at this public declaration of their intimacy rose from her body to flood her neck and face and even her bare arms. But she loved the warmth glowing in his dark eyes.

Etienne brought a portable cassette player from his room, and plugged it in. Nance Marie gave him the tape and soon an exciting beat filled the room, stitching together the burst of lively talk and laughter. Nance Marie was telling them she was going to send the cassette to a New York agent.

"What will you do if he asks you to come to New York?" Armand's brother-in-law, Maurice, asked him.

"Go fishing," Armand said promptly, and Papa LeBlanc laughed uproariously.

"I'll go to New York with you," Picou told Nance Marie. He grabbed her around the waist and began dancing with her in the lively Cajun folk dance Jessica had seen at the *fais-do-do*.

Jocko, who was standing rather shyly at Jessica's side, said under his breath, "The Cajun jitterbug."

For some reason, the young man she had given a ride to came to Jessica's mind again. Papa LeBlanc, she realized, could very well be the "laid-back Cajun" he had said he disliked. *Pépère*, Armand's grandfather, was closer to the earlier generations of hardworking fishing and trapping Acadians who had forged a way of life in the beautiful desolate wetlands. Etienne, who preferred to be called Steve, and Claire's young man were of the generation that wanted neither the demanding hard labor of the old ways nor the "good times" with which their elders defied the poverty bred by their isolation from mainstream life in America. They wanted to be part of that mainstream.

And Armand? He was one of those who felt a pride in Cajun traditions and was carrying them to a new generation of Americans, eager to learn more about the corner of their broad land. Armand was a perfect blend of the old and the new, Jessica thought, her heart swelling. Ambitious for the future and critical of the past, yet caring for what was good in it, and especially for the family ties that were so important to his people.

She looked for Claire, but didn't see her. In a flash of intuition, she knew that Hugh, the angry young man who wanted to go to Saudi Arabia, was the man Claire really loved. She suspected that the young woman's flirting and her party-girl image were a deliberate camouflage of that love.

After both sides of the tape had been played, Mama LeBlanc called everyone to come and get some shrimps.

"It's just an appetizer," Armand warned Jessica. "She'll expect you to eat jambalaya later."

The shrimps were served cold. They had been marinated with raw onion rings in a mixture of mustard and horseradish with olive oil and vinegar and a splash of the inevitable hot peppers sauce.

"It's Mama's own recipe for rémoulade sauce," Armand said, holding up a shrimp on the tines of his fork and examining it with a sensual pleasure. "She says the secret is to peel the boiled shrimps while they're hot, and quick put them in the sauce, anh? She says that way they drink the seasonings."

He leaned toward Jessica and offered the shrimp like a flower to her lips, and smiled into her eyes when she took it between her teeth. "Good, no?"

"Umm, delicious!"

His eyes were full of sparkling promises.

The evening broke up soon after dinner when Danielle announced she must put the children to bed. Armand followed Jessica's car home, and her eyes lifted often to her rearview mirror to watch the lights following every turn she made. Each time she saw them, her tense anticipation of the moment when they would be alone rose higher. Her heart was beating fast and her mouth felt dry.

They slammed the doors of their two cars almost together. Armand put his arm around her waist and their hips touched as they walked across the grass, exciting her unbearably. She could sense his mounting passion like vibrations in the thick air. Inside her house, Armand kicked the door shut behind them, and they melted together, devouring each other in kisses.

He stopped long enough to murmur, "I thought this time would never come."

Then he picked her up and carried her into the bedroom, and for the first time since she had rented the little house, Jessica did not sleep in it alone.

CHAPTER TWELVE

JESSICA OPENED HER EYES and stretched luxuriously, unhampered by any nightclothes. In Louisiana's steamy summer she had taken to sleeping nude with only a sheet covering her, so her state of undress was normal. But her gaze fell on a bare brown shoulder, strong and muscular, curving smoothly into a neck partly hidden by curling black hair that tumbled over what was visible of an ear.

Armand!

She lay very still, savoring the pleasure of waking in her own bed beside him. Memories of the sensual delights they had shared during the night streamed through her consciousness. She was tempted to blow gently into the shell of his ear, but he was sleeping so soundly! And it was Sunday. The whole lovely day lay ahead of them.

She eased herself out of bed and went to the kitchen to put on some coffee, then went to the bathroom to take a shower. When she was dressed in a clean pair of shorts and a T-shirt, she began stirring eggs for an omelet. Presently Armand came padding out of the bedroom, wearing nothing but a sleepy look and his shorts.

"Here you are," he said huskily. "I was afraid I'd been dreaming." He held out his arms.

"You weren't dreaming." Her words of assurance were muffled against his solid chest, with his heart beating strongly beneath her ear. He held her so gently that she felt cherished and safe.

But when he murmured, "This is where I want you, always," she pulled away. Always?

"Breakfast will be ready when you've showered," she warned him, and he turned obediently away.

She set the table and poured orange juice and when she heard the water turned off in the shower, began heating the pan for the omelet. She turned it out just as he returned, his hair in unruly curls from the dampness.

They were sitting at the kitchen table over a second cup of coffee when Jessica said, "I want to read something to you." She picked up a small book and turned a few pages, then began to read.

At low tide, the wind blowing across *Spartina* grass sounds like wind on the prairie. When the tide is in, the gentle music of moving water is added to the prairie rustle.... You can hear the tiny, high-pitched rustling thunder of the herds of crabs moving through the grass as they flee before advancing feet....

Armand listened to her soft but precisely edged northern voice and watched the lips whose touch was sweeter to him than cane syrup, and thought the words she was saying made a kind of music. Listening, he could see the wind blowing across a waving sea of salt grass and hear the thin call of the marsh wren. But she was in his inward vision, too, sitting on the deck of his boat with the marsh at her back and her golden hair spread out to dry in the sun. It was at that moment, he knew now, that he had fallen in love with her.

"That guy knows the marsh, anh?" he said companionably. "I've heard that tee-thunder!"

She nodded, smiling at him, savoring the notion of *petit* or little thunder. Fluttering the pages, she said, "Listen to this. It's about the mating dance of the fiddler crabs."

"Yes?" Armand's eyes gleamed.

Uca minax, the largest crab, stands on his back legs and holds his fiddle halfway in the air, then suddenly waves it up as far as possible and jerks it back down in several stages.

Armand nodded, laughing.

Uca pugnax holds his fiddle in front of his mouth, raises himself up off the ground slightly and moves the fiddle diagonally upward, then returns it with several jerks. When females are present, he also curt-seys to them, moving his body up and down.... Hundreds of males stand by their burrows and wave, their eyes raised high on their stalks, looking for a passing female. The bowing and leading of possible brides into the burrow alternates with rushing at nearby males and fighting battles with the large claw....

"Exactly," Armand said. "Exactly right. But I never heard those names for crabs before."

"They're scientific names, used to distinguish different species. It's Latin."

"Anh!" His eyes lit with comprehension. "The priest used to talk Latin. I've seen just w'at this fella describes. Who is he?"

"The book was written by a man and his wife who have made a study of salt marshes. When you've finished your literacy workbooks, you'll want to read it all."

"A man and his wife," Armand repeated dreamily. That had a pretty sound. He had a delightful vision of leading Jessica into his burrow.

"There's more to reading than I *thh*ought," he said. "I thought if I could read the newspaper and the contracts I sign, it would be enough. But there's more out there, isn't there?"

"Much more. So much more," Jessica agreed.

"And you will help me find it," he said, capturing her hands so that she had to drop the book. "Because you love me, anh?"

"Because I want you to have it, all of it," she said warmly.

"And because you love me."

She wanted to run her fingers along the clean pure line of his jaw, but he kept her hands locked in his. "Because I know how much pleasure it will give you, Armand."

"And you love me." His gaze was strong and caring, demanding an answer.

"And I love you," she said unsteadily.

Armand looked at her with unmasked delight. Her face, framed by her gold silk hair, was radiant and her eyes were the warmest blue. Her smile was tremulous with love. He had never seen any woman so beautiful, and she had admitted that she loved him.

He stood up, still holding her hands, and pulled her to her feet. There was no more talk of reading that day.

But that week the lessons in reading and writing were resumed. A lesson often ended with Jessica reading a chapter from *Life and Death of the Salt Marsh*—and was nearly always followed by making wonderful love.

LUCKILY ARMAND was not there the evening Jessica's mother called in acute distress because she had seen Russell and heard from him that his trip to Louisiana had been a disaster. For once Patricia Owen's facade of objectivity had cracked.

"How could you do that to Russell," she demanded, "after his years of devotion to you?"

"Mom, do you remember when you used to tell me to 'follow my heart'?" Jessica asked her.

"That was when I couldn't imagine your heart leading you to an uneducated man!" Patricia said bitterly. "Tell me, have you—"

"Yes. We have a relationship," Jessica said.

"But you aren't planning to marry him!"

"No. Just now I'm happy with things as they are."

Her mother's silence was eloquent.

"I *am* happy, Mother," she said softly.

"I'm sorry I can't say that," Patricia Owen said at last. "I think you've treated Russell shamefully."

"Russ wouldn't want me to pretend something I don't feel."

"Good night, Jessica. I'll call again when I am not so upset."

"Good night, Mother. I love you," Jessica added, but her mother had hung up.

IT WAS ONLY a few nights later, after they had made love, when Armand said out of the blue, "Where you want to live after we're married, anh?"

Jessica went absolutely still in his arms. "Married!"

"It's something people in love do," he said, amusement coloring his voice. "The priest says some words that tell them they can move in together and have *bébés*."

A kind of panic filled her. "Nothing's been said about our getting married!"

"I'm sayin' it now. It's time we had a talk with Père Naquin, anh?"

"Armand—"

"You think this house is big enough for two people? Me, I think we should have a bigger kitchen. And I guarantee it's not big enough for *bébés*."

Jessica raised herself on an elbow. "Hold it, Armand!" she said. "Nobody's asked *me* if I want to get married."

"Don' you want to marry me?" Armand said with his most ingratiating smile.

"I'm not even thinking about it," Jessica replied.

He looked so stricken, that she hedged, "Not yet, anyway."

"W'y not?"

"It's too soon. We don't know each other well enough."

"When will we know each other well enough?"

She traced ovals on his chest, curling the dark hair around her index finger. Unconsciously she made a half oval to the right, then to the left....

"When I can read and write?" he asked her, his gaze suddenly sober and perceptive. "Is that it?"

"Part of it," she said.

"Or when I've read a thousand books?" There was a trace of hurt in his tone.

She threw her arm over him and laid her head on his chest. "Armand, do you remember every single thing I've said to you?" she asked remorsefully.

"Everything you say and do is important to me. Don' you know that yet?"

"You mustn't say such things. Don't even think like that."

"W'y not?"

"Because you're putting too much importance on what I say. I don't want to have to stop and think before every word—"

He interrupted her. "Do you love me?"

"Yes," she answered with no hesitation.

"Then w'y won't you mar—?"

She put her hand over his mouth. "Please don't say it, Armand. Don't even think it. We're so different. Our backgrounds are so totally different."

How long could this fevered desire last without the solid basis of shared interests—the thought shattered on the obstacle of her failed engagement to Russell, whose background was identical to hers. If that love could not survive a long separation, how could this wild hunger for a man so entirely different from anyone she had ever known before endure?

He grabbed her hand away from his lips and said, "But I want to think about it. I want you to think about how important is this difference between us, really? You say you love me."

"Are you happy, Armand? Are you happy now?"

"I've never been so happy, me!"

"Then don't ask for more. Please?"

Her hand smelled of some flower-scented lotion, and it was sending a delicious fog through him, beguiling his senses. He grabbed her hand and began kissing his way up her arm, with the most delightful effect on her, until he reached the soft area around her breast, and she moaned with pleasure. Things developed with a beautiful logic from that point, until he had her astraddle him with her long yellow hair falling over him like a golden tent, and was thrusting into her once more, pouring out the love she would not let him express in words.

THE FOLLOWING WEEKEND Armand asked Jessica to go
with him to a local nightclub where the band was playing.
"That agent Nance sent a tape to in New York wants a
video," he explained.

"Are you going to send him one?"

"Nance Marie has hired a team that used to do camera
work for the oil companies. They'll be filming the band
tonight."

It was a more sophisticated bistro than the dance hall in
the country where they had attended the *fais-do-do*. But as
before, Armand's family was present to support and
monitor the band. Marie and Danielle and their husbands
were there. Mama came with Papa LeBlanc, and she
danced with a zest that Jessica found charming.

As usual, they formed their own little group on the floor
between dances. In his open hearty way, Papa LeBlanc
greeted Jessica with "When you an' Armand gonna see
Père Naquin, so you can give me a *joli blon' bébé* to
bounce on my knee, anh?"

Jessica stiffened, and could not produce an easy answer.

"Papa!" his wife reproached him, but Claire's eyes
glittered oddly.

"Don't hold your breath, Papa," she said.

Jessica danced with each of Armand's brothers-in-law,
but mostly she sat near the band and watched the cameraman work, as they got the performance of several numbers on videotape.

Claire's date was sharply dressed with blow-dried hair in
the best anchor newsman style, and Claire looked beautiful. Jessica tensed when she saw the young man named
Hugh. He had apparently come alone and he was not
dancing. He stood on the edge of the floor, watching

Claire and her date with burning eyes. Looking at his expression, Jessica could almost smell explosives.

Claire was behaving outrageously, Jessica thought. She must have felt Hugh's gaze like a hot wind, but she pretended not to see him, all the while managing to flirt with her date with all the finesse of a ten-year-old child begging for attention.

Jessica had noticed both Mrs. LeBlanc and Marie speaking to her as if in warning, but both Armand and his father were too occupied, Armand with leading the band and his father with helping the camera crew get what they wanted, to notice Claire's behavior.

Jessica unobtrusively made her way across the floor to where Hugh stood. "Hello," she said. "You didn't call me, but I asked about jobs at the lab."

He looked surprised and actually flushed with shyness.

"I talked to the director about you. There's no opening at present, and he has a long list of applications. I'm sorry."

He nodded gloomily. "Thanks for trying."

"But he said he'd keep you in mind, Hugh. He said when an opening comes up and they want somebody in a hurry—well, the list shortens all at once. Because many applicants are no longer available. They've found other jobs or—"

"I get the picture," he said. "I've heard it all before."

They were jostled by a whirling couple, and Jessica said, "Shall we dance?"

He gave her a quick questioning look, but she just held out her hands. He took one and put an arm around her waist. As they began moving to the music, she said, "I was surprised to see you here, because I remember what you said about letting the good times roll. Or did you come to see Claire?"

"I never should have talked to you like I did," he said, with an angry edge to his voice. "All right, I did hear she was coming with that *byok* tonight. He looks good, but he's a rotten SOB, Miss Owen. She shouldn't be going out with him."

Jessica said firmly, "I'm sure Claire can take care of herself."

"Don't worry! I left my knife at home."

"I'm glad of that," Jessica said lightly. "Because if looks could kill—"

"I won't promise not to work him over with my fists," he muttered, "if he says or does one thing out of line."

"Claire must care a lot for you, Hugh."

"Why on earth would you think that?"

"She acts like a girl who is trying too hard to deny that she cares."

He shook his head decisively. "If she loved me, she would have married me and gone wherever my job took me. Isn't it her place to do that?"

"Don't ask *me* that question," Jessica said. The music was fast and now that Hugh was not thinking about his dancing, he was guiding her in perfect rhythm. "I refused to leave here, too, because it meant leaving my job."

"Claire isn't a career woman like you, Miss Owen. She wants to get married and have babies? But she also wants to live and die in the parish she was born in. Her children must be raised here just because she was? Does that make any sense?"

"Not to me," Jessica admitted. "But then I'm not Claire."

"Sometimes I wish Claire was like those old bra-burning feminists," he muttered. "They would have gone to Timbuktu! Whatever happened to them, anyway?"

Jessica laughed. "I"'m not sure they would have gone with their men. Anyway, their daughters think the battle of the sexes was won."

"They don't know girls like Claire with swamp water in their veins! I wish Claire were more like you, more willing to explore new paths."

"Every woman, even if she's willing to take chances and explore new paths, dreams about finding her special man," Jessica said softly. "I think you're that man for Claire. And if you didn't care for her, you'd be in Saudi Arabia now, right? Why don't you ask her for a dance?"

"And talk about what? Our abandoned wedding plans? I know just what would happen. I'd tell her what I think about her date and that would tear it. Miss Owen, without a job I can't even ask her out."

The music ended. He thanked her for the dance and left her. Jessica looked across the floor and saw Claire's dark unhappy gaze following him.

When the band took a break, the musicians came to the table where Jessica sat and pulled up extra chairs so the two cameramen could join them. They were discussing the video. Nance Marie was asking eager questions of a technical nature.

"You need a professional editor," one of the cameramen said, and suggested a man he knew in New Orleans.

It was Nance Marie who asked for his address. It was she, Jessica saw, who made most of the suggestions, although she put the decisions to the whole band. While Armand was the band's leader, Nance Marie was obviously taking over as business manager.

Jessica remembered what Mama LeBlanc had said. "Nance Marie has ambitions. She will not stay in the bayous, that one.... She go. An' try to take Armand."

But Armand has swamp water in his veins, too.

It was decided to let the cameraman take the films back to the city with him and turn them over to an editor he knew, who would return the edited videotape to Nance Marie. She would then send it to the agent in New York.

"Nothing will come of it," Armand told Jessica. He had lingered at the table after the others got up to return to the stage and their instruments and cameras. He hesitated. "I saw you dancing with Hugh Broussard."

"Yes. I was trying to persuade him to dance with Claire."

Armand raised his eyebrows. "You want to see another big fight?"

"Why can't those two kids admit they're in love?" Jessica mused.

"I think Claire's sorry she broke up with him. Hugh, he don' come 'round, and she thinks he doesn't care anymore. But I think he's lost his self-respect because he can't get a job. Me, I don' know w'at else I can do. Any chance you can get him something at the lab?"

"It doesn't look very hopeful."

Armand finished his can of soda, and stood up to rejoin the band. "Tonight," he said softly, just for her.

When the band started playing again, Jessica went to the women's lounge. To her surprise she found Claire there among the women combing their hair and renewing their lipstick. The sound of music was emptying the lounge. In a few moments they were alone at the mirrors. Claire's eyes glittered brightly but there were dark shadows under them, as if she were not sleeping well.

"I saw you dancing with Hugh," she said, looking at Jessica's reflection. "You were talking about me, weren't you?"

"Yes. Hugh told me you broke your engagement to him because you didn't want to leave Louisiana. Is that true?"

"Not quite," Claire said. "I didn't want to leave my family."

"I can understand that it would be difficult," Jessica said. "Your family's wonderful! But isn't giving up the man you love a high price to pay?"

"It may seem high to you. But oh, Jessica, I don't think you do understand! You haven't had the experience of growing up in an extended family like ours, have you?"

"No," she admitted. "There was only my brother and me." And a mother who cared more for her little patients . . . If her father had not begun taking her with him into the marsh, she might have become one of those lost teenage girls who make up the tragic statistics.

"Do you know," Claire said, "that I could have moved into any one of my uncles' homes and felt just as protected and loved and *connected*? My cousins were as much at home in my house as their own. And we all had *Mémère* and *Pépère*, too. Every child should have that kind of family support."

"But how many do?" Jessica said. "You were fortunate."

"I don't want to raise my children in a strange, frightening country where the language is just a clatter in our ears and there is no one but me to cling to because their daddy is always at work."

"There are other Americans working in Saudi Arabia, I'm sure."

"But they're not family."

"You mean they're not Cajuns."

"How can they understand us when they know nothing about us, or what we've endured here in this lost land? Suppose something happened to Hugh? What would become of me and our children?"

"You'd come home. But really, Claire, people are people wherever they have to live. A group of friends can become very like a family. We're rather isolated at the marine biology facility, actually, down there at the edge of the marsh, and many of us are away from our families. But our work is a bond."

"No, you don't understand, do you, how an extended family can bond together, the way we all came together to support Armand's tremendous effort to get his first-class shrimp trawler because it was so important to him. You don't understand how deep our roots go, the deep ties that go back for generations—"

"I *do* understand!" Jessica cried, offended. "Why do you think I can't understand? My mother can trace her family back to the *Mayflower*! And she's damned proud of it."

"Yeah? How many of your cousins has she mothered from time to time? How many are like sisters to you?"

"I don't have that many cousins," Jessica said stiffly, "because we don't have such large families. Besides, my mother has always had her own career."

Claire capped her lipstick and put it away. "You should be one of us now, if you truly love Armand. But you're not, are you? You're different. Are you going to marry my brother?" she demanded. "Or are you just interested in sleeping with a handsome Cajun fisherman?"

Jessica stared at her in shock.

Claire flushed to the roots of her dark hair. "I'm sorry! I shouldn't have said that, Jessica. I always get a little crazy when I run into Hugh. I wish *he* could be happy trawling for shrimp!" She picked up her comb and tucked it in her clutch, and left Jessica standing in front of the mirror as the door swung shut behind her.

CHAPTER THIRTEEN

ARMAND WAS WORKING on his boat. He had installed a new shelf for the more powerful CB radio the club engagement in New Orleans had enabled him to buy, and was giving the piece of cypress several coats of waterproof varnish. In spite of the lowered windows in the wheelhouse, the sharp petroleum odor of solvent was strong.

While the varnish dried, he puttered with some small adjustments to correct problems that had shown up during *Cajun Pride Too*'s shakedown trawls. As he worked, he now and then broke out in song. But his mind was neither on his work nor on what he was singing.

All unaware, he was singing the lyrics of that old favorite, "Jolie Blon'," because he was thinking of Jessica and trying to understand her refusal to marry him.

He was nearly thirty. As his parents' oldest child, he had helped them through the hard times, when his father had lost his boat in a terrible storm and suffered a heart attack. Claire and Etienne were babies then. Now those two were almost grown, and he had his own trawler, as fine a Lafitte skiff as there was in the bayous. He could put bachelorhood behind him and start his own family.

He had found the woman he wanted for his wife. He wanted to live with the sound of her cool voice and her teasing laughter. Life was wonderful since they had become lovers, but it was growing more difficult each time he left her to go back to his parents' house. He wanted

Jessica in his bed every night, and not just so he could make love to her, as splendid as that was.

He wanted to open his eyes and see the gold shawl of her hair spilled on his pillow and draw in its fragrance with his waking breath. He wanted to waken and put his hand on her silken skin while he kissed her awake. He wanted her to share other early mornings—and sunsets—in the marsh on his boat. He wanted to give her his seed, and see a tow-headed girl and a curly-haired boy running through their very own house.

He knew that she loved him, and he knew now that she had ties to no other man. Her strongest ties were to her career, but he did not see that as a threat to their happiness. He knew enough about what she was doing to share her absorption in her work, and he would never demand that she give it up. The marsh gave them both their living, and her enjoyment of it enlarged his own. So it must be his lack of education that was keeping them apart.

Well, he could learn. He had already learned much from her! One day he would read that beautiful husband-and-wife book about the marshes aloud to her, page by page, from cover to cover!

He heard the click, clack, clack of high heels on his deck, and called, "Claire?"

"Hey!" It was Nance Marie's voice. She came through the galley and bunk room and stood beside the wheel for a moment, watching him brush another thin coat of varnish over the new shelf. Her eyes were gleaming and an attractive flush colored her face.

"W'at's up?" he asked.

"You know that video I sent to New York? The agent who wanted it says he's got a spot for the band in a New York club! Starting weekend after next."

Armand stood back from his work, and looked at her. She drew in a deep breath, revealing her state of excitement. Clearly she wanted him to take the band to New York, but the thought filled him with a sort of leaden dread.

Anyway, it was impossible. He would be heading out for the offshore trawling as soon as the white shrimps were mature.

"So?" he said.

"Oh, Armand, you're such a cabbage head!" she exclaimed. "Why aren't you as thrilled as I am? It's our big break!"

"Nance, the fall season opens soon. That's w'y I built my new boat, anh? So I could go offshore after the big, big ones?"

"He says it's only for a couple weeks. You can be back in time for the opening."

"Two weeks? You want us to travel so far for two weeks?"

"It's a showcase, see? Oh, please, Armand, you don't know how much I've wanted this chance to find out what I can do in the big time!"

Armand studied her. He understood better than anyone how much singing meant to Nance Marie. She was damn good at it, too. "I've seen New York on TV," he mused. "Maybe that's close enough, anh?"

"It can't be all bad," Nance coaxed. "They buy our shrimps up there. And they like zydeco."

"I won' know my way aroun'." He had progressed with reading, but street signs in a strange city? In New Orleans he knew the landmarks and could ask directions. New York would be foreign country.

He dropped his brush in a coffee can of cleaner and wiped his hands on a rag. "I wonder, would the professor go with us?"

Nance Marie's expression changed. "She's got classes going, hasn't she? Anyway, I can read the contracts. Who needs her?"

"I do," Armand said soberly.

Nance Marie looked at him for a long moment. He could almost see her mind working. If it took the *jolie blon'* professor to get him to New York, she would go after the professor. But he was sure Jessica couldn't get away. Not in summer.

"Picou's counting on making the fall opening, too," he reminded Nance.

"Oh, Picou," she said. "I can handle him." Her brows drew together in anxiety. "Please say yes, Armand. If I don't call the agent back, he'll look for another band."

"I'll ask Jessica tonight," Armand promised.

He spent almost every evening with her, now that the first half of the shrimp season was over, but after that first time in her house, she wouldn't let him spend the night, and it was frustrating him.

"We have to observe the proprieties," she insisted, although he knew Estelle Thibault, her landlady and close neighbor, was perfectly aware of their relationship and took much pleasure from her knowledge.

That evening he told Jessica about the proposed two weeks in New York, before they started on the workbook and while they were eating hamburgers she'd prepared. "Nance Marie is ready to travel. I told her I'd do it if you'd go with us?" He gave her a glance, half humorous, half questioning.

"You know I can't." Jessica studied his expression. She was beginning to know him a little better. "You don't really want to go, do you?"

He shrugged. "W'at would I do in New York?"

She saw that the idea of going to a strange city intimidated him, and realized more fully what a handicap an inability to read could be. If one had trouble reading a newspaper, or directions... She could understand his dilemma because she had experienced a small culture shock that summer she traveled to Europe alone.

To hide the twist of painful empathy his handicap always aroused in her, she protested, "So you told Nance Marie you'd go if I'll go? That's not fair, Armand."

He grinned ruefully. "She knows I've got work to do on my boat before I take it out again. But Nance is ambitious, anh? She thinks this is her big chance."

"It could be," Jessica agreed. "And she's a very good singer."

Armand nodded, looking worried.

Jessica was still troubled by Claire's challenge the night the band had made the video. *Or are you just interested in sleeping with a handsome Cajun fisherman?* The implication that she was only looking for cheap thrills had hurt.

Mrs. LeBlanc had taken her relationship with Armand very well—better, in fact, than her own mother had. Armand's mother had also taken her refusal to marry him in stride. But Claire had not. Claire was unhappy herself, and she had recognized her brother's growing unhappiness because Jessica refused to marry him. The result, it seemed to Jessica, was that Claire saw her as playing at love, or worse, at lust. It was ironic, in view of Claire's enthusiastic "smelling the flowers," as one of her sisters had put it.

Jessica sensed Armand's frustration with their relationship, but she didn't know how to resolve the problem. She didn't have enough faith in a marriage between two people from such different backgrounds to believe it could last, yet she loved Armand too much to let him go. When she thought about telling him that the reading and writing lessons had to end, and that he must stay away from her, she knew she could never do it and make it stick. Her resolve would melt the moment he touched her.

At times she was tempted to say yes when he urged her to marry him. Just to take the plunge and see what happened, *laisser les bon temps rouler*. But her upbringing wouldn't allow her to be "laid-back" about something as important as marriage and having children.

If only she *could* go to New York with Armand! It would be an opportunity to test their relationship. Out of his environment, without the glamour of local color and traditions that were intensely romantic, wouldn't she be able to see him more clearly? Knowing that her parents would disapprove of marriage to him had not changed her feelings for him. They were of another generation, after all. She was no longer their child. She was her own person, and she needed to find out for herself just how strong her relationship with Armand was.

All at once it seemed very important for her to see him in her native environment. If she could see him more objectively, as her mother would say, maybe she would be able to find the strength to do what must be done—either marry him, or free him to marry someone else.

Someone like Nance Marie, she thought, a ripple of jealousy stirring within her.

"When do they want your band in New York?"

"The first two weeks in August."

She groaned. "The last of my second summer session. I'll be teaching *and* taking students on field trips."

He nodded, watching her closely. "I know."

"When do you open?"

"If we take the job, we'll open the last Saturday in July."

Jessica said slowly, "Maybe I could fly up with you for the opening—just for the weekend . . . ?"

Armand grabbed her and whirled her around the kitchen table. "Then I'll do it!"

She collapsed against him, laughing breathlessly. "I said maybe, Armand."

"But you'll ask, anh?"

"I'll ask Dr. Tarbell if one of the others can substitute for me on that last Friday. That will give me three days." Hardly enough time, but it was the most she could hope for.

"I love you, Professor!" Armand gathered her close for an enthusiastic kiss that led to one pleasant thing after another, and finally eliminated all thought of the workbook for that night.

EARLY ON THE LAST FRIDAY in July, the band drove to New Orleans International Airport in two cars. Jessica and Armand took her little car so she could drive home in it Sunday evening when she returned. Jocko took the others and the luggage in Armand's car.

In the terminal, waiting to board, Jessica learned with some surprise that only Jocko had flown in a large jet before. He had once been with a band that had played in Chicago and Nashville. He had even visited New York for a brief time.

Smaller planes flew in and out of the bayou towns, and helicopters had once been familiar sights over the marshes as they ferried oil company executives to the offshore rigs, or carried coast guard patrols. But this was a new experience to all but the drummer. Armand and Nance Marie were giddy with excitement. They couldn't stop talking, and paced around in the terminal, neither of them able to sit still.

Picou was plainly apprehensive. He looked out through the tall windows at the large aircraft waiting for them, and said distrustfully, "Dat arrow pleen look just too big to git off de groun', don' it?"

Jocko laughed at him, and teased them all, enjoying his superior experience.

Jessica had booked their seats all in the same row, three on the left side of the aisle, and two on the right. As they entered the plane, the pilot, resplendent in his blue and gold uniform, stood beside the flight attendant who was greeting them. Behind him, the door to the cockpit stood open. Armand glanced in at the instrument panel, and whistled, "Some wheelhouse you got!"

The pilot laughed. "You're a fisherman, right?"

"Shrimper," Armand said, with his infectious grin.

"Welcome aboard."

Armand looked approvingly at the compact little galley and at the overhead lockers as they walked down the aisle to their seats. "It's built shipshape, like my boat, anh?"

They had brought their musical instruments as carry-on baggage, all except the drums. At first Picou resisted turning his fiddle over to the flight attendant, but finally trusted her with it.

In the tense moments when the plane raced along the runway, gaining speed for takeoff, Picou, who sat just across the aisle from Armand, grabbed his armrests and tucked his chin down on his shirt. It occurred to Jessica that he might be praying.

She and Armand had taken the pair of seats on the right. He held her hand tightly, smiling down at her in a silent invitation to share the pleasure of his first experience with him. She heard Nance Marie let out a soft, "Ooo!" as they left the ground and below them the buildings, the highways and the cars moving along them began shrinking into miniatures of themselves.

After a hearty breakfast was served, everyone was more relaxed. They were above the overcast now and in brilliant sun, looking down on a fluffy white layer of clouds. The attendants were charmed by Armand and convulsed at Picou, at his worry over his fiddle, his distrust of the "arrow pleen" and his deep bayou country expressions.

"Pop me a kang of sody pop?" he asked one of them, and she teased him about it for the rest of the trip.

They were losing time as they flew east, and it was late afternoon when they first glimpsed the towers of Manhattan. Jessica experienced a rush of nostalgic emotion seeing them. For so long the sight had meant coming home. It was clear and hot down there, according to the pilot's weather report. The low orange sun was reflected from thousands of windows in the fantastic New York skyline. The sight was so impressive that it silenced the foolery the members of the band had been using to pass the time.

Their nervous anticipation grew as the plane circled, awaiting permission to land. At last they glided down and touched ground smoothly. When they filed off the plane into the bewildering horde of travelers at La Guardia Airport, the poetic beauty of the towers was rudely shattered by the reality of a large city. With Jocko's help, Jessica led them to the bus that offered transport into Manhattan, and in a short time they were at Grand Central Station, peering down the canyons of the city while awaiting a taxi.

"What do you think of it?" Jessica asked Armand.

"It's like N'Orl'ns, only bigger, anh? But w'y is everybody running when it's so hot?"

"Good question!" Jessica said, as they all climbed into a cab. She was discovering that in spite of how hard she had worked since joining the staff at the lab, during the months she had been in "laid-back" Cajun country she must have adjusted to an easier pace.

Her ears, accustomed to the sound of the wind, the lonely birdcalls of the marsh and the quiet concentration in the laboratories, were assaulted by the sheer volume of noise generated on a city street by moving cars and buses and the shuffling of thousands of feet. The talk and laughter of people passing by, punctuated by a shout or the toot of a horn or a siren, the hammering of construction somewhere on another street—it all combined into a background roar that she had almost forgotten. The life surging along the streets they were passing through pulsed with energy.

"New Yorkers always in a hurry," Jocko murmured.

"W'y?" Armand asked.

"To make money, what else?" said their cab driver in an irritated tone.

Jessica had engaged a suite at the Royalton, with separate rooms for Armand and herself. When she called her mother to tell her they had checked into the hotel, her mother was disappointed that she was staying downtown. "I'd assumed you'd be coming home."

"I'm only here for two nights, and I'll be staying up late and sleeping late. It'll be more convenient to stay with the band. I hope you and Daddy and Norm can come to the opening?"

"I'm not sure about Norm, but I've reserved a table. Will you bring Armand to the apartment for dinner tonight? I've invited some of your friends who want to see you."

Russell? Immediately Jessica suspected her mother's motives. But wasn't this just what she wanted, to see Armand in her old environment, among her old friends? At any rate, tonight was impossible. "Mother, the band will want to look over the club and rehearse. Tell my friends to come to the opening tomorrow night."

"You'll be able to lunch with us tomorrow, won't you?"

"I've promised to help the band. That's why I came. They don't know their way around, and there's going to be lots of business to tend to, getting set up and all."

"Then how about supper after the opening?"

"Wonderful. We usually all go somewhere to eat."

"Here, I think," said her mother. "It will be easier to visit. I'll have some food sent in." She sighed. "Somehow I can't see you as a groupie, following a rock band, Jessica."

"It's not a rock band!"

"Whatever," said her mother. "I just can't imagine you in that role."

Role? Like Russ, her mother thought of Armand as an aberration in her otherwise normal behavior.

"Imagine it," Jessica said, and hung up.

THE CLUB WHERE THEY PLAYED was an obscure place on Forty-seventh Street, long and narrow, with a small stage jutting out from the wall halfway back and a handkerchief-size dance floor almost cutting the room in two. By eleven o'clock, so many people were milling around as new customers were attracted by the different sound of the music that dancing was impossible. No more tables were available, so newcomers stood in the entrance and listened.

Jessica and her parents and their guests were at two tables just to the right of the dais. To Jessica's relief, Russell had not come with them.

The manager stopped by, obviously pleased with the crowd the new band was drawing. "Zydeco's the new sound," he told them. "Everybody's talking about it. Everyone wants to hear it."

Its rapid, syncopated beat had the listeners tapping their toes and snapping their fingers. When Nance Marie and Armand sang their fast-tempo, minor-key duet "Why Does Love Got To Be So Sad?" the applause was enthusiastic. Armand, as well as the others, seemed stimulated by their reception. Jessica thought their music had never sounded better.

Just before the first scheduled break, Armand put down his guitar and picked up the small homemade squeeze box that had been *Pépère*'s, and Jocko stepped away from his drums and held up a triangle.

"We're going to play an old-time Cajun song the way my *grandpère* played it," Armand told the audience. "It's called 'Jolie Blon',' which means 'Pretty Blonde.'"

With the drum silent, the talk in the room stilled. Jocko beat out the simpler rhythm on the triangle, and Picou's fiddle took the melody with Armand embellishing it on his accordion. Flashbulbs went off. When Armand and Nance Marie swung into the lyrics, Armand looked over at Jessica, who sat with her blond hair tied up in a ponytail, his eyes promising her his love for all to see.

She was moved almost to tears, as all the things she loved about him crowded into her mind: his humor, his tenderness, his infectious joie de vivre, his serious and dogged study of the lessons she set before him, his sensitive appreciation of the incredible marsh life they had both investigated in their separate ways.

"That's the kind of music my people made," Armand said, acknowledging the applause. "They played it and danced to it to forget their hard life, because they were pioneers in a mean land that was mostly swamp, and they came wit' empty pockets, anh? But that didn't keep them from letting the good times roll."

With that, the band swung into a fast zydeco rhythm to which they all shouted, "Ya, ya!" They soon had the listeners shouting with them.

The agent who had arranged the engagement was holding court at a table to the left of the stage, and Nance Marie spent the break the band took with him. Armand came over to greet Jessica's parents, and meet their guests, who were college friends of Jessica's. Her brother, Norm, appeared with a camera in his hands. His had been one of the flashbulbs popping.

Jessica surprised and embarrassed Norm by giving him a hug that would have been taken for granted in Armand's family.

"Armand," she said, her eyes shining, "this is my brother, Norm."

Armand grabbed Norm's hand and said, "I'm glad to run up wit' you, Norm! The professor, she talks about you."

Norm's face registered shock. "Jessica?" He looked dubiously at her. "You call her the professor?"

"Anh! You're a professor, too, no?" Armand laughed, and as always his easy laughter brought answering smiles. Beside Norman's slight figure and pale bespectacled face, he looked bronzed and radiantly fit. "You didn't hear our music yet?"

"Yes, I've been listening up front. I couldn't even get inside until you stopped playing. That *jolie blon'* song you played wasn't zydeco, was it?"

"*Non*, I grew up hearing that song. I learn' it from my father, and he learn' it from his *pépère*."

"They were all musicians?" Norm asked.

Again Armand's laughter rolled out. "*Non*. But a shrimper, he has time for singing and dancing, because the season, he's short?"

"This is Armand's first visit to New York," Patricia Owen told Norm. "He's going to be here for two weeks. Perhaps you can show him around one day? What would you most like to see in New York, Armand?"

"The fish market," Armand said promptly.

Sharon, the dark-haired beauty who had been Jessica's roommate at college, giggled.

"Actually, that might be interesting," Norm told Armand gamely. "It's pretty much of a tourist spot now, but they've got some good seafood bars down there, if you like shellfish."

"Serving the shrimp me an' Picou trawl for, anh?"

Norm looked so uncomfortable that Jessica glanced down into her glass of wine to avoid his eyes. Had he forgotten Armand was a fisherman, or hadn't he expected Armand to be so forthright about what he did for a living?

She did not know whether she was more embarrassed for Norm, who was obviously in shock after hearing Armand speak for the first time, or for Armand, who was being so blatantly provincial before all her friends.

Thankfully it was time for the band to play again, and Armand left them to return to the stage.

CHAPTER FOURTEEN

THE OWEN'S APARTMENT in the East Fifties was crammed with guests. They were gathered several deep around Armand and Nance Marie, plying them with questions about zydeco and Cajun country.

Jessica's ex-roommate, Sharon, was telling Armand, "You don't talk like most Southerners."

She was amusing herself and her friends at Armand's expense, Jessica knew, resenting her. She should have known how it would be, and just how sensitive she would be to any implied criticism of the man she loved.

Armand asked, "How do mos' Southerners talk, Miss Sharon?"

Sharon fluttered her dark eyelashes and drawled, "Oh, sort of soft and slow."

Jessica, watching, thought, *She's not immune to his masculine attractions, either!*

He sent an amused glance over Sharon's shoulder at Jessica, a few feet away, before he answered. "Me, I t'ink New Yorkers talk funny."

Sharon challenged him. "How do you mean, funny?"

"Like knives flashing, anh?"

Her eyes opened wide. "Knives!"

"Long knives?" he suggested. "Like in those late-night movies?"

Jessica laughed aloud. He was having his own fun! All Louisianians had been raised on stories of long-ago duels behind the cathedral on Jackson Square, or under the oaks on some bayou bank.

She stood with her back to the tall windows, through which one could step out on a balcony overlooking a slice of cityscape. Later when some of the guests had left, and Armand was free, she would take him out there and share with him the view that had been hers growing up in this Manhattan apartment.

Across the room, she saw Russell the moment he stepped in from the foyer, looking self-assured and very much of the city. His grooming was the kind that signaled success—the blow-dried hair, the button-down collar with the perfect tie. She watched as he cased the crowd, located her, then made his way toward her, stopping once to speak to her mother.

"Are your friends enjoying their fifteen minutes of fame?" he asked when he reached her.

"Wouldn't you? They were very well received, Russ. You didn't hear them."

"I saw no reason to repeat my New Orleans experience." He looked at the band with a baffled expression. They were still wearing the clothes in which they had appeared at the club, Armand and the other men in jeans and loose white shirts, open almost to their waists, and Nance Marie in a low-necked peasant-style cotton dress. Simple but sexy.

Nance Marie had brought the agent with her to the apartment, and he was at her side.

"Is Fitzhugh representing them?" Russell asked Jessica, indicating the small dark man, who was talking very fast with excitable gestures.

"Yes," Jessica said. "You know him?"

"I know who he is. A high-powered agent."

"He's been telling Nance Marie they should dress punk, but she soon squelched that, and I think she's right. She's really very shrewd, Russ."

He turned his back on her mother's guests and looked at her steadily. "When am I going to see you alone?"

"I'm going back to Louisiana in the morning. I have to work Monday."

"I see," he said after a long pause. "Can I drive you to the airport?"

Jessica shook her head. "Thanks, but I'll take a cab from the hotel." As his face began turning a fiery red, she bit her lip. Apparently he had not been aware that she wasn't staying in her parents' apartment. She explained, "The band has a suite at the Royalton, and I wanted to be near them."

"I see," Russell said again stiffly. Deliberately he turned his back on her and hunted up Norm. After a few minutes of conversation with her brother, he left the party.

Jessica's father came over to her immediately. "Did I just see you send Russell packing?" he asked.

"Oh, Dad!" Jessica's voice had a tiny catch in it.

"Never mind," he said quickly, and began asking about her work at the lab and his friends there. They hadn't had much opportunity to talk, and Jessica launched into an account of what was going on among her colleagues. Since his visit there, her father had interested himself in the environmental problems Louisiana was facing.

Talk of the environment led to the topic of the state's important fishing industry, and soon Jessica was telling her father about Armand's first shrimp season aboard his new trawler, *Cajun Pride Too*.

"How did he do?"

"The catch was smaller than last year," she admitted. "Armand's pinning his hopes on the fall season, when the white shrimps mature."

Her father nodded. "Armand's quite a fellow. I like him, Jessica."

She felt the threat of quick tears at this expression of understanding.

And then he said, "But what's all this rock band bit? He's not serious about it, is he?"

"Nance Marie is serious about it," she said, and her father's glance sharpened. "It's more like a hobby with Armand. And it's not exactly a rock band."

"I'm glad," he said. "I found the music, uh, interesting."

Suddenly Jessica felt very tired. Armand thought the applause he received at the club meant her family and friends were accepting him. He didn't realize that a rock star was just as far out of their orbit as a man who depended on fishing for a living. Jessica was expected to fall in love with a professional man, someone like Russ, or at least another scientist.

When a friend approached her father and engaged him in conversation, Jessica slipped away, wanting to be alone for a while. At the moment the friends her mother had invited, all very curious about Armand, were talking with him and Nance Marie. Unnoticed, Jessica threaded her way through the conversational groups and went down the hall to her old room.

It was little changed. It had always been kept ready for her when she was away at college, and this time someone—her father, most likely—had laid out a new article about the salt marshes on her bedside table.

She picked it up and was examining it when Armand appeared in the doorway. Seeing him here in this intimate setting was curiously unsettling. He exuded the same strong masculine vitality that had impressed her the first time she saw him on his boat deck, and it was even more striking in these surroundings. She smiled at him, conscious of the quickening of her pulse.

"I saw you leave." He looked around him with genuine interest. "This is your bedroom, anh?"

"This is where I grew up, Armand." He brought a current of energy into the four walls that enclosed her private space, a dynamic something that until now had been lacking.

He was examining the books in her bookcase. He puzzled out the title of one book phonetically: "Litt-ul Women?" He gave her a triumphant grin. "*Little Women*!"

"It was my favorite book when I was a young girl."

"W'at's it about?"

"It's about this wonderful family of girls—and I didn't have a sister."

His eyes were warm and understanding. "You have sisters now. Four of 'em, anh?"

"Four?"

"You haven't met Sister Catherine yet, the one who's in the convent in N'Orl'ns. She'll love you, Professor."

Her heart melted.

Armand turned to the pictures on her walls, standing a long time before an enlarged print of the sun setting over the New Jersey marshes.

"My father took that one," she told him. "I've always loved it." She took it off the wall. "I think I'll take it home with me."

His eyes flashed a silent message at the word *home*. At last he came back to where she stood watching him, and took her tenderly in his arms. The tobacco smoke of the club still clung to his shirt, mixed with the perspiration he had worked up on the stage, and there was not a hint of the salt of the fisherman that had always tied him in her mind with the marshes she loved. But the feel of his arms around her and the way she fitted into them were wonderfully familiar. He kissed her deeply.

She felt his body warmth through her clothing, and experienced that sensation of fusion with him. Her heart was racing, and she could feel the strong pounding in his chest that combined with her own heartbeat in a rapid zydeco-like syncopation. A weakness hit her knees and traveled up her thighs until she swayed against him.

He left her so suddenly that she staggered and sat down on her bed. With a purposeful step, he picked up the chair at her dressing table and wedged it under the doorknob.

When he turned back to her with naked desire blazing in his eyes, her swift arousal astounded her, but she pushed herself to her feet. "No, Armand! Absolutely not! Not now."

He couldn't tell her why it was suddenly so important to him to have her here in this room at this precise moment. Part of it was his exhilaration over the exciting reception of his band. He was still high on the enthusiasm of their audience. But he also understood that another part had to do with how close he felt, in this girl's bedroom, to the Jessica he had not known.

Perhaps here in this very personal place, he could penetrate the mystery of her cool power over him. Here amid the books and possessions that must be clues to what had shaped her, he could plumb the depths of that sometimes icy reserve with which she concealed a volcano of warm womanly passion.

Ignoring her protest, he drew her into his arms again. "In N'Orl'ns you took my hand?" he murmured. "And put it where you wanted it, anh?'' He lifted her hand and placed it between his thighs.

She gasped, and then in a frenzy of haste they were rearranging their clothing until he could touch her, throbbing, there where she wanted him. Her pulse was pounding, she was terrified of being discovered, yet never had she wanted him more urgently, or felt his desire more potently. He tipped her over on the bed and made one plunge into her, then sprang up, pulling her to her feet. Dimly she realized someone was walking down the hall.

''We'll continue this at the hotel, anh?''

''Damn you, Armand!''

He laughed exuberantly. ''I love you, Professor.''

NORM PICKED HER UP the next morning to drive her to the airport. Her mother had suggested it, and Jessica realized why immediately. It was very early on Sunday morning, and the streets were uncommonly free of traffic. Norm started in on her as soon as he pulled away from the hotel.

''The folks are very hurt, Jess,'' her brother began. ''Couldn't you have spent the nights at home?''

She and Armand had made love for the last time just before she got up and she still could feel his physical presence. Besides, her mind felt drugged from lack of sleep. She was in no mood to accept her brother's recriminations. *He* didn't live at home!

''I wouldn't have had any more time with them. I've been with the band from early morning until late at night.''

''Was that necessary?''

''Armand needed me. There were contracts to sign, insurance forms to study. He doesn't read all that well. Oh, he's learning fast, but he wouldn't have come here with his band if I hadn't come with them.''

Norm shook his head. "You're throwing yourself away, Jess," he said. "You, of all people—with a guy who can't even read a newspaper!"

She was suddenly furious with him, and with her mother, who must have put him up to this. "Butt out, Junior," she said. "This is one time when you don't know what you're talking about!"

His anger was just as swift. In seconds, they had reverted to their childhood, when Norm had been "the pest."

"You're probably stupid enough to marry the jerk! It would serve you right," he flung at her. Then he added more gently, "I think Pop could accept it, but it would break Mom's heart."

As quickly as it had sprung up, her anger died. She didn't want to quarrel with him. She said more quietly, "You know I don't want to do that, Norm. But this is something I must decide for myself. I'm nobody's 'little girl.' You understand that, don't you?"

"Yeah, I guess," he said finally.

"And if I do marry Armand, it's not going to break Mom's heart. It isn't her heart that's involved, it's pride. Pride of family. She knows I love her—I love you all—and I know she loves me, although she works hard at not showing it."

"Yeah, you're right about that," Norm said wryly. "You *are* planning to marry the guy, then?"

"His name is Armand," she said firmly. "No, I'm not planning it. I love him, but I just don't know, Norm."

He reached into the breast pocket of his jacket and pulled out a Polaroid snapshot. "This is the best shot I took last night. Thought you might like to have it."

It was a color photo of the band, taken while they were doing the oldie, "Jolie Blon'." Armand was playing the traditional Cajun squeezebox and looking off to one side—probably at her, she thought, remembering that revealing expression of love with a catch in her throat.

"Thank you, Norm," Jessica said, touched. When he drew up at her terminal, she leaned over and kissed his cheek. "I hope you get acquainted with Armand while he's here," she said. "He's really a great guy."

Norm made a face. "I promised to take him to the fish market, remember?"

Jessica laughed. "I'm sorry I'm going to miss that."

"Take care, Sis." He hugged her briefly.

Jessica threw the strap of her carry-on bag over her shoulder and went into the terminal.

It was a long lonely flight back to New Orleans, and she had to fight off a depression that filled her with a strange foreboding. Seeing Armand in her old environment had not been the revelation she had hoped for. She was as undecided now as she had ever been about the risks of marrying him. He had carried his glamour of individuality and all his local color with him, and Sharon and her other friends had been bemused by it. His attraction for her had not been dulled, but an apprehension had been added.

She had hated to leave Armand, and two weeks apart from him seemed an unbearably long time.

Anything could happen in two weeks.

THE VERY AIR SMELLED different in New Orleans. As she waited for the shuttle to the parking lot where she had left her car, Jessica drew into her lungs, with the ever-present automobile fumes, the scent of roasting coffee and the pervasive perfume of Southern gardens. In another half hour, she was out on the River Road, heading west.

Crossing the Mississippi, she saw the traffic of barges on the mighty river and heard their mournful horns. Her appreciative eye took in the lush green foliage that appeared along the highway after she left the bridge, and the empty space that seemed restful after the frenzied activity of New York streets. The breeze flowing in her open windows brought a damp whiff of the swamps that lay just out of sight of the highway.

She hummed to herself as she drove the hundred miles to the fishing village on the bayou, where her little house welcomed her with a silence that seemed uncanny after the constant rumble of background noise in a big city. This was home, she thought, glancing around—not her carefully preserved room in the apartment on Fifty-seventh Street. She was glad to be home, and looked forward to returning to the lab. But more than anything else, she looked forward to Armand's return.

Two weeks, she thought, sighing, and picked up the phone to call Mama LeBlanc.

A couple of evenings later, she sat at the big table in the LeBlanc kitchen, describing the band's opening night for Armand's family. She had brought the snapshot Norm had given her, and excitement had traveled around the table as Armand's parents, and *Mémère* and *Pépère* examined it. Norm had captured some of the audience around the stage, and their rapt enjoyment of the music was easy to see. The reaction of Armand's family to that was, but of course! Naturally! It was Cajun music, wasn't it?

Etienne came into the kitchen and looked at the picture closely. "Hey, I can play the *fer*!"

"Anh!" his father exploded. "You think so? You so *fonchock* stuck-up, *Pépère* couldn't teach you to play the accordion."

"I'll show you," Etienne retorted. He left the room and came back with the iron triangle, beating out a rhythm on it with its metal rod.

They laughed at him, to his obvious chagrin. Later, when Jessica was repeating her story for Marie and Danielle, whom Mama called to come over, she could hear Etienne in his room, playing the tape the band had made, and striking the triangle along with it.

She missed Armand with an ache that was almost a physical pain, but here with the people he loved most, she felt their love for him reach out and include her in their close family group.

"I suppose Claire is out dancing tonight?" she asked, wondering if she would feel as accepted if Armand's youngest sister were there.

Mama LeBlanc nodded, but she looked concerned.

"That idiot!" Papa LeBlanc growled.

Mémère muttered something in French.

"They're both stubborn," Marie said.

Jessica glanced questioningly at Marie, who explained, "Hugh Broussard. Claire broke down and called him, and he wouldn't come to the phone."

"Oh, no!" Jessica said, aching for Claire.

Mama LeBlanc nodded, her lips tight. "I worry about her, Jessica."

"She stormed out of here tonight, boiling mad," Danielle said.

"I'm gone over to that dance hall purty soon and fin' out if she's fizzed up another fight," her father said. "She's jus' tryin' to get Hugh's attention. Me, I could knock those kids' heads together, I guarantee."

Shortly afterward, he and Etienne left in his pickup to ride over to the dance hall, and they had not returned when Jessica left.

Her week was a busy one. It was the last big class of the season. The next group would be mostly graduate students, and she spent her evenings preparing a program for them.

When Saturday came around again, Armand telephoned. "I've missed you, Professor." His voice traveled over the wires to her ears like sweet music.

"I've missed you," she confessed.

"I've wanted to call every night, *chére*, but when you're home from the lab, the band is already setting up at the club. Our times are all crisscrossed, anh? Anyway, there was nothing to say but 'I love you,' and you know *thh*at."

"But I never tire of hearing it. I love you, Armand."

"Me, I've been studying since you left," he said with pride and enthusiasm. "And I bought myself a dictionary."

"Great!" She thought she couldn't love him more.

"We're flying home a week from today. One more week. I'll never want to go anywhere without you, my little mud hen. I miss you too much. How would you like to go to France with me?"

"France!" That jolted her. "Slow down, Armand. You're going to France? When?"

"I don' know. That agent of Nance Marie's is saying he can arrange a tour for the band over there."

"What?" Jessica almost screamed.

"He says Frenchmen are eentrigued by zydeco. Can you believe it? Nance is all excited. Jocko's been there—that fella's been everywhere, anh? Picou's not sure he wants to fly again." He chuckled.

"Damn that agent," Jessica exploded. "Damn Nance Marie!"

"Hey!" he said. "W'at's up?"

"That's what I'd like to know!" she cried. She was surprised to feel a tremor in the hand holding the receiver to her ear, astonished at the way she was reacting, but she seemed to have no control.

"Wouldn't you like to see France, Professor?"

"I've seen it. And I can't get away long enough for a tour."

"Well, I haven't seen it, my *jolie blon',* and I've always wanted to. Papa always used to say when he had a real good catch some year he'd take us all. It's where our people came from in the beginning."

"Nearly three hundred years ago! What do you have in common now?"

"Mebbe that's w'at I want to find out, *chére.* Besides, this fella says we'll make good money, and that sounds good, don' it? Don' you want me to make more money?"

"What about your new boat? Are you going to let it just sit there in the bayou? And what about me? Nance Marie can go chasing across the Atlantic with you, but I can't, if I want to keep my position."

"Are you jealous of Nance Marie, *chére*?" He sounded almost pleased.

Furious, she shouted, "I'm not jealous!" and then stopped, wondering what had happened to her ingrained reserve. She had completely lost control. She *was* jealous! She couldn't stand the thought of Nance Marie and Armand traveling together through France.

"I think," she said unhappily, "that I have more in common with a fisherman than a rock star!"

"Zydeco isn't rock," he said, sounding offended. "It's Cajun."

"All right, Cajun rock! What I said still goes."

"Let's not quarrel, *chére,*" he coaxed, his voice so tender that it melted her. "I'm coming home next week, whatever. And I'm going to take *Cajun Pride Too* out this fall. I love you, Professor."

"I love you," she whispered, almost in tears.

"Then marry me, Jessica."

She didn't sleep that night. She had hung up the phone, pretending she hadn't heard Armand's last words. She was too afraid it was an ultimatum. What was happening to them? What had happened to him in New York?

Russell's remark came back to haunt her. *Are your friends enjoying their fifteen minutes of fame?* Had success changed Armand? She was changing! She hardly knew the person who had screamed at Armand over the wires.

Jessica had finally dozed off, near daybreak, when the telephone rang in her kitchen. She dragged herself out of bed, wondering who would call her this early. She remembered that it was an hour later in New York.

"Hello?" she said, wondering whether she would hear Armand's or her mother's voice.

But it was Mama LeBlanc who cried, "Jesseeca!" in tones of tragedy, and then launched into a high-decibel mix of Cajun and English that was totally incomprehensible.

"Slow down," Jessica begged her. "I can't understand you."

Another stream of high volume sound assaulted her ears. All she got out of it was "Claire" and an impression of terrible anxiety.

"Etienne!" Jessica shouted into the phone, "I mean Steve. Get Steve."

"'*Allo*, Miss Jessica," he said finally, sounding calm but very serious. "Mama's very upset because Claire didn't come home last night. You haven't seen her, have you?"

"No," Jessica said. "I haven't seen Claire since I came home from New York."

"Mama's wild. She and Papa have been phoning all her friends. She wasn't with any of them last night. Nobody's seen her."

Jessica felt her stomach slide down like a fast elevator. "Tell your mother I'll be right over."

"Thanks, Miss Jessica. Marie's coming over, but Danielle has her kids to take care of. I'm goin' out with Papa now to look for Claire."

"Where?"

"Good question," said Etienne. "We thought she went to the same dance hall as last Saturday night. But nobody Papa talked to saw her there, and the guy she told us was taking her says he didn't have no date. Papa says he can't sit by the phone any longer. Mama wants me to go along so he won't smash himself up. Or somebody else."

"Tell them I'll be there as soon as I can get dressed."

"Okay."

Jessica put down the phone and went to get some aspirin for the fierce headache that was already developing. She hastily pulled on shorts and a T-shirt and brushed her hair, feeling a little sick because of the picture that had flashed into her mind as Etienne talked. Where had it come from? She tried to put it out of her mind—a haunting vision of Claire's pretty face staring sightlessly up through a foot of black bayou water.

CHAPTER FIFTEEN

JESSICA FOUND Mama LeBlanc sitting at the kitchen table, uncharacteristically quiet, with tears rolling down her cheeks. *Mémère*, looking wizened and fragile, was at the stove, making a fresh pot of coffee. Marie had arrived, and was on the telephone.

Jessica sat down beside Mrs. LeBlanc and held her hand. "I'm certain Claire is all right," she said, wishing she could be as sure as she sounded.

"She never stay away wit'out telling me," Mama LeBlanc said brokenly. "She's good girl. Somet'in' wrong, wrong."

"Did she tell you where she was going?"

"She say to dance!" Mrs. LeBlanc became so agitated that once more Jessica could not follow her speech. She looked to Marie, who had hung up the phone.

"All we know is that she had a date. We were all here last night, talkin' an' carryin' on, like we do. Claire waltzed in and kissed Mama and said, 'I'm goin' now.'" She shrugged. "Mama was busy at the stove, and never did see who came for her. When we discovered she hadn't come home last night, we started checking, and none of us had seen her date."

"But she left in a car?" Jessica asked.

"Well, she must have. Mama thought she was going out with Henny, so Papa called him, but he said he didn't have a date with her and he didn't see her last night. So Papa began calling her closest friends. Nobody had seen her at any of the places the young crowd hangs out. So he called Father Naquin, and learned that she hadn't gone to him. Next he began calling all our relatives, anybody she might have gone to. Nobody's seen her."

Jessica's feelings of dread and apprehension were growing stronger by the minute. "Someone must have been driving the car that took her away."

A look came into Marie's eyes, and Jessica regretted having put it there. "I never thought—but I don't remember hearing a car drive off." She rejected her fear with "But we were so noisy—"

"Have you checked to see what she took with her?"

"To a dance?" Marie said. Then she stood up. "Come on, let's go look."

Jessica followed her into Claire's bedroom. Neat and sparsely furnished, on this Sunday morning it seemed to exude a sad aura of desertion. Marie lowered her voice so her mother and grandmother would not hear. "Papa is very upset. He wanted to go to the police, but *Pépère* reminded him that Claire is over eighteen. Jonquile says that anyway the police have no reason to consider her missing until more than one night has passed.

"He brought me over here and then went down to the bus station to try to find out if she bought a ticket."

"Where would she go?" Jessica asked.

"She could go to our aunt in New Iberia, or she could go to Sister Catherine's convent in New Orleans. Papa's called them both, but she still could turn up there."

Marie opened Claire's closet, and began pushing hangers to one side. "Maury's out looking, too. *Pépère*'s over at his trailer in case she calls there. Danielle said she'd stay home with the kids. They'd only get on Mama's nerves right now."

She had reached the end of the closet rod. "I can't see that anything's missing here except the dress she had on." Slowly she gazed around the room, frowning. "She usually keeps a flashlight on the table beside her bed . . . but somebody could have borrowed it."

The telephone was ringing, and Marie hurried out of the bedroom to answer it. Jessica stayed behind, trying to put herself in Claire's mind, hurt and humiliated by Hugh's refusal to even talk with her. What would she have done? Where would she have fled to escape her torment?

She checked all the surfaces and opened the drawer in the nightstand. No flashlight there. Could Claire possibly have taken it with her? And if she had, why? Her own feeling that something was wrong intensified. Jessica got down on her knees to look under the bed.

She did not like what she was imagining: Claire walking. Alone, with a flashlight. It didn't sound like she was going out on a date. Nor running away, if she took no clothing. Claire had obviously been unhappy, but—oh, dear God, not that unhappy! If their search ended in tragedy . . .

Jessica thought of Armand's pain first, then that of all his big devoted family. Claire was their baby. So pert and sassy! Jessica's throat tightened, and she fought for self-control before going back to the kitchen.

Marie was saying, "Mama, did you borrow Claire's flashlight?"

"*Non*, it's in her room. There's another in the pantry, eef you need."

Marie looked significantly at Jessica. "That was Danielle that called. She said Jonquile and Maury are checking other nightclubs in the area, asking if anyone saw her among the dancers last night. She said Papa's going around to the houses of all her girlfriends, anyone she might have stayed over with. He thinks they could lie to him over the phone. He plans to visit every man she's dated. But why would she want to worry us like this? It isn't like Claire.''

"Will he go to see Hugh Broussard?" Jessica asked.

Marie exclaimed, "I hope not. He's so angry, he'll tear him limb from limb!''

Mémère poured coffee for everyone with shaking hands, and they sat around the table, drinking it in a brooding silence.

Jessica was thinking about Claire's telephone call. It must have taken courage and great sacrifice of pride to call Hugh. Jessica wondered whether she had been going to offer to leave the country with him, after all?

His refusal to speak to her would have been devastating. She tried again to put herself in Claire's place. What would she have done?

This time the answer was clear. She wouldn't have thrown herself in the bayou!

Nor would Claire! She had seen that terrible fear leap into Marie's eyes to match her own. But the more she thought about it, the less she believed in it. Claire was proud, and she was stubborn. She was not one to give up hope.

"They were both stubborn," Marie had said.

Jessica began trying to recall everything she could of her conversation with Hugh the day she had given him a ride. She had not been successful in finding him a job, but he still hadn't left town.

And leave Claire? he'd said. *I guess I'll always worry about her.* That sounded to Jessica like a man in love.

And Hugh knew Claire well. *She's acting like a woman on a motorcycle riding around in circles, not knowing how to turn the damn thing off.*

When she had an opportunity to talk to Marie alone, Jessica said, "I think we should call Hugh Broussard."

Marie shook her head. "Papa and Mama both blame him for Claire's unhappiness."

"But wouldn't Hugh have some idea of what Claire would do, where she would go?" Jessica argued. "After all, he must know her pretty well."

"If he wouldn't talk to Claire, he won't talk to me. He thinks we cost him his fine job with the oil company, you know."

"Just the same, he wouldn't want anything to happen to Claire. I think he cares for her. Let's talk to him, Marie."

"I've got to stay with Mama and *Mémère* until someone comes back."

"If you'll tell me where he lives, I'll go see him," Jessica offered. "All he can do is tell me to mind my own business."

Marie ran a hand through her dark hair in a gesture that reminded Jessica of Armand. "You could get away with that better than any of us could," she agreed, with a wry smile. She gave Jessica directions. "Everybody lives on the bayou, so you can't miss it. Just look for R. Broussard on the mailbox. You'll see lots of Broussards," she warned.

After telling the two older women that she would be back, Jessica went out to start her car. The sun had reached it, and the vinyl seat and the steering wheel were painfully hot. She started it and turned on the air conditioner. She wished Armand were here. Perhaps she should have called him and asked his advice before meddling in Claire's explosive affair.

Well, she was committed now, and she felt a pressure to hurry, to prevent something tragic from happening. She could at least warn Hugh that Claire's father was violently angry at him, as well as desperately worried about Claire.

The morning air was still. The strands of moss festooning the trees hung limply. Dragonflies hovered over the bayou, mirrored in its unbroken surface. Gradually the car cooled until it was bearable.

Jessica drove slowly, reading names on the mail route. It was still early, but men were already puttering on their boats tied up at the small docks on the bayou, or sitting, still in their Sunday clothes, on the shaded verandas facing the water. Children and dogs ran happily back and forth across the road, between the houses and the docks.

She was in luck. Hugh Broussard was just stepping from the dock in front of his house into a small outboard motorboat when she spotted him. She pulled off the road and stopped. "Hello, Hugh," she called.

He stared at her for a moment. He didn't look happy to see her, but he waved. She jumped out of the car, taking her purse and her keys, and ran down to the dock.

"Claire didn't come home last night," she said, not wasting time in leading up to what she had to say. "Do you have any idea where she might be?"

"Why should I?" he asked, scowling.

Jessica chose her words carefully. "She didn't have a date last night, Hugh. She left the house alone, and I believe she was walking, with a flashlight. And she hasn't come home." She added, "She was upset because you had refused her call."

Hugh said nothing, still regarding her with that black scowl.

"Do you have any idea where she might have gone?"

"I might," he said, after a silent half second. He stretched out a hand. "You'd better come along."

Jessica took his hand and stepped carefully into the boat. He untied it and went to start his motor. Moments later they were cutting a wide wake down the bayou.

They soon left Chauvin behind them. She didn't realize immediately that the bayou had forked because things looked different seen from the water than from the road she followed to work. But there were no houses here. Hugh slowed and moved ahead cautiously. Presently he cut his motor and let the boat drift toward the bank. There was a strip of mud there that showed the marks of a small boat, possibly a rowboat, sliding down into the water.

Hugh revved his motor, returning to the center of the waterway and continued on his way. Ahead of them was the marsh, mostly flooded here, with a few clumps of grass standing high. But directly ahead of them the flat grassy horizon was broken in one spot by a clump of oak trees. As they neared it, Jessica saw that it was an island of high dry ground in the marsh, covered with oaks half-killed by the moss that draped them so heavily that the space they occupied was curtained off from both the sun and the wind.

"How could Claire come here?" Jessica burst out, unable to contain the questions buzzing in her head any longer.

Hugh pointed to the bank he was approaching. There was no dock, but a small, flat-bottomed boat had been dragged up out of the water into the grasses. "She came in that."

"You know she's here?"

"That's our pirogue." He cut the motor, letting the bow of the boat nudge the bank, and jumped out to drag it up on the mud beside the canoe. "You'd better stay here while I get her," he said. "She's in our secret place. No one else knows about it."

Jessica nodded. He wiped his hands on his trousers and began trotting toward the trees. In moments he had disappeared behind the curtains of moss.

She waited under the awning that stretched over the midsection of the boat and protected her from the direct sun. The ripples of their wake lapped gently against the stern for a little while, and finally died. The bayou grew still again, with no discernible tide. Mosquitoes buzzed near her ears, and she searched her purse for a piece of paper large enough to fan them away.

The birds frightened up by their motor settled back down in the trees and on the marsh, and the only sound was the click and rustle and buzz of insects in the grass, a sound that seemed to emphasize the heat.

From time to time Jessica looked at her watch. What had Hugh found in the ghostly rooms behind the moss disguising the skeletal oaks? What was happening?

She was very hot. Now and then she trailed her wrists in the water, which was cooler than the air.

Nearly an hour passed.

Jessica had decided to climb out of the boat and go up the grassy bank to face whatever was behind the trees, when the two of them came through the moss draperies, Hugh with his arm around a tearful Claire. Her face was swollen with heat and tears and mosquito bites, but in spite of that it had a new serenity.

Looking at her, Jessica knew what it was that had subconsciously urged her to go to Hugh Broussard. It was something Armand's father had said earlier in the week, when Jessica had dinner at the LeBlancs'.

Claire had finally succeeded in getting Hugh's attention.

THEY SPED BACK up the bayou, with Hugh at the rudder and the pirogue Claire had used tied on behind, bouncing in their wake.

"I think you should go with us to the LeBlancs'," Jessica told him. She refrained from reproaching Armand's sister or asking for explanations. The important thing was to get word to her family that she was safe.

"You can talk to Claire's mother first, if you wish. The men are out searching for Claire."

He nodded soberly.

He seemed to understand what Jessica was saying. She hoped he could talk fast enough to keep Papa LeBlanc from losing his temper when he came home.

Claire seemed aware of nothing but that Hugh was with her, holding her close, although tears were still coursing down her cheeks. Jessica's heart swelled with sympathy and a fearful hope for her happiness. It was obvious that they had taken time to talk out at least one of their problems. They knew they wanted to be together.

With some apprehension, Jessica walked with the two lovers along the veranda to the LeBlancs' kitchen door, then remained at the door while Mama LeBlanc, sobbing with happiness, embraced both of them. She hugged Jessica then, her garbled language not making much sense, but her emotions easy to understand. Marie was on the telephone to Danielle, telling her Claire had been found, and to let the men know if they called.

"Is Papa very angry with me?" Claire asked.

"He'll be happy," Marie reassured her. "He said you were both so stubborn he'd like to knock your heads together."

Hugh laughed nervously.

"Where did you go?"

Claire exchanged a loving look with Hugh. "To our secret place. You won't tell, Jessica?"

"Never," Jessica promised.

Mémère took Claire off to her room, clucking in French at her mosquito bites, and insisting that she get some rest. Jessica prepared to leave and offered Hugh a ride, but Hugh shook his head.

"I'd better wait and see Mr. LeBlanc."

Jessica nodded her approval. She went outside and started her car. She was crossing the bridge to her side of the bayou when she realized with a feeling of surprise that Sunday was only half over. She wondered what Armand was doing in New York, and as soon as she unlocked her door, went to the telephone and called the Royalton Hotel.

Armand was not in his room, the operator reported. Jessica asked her to try the other rooms occupied by the band. Nobody answered. Then she had Armand paged.

He was not in the hotel.

They were probably all out sight-seeing together, she thought. And why not? New York was an education in itself. Wasn't that what she wanted for Armand?

Nevertheless, the excitement of the morning, and the frustration she felt because she wasn't able to tell Armand about the commotion Claire had caused in the family by slipping away, had left her feeling very let-down.

She didn't know whether Claire or Hugh had straightened out their relationship, but Claire was obviously happier. In contrast, Jessica's problem seemed to be getting more complex and more worrisome.

She had a nagging feeling that if Armand agreed to go on tour with Nance Marie in France, it would signal the beginning of the end of their relationship. There was so much pain in that thought that she rejected it. But neither did she enjoy feeling like a dog in the manger.

How long could she go on, enjoying Armand's love but refusing to give him the commitment he wanted?

The rest of the hot, sun-filled Sunday stretched interminably ahead of her. And she was very lonely.

CHAPTER SIXTEEN

ARMAND'S FIRST GLIMPSE of his home state was of the forked mouth of the Mississippi River spilling brown silt into the greenish-blue waters of the Gulf.

His plane had swung south over the Gulf, and as it lost altitude it flew over the marshes southwest of New Orleans. He leaned to look down from his window on the bayous below, winding lazily through the grass in an intricate pattern of canals and lagoons. Here and there he saw a lonely house on stilts, far from its neighbors. He felt a deep affection for those unknown marsh dwellers, because his longing to be down there himself was so intense.

For two weeks he and the members of his band had been living practically in each other's pockets, with the din of the city, night and day, in their ears. He liked them all; he enjoyed Jocko's worldly sanity and Nance Marie's bubbling enthusiasm, even Picou's dogged pessimism, but he needed to get away from them. New York was exciting, but there the other people crowding one were an irritant, like an itch. A marsh dweller's neighbors were unseen yet closer, because they were prized.

He felt a deep need for the isolation of the marsh. To be alone, with the grasses and the limitless horizon and the snowy-plumed egret soaring overhead in the lonely sky, and the deck of *Cajun Pride Too* under his feet... Alone with Jessica.

It was Saturday, so she would be home. He called her from the airport. "It's the dark of the moon tonight, Professor," he told her, when he heard her clear crisp voice. "Will you go out on the marsh wit' me?"

She answered, "Yes," without hesitation.

That's my woman, he thought. Oh, *Dieu,* how he loved her! "I'll be there in two hours."

"Welcome home," she said softly. "Oh, welcome, Armand! I'll fix something for us to eat."

"Fix a little somet'ing we can take wit' us," he told her, and went to pick up his car. When the band's luggage had been stowed in the trunk, he tossed Jocko his keys and handed Nance Marie into the front passenger seat. He crawled into the back with Picou to take a nap, as best he could with his guitar between his knees, while Jocko drove them back to the bayous.

He couldn't sleep, after all. He hadn't been able to sleep on the plane. His head was a beehive, swarming with thoughts of Jessica, thoughts that made his body throb with impatience. By the time he had taken the wheel and delivered the other members of his band to their doors, his nerves were quivering. To his dismay, both his married sisters were at the house, and Etienne was dispatched to the trailer to bring *Mémère* and Pépère to welcome him home.

He was greeted like a conquering hero, with Papa and his sisters hugging him, and Etienne pounding his back. One of Danielle's toddlers grabbed each leg. Laughing, he pulled them with him as he waddled over to his mother. She and *Pépère* were laughing, too, but old *Mémère,* so fragile she trembled, was crying.

He could not get away without hearing how Claire had run off to a secret rendezvous only Hugh Broussard knew about, and how Jessica had been smart enough to guess that Hugh would know where she was hiding, and had brought the two of them back home.

"So is Claire's wedding on again?" he asked, noting that Claire was the only one not there to greet him.

"Hugh still doesn't have a job," Danielle reminded him.

"But at least, they're speaking," Marie put in.

Etienne said, "Hey, the next time you go to New York, I want to go, too, and play the *fer*."

"Anh! You finally decide' you want to be a dumb Cajun?"

"If they dig our music in New York, why shouldn't I?"

"Now you gettin' smart," Armand told him. "You still gone bug us about calling you Steve?"

His brother flushed. "I answer to Etienne, don't I?"

"Okay, Steve."

Etienne beamed.

Armand finally got away without his brother, who wanted to go with him every time he took the boat out. He ran down to the dock, untied *Cajun Pride Too*, and started her engine. It just purred. A short time later he was tying up at the dock Jessica shared with her landlord.

When she opened the door, he stood still for a moment, feasting his eyes. Her pale hair shone like the gold of a sunset over the marshes and her eyes were the warm deep blue of the Gulf on a cloudless day. She was like no one else, and she was incredibly beautiful. When he opened his arms she fitted into them as if *le bon Dieu* had made her for him. Which, he thought, was quite likely.

"*Chére, chére* Jessica," he said, holding her close, and wondering if he could let go of her long enough to take her out on the marsh. He wanted her, wanted to taste her, to caress her everywhere at once, to fuse his body with hers. He slipped his hand down the front of her shirt and gently found her hardened nipple, and his longing almost over-whelmed him.

"We could have missed finding each other, anh? How could I live without you?" He tore himself away from her warm welcoming lips, and asked, "You ready? If we don' leave now, Professor," he threatened, "I'm gone carry you into your bedroom. Tonight I want you with me on *Cajun Pride Too*, anh?"

My two loves!

Flushed and looking wonderfully happy, Jessica picked up a basket from the kitchen table and went out with him, locking her door. She was wearing white shorts and a white shirt, and her beautiful legs were long and golden in the waning sunlight as she took his hand and stepped aboard the boat.

She left her basket in the galley, and they went through the cabin. He stood at the wheel with Jessica at his shoulder, looking through the windshield as he steered the boat down the bayou. The smell of the salt marsh with a hint of diesel fuel from his engine was familiar and deeply satis-fying. He drew it into his lungs in a deep breath.

"It's good to be home," he said. "Me, I couldn't ever live away from the marsh."

"Does that mean you won't go to France?" Jessica asked.

"Anh! We have to talk about that." But he didn't say any more.

They passed other boats tied up to the banks, and they waved back to those who hailed them from the shore.

"Where you go?" a man called. "It's too soon for the shrimps, man."

"We make a ghost run," Armand shouted through the open side window of his wheelhouse.

"You *fooyay* to waste all that fuel!" the man shouted back.

They glided past the houses on stilts, past the marine biology laboratory, past the end of the road where the marsh began, and headed into the shallow waters of the lagoon. When the last buildings had disappeared, and the sun was sinking into the marsh to their right, Armand cut his engine. The boat drifted to a stop in the still water and a profound quiet enveloped them. The only sounds were the soft lapping of their dying wake against the hull and the plaintive call of a curlew hidden in the marsh.

"W'at you got in that basket?" Armand asked.

They went back through the cabin and Jessica picked up their supper. She had brought sandwiches and fruit and a bottle of wine. She filled two wineglasses. They sat cross-legged on the deck and ate and sipped wine, while the sun dropped below the horizon and darkness gradually erased its bright afterglow.

The air was balmy and moisture-laden, redolent of salt marsh odors. The night had come on so gradually that they didn't miss the day when it was gone, and Armand postponed putting on his running lights. Stars twinkled overhead but there was no moon. A powerful magnet was drawing them together, but Armand resisted it. Not yet, he told himself.

He picked up a crust of bread that had fallen from his sandwich. "Watch this," he said, and crumbled it and tossed the tiny fragments of bread overboard. Each crumb became part of a bright shower of sparks, and as they fell through the water, a school of minnows flashed upward to reach for them, each tiny fish outlined in light.

Jessica exclaimed softly, and leaned over the rail to watch. She cried out again at what she saw. The whole bottom of the boat's hull was outlined in the water below

the surface by the phosphorescent glow of bubbles clinging to it. She looked up at him. Their gazes met, and
without another word, they began removing their clothing.

Armand went into the water first, and Jessica exclaimed aloud at the flashing beauty of his body outlined
in phosphorescence and followed by a trail of sparks. The
little fish made streaks of light as they darted away. She
slipped over the rail and glanced down to see her own legs
and feet outlined in light before she went under.

Armand was treading water near her when she surfaced
again. "Perfect," he said, looking at the exquisite curves
outlined by glowing sparks.

"This is unreal," she said, her voice unsteady as her
wide eyes traced the golden outline of his body.

"You've never seen this?" He was moving closer. "It
happens in fall, eef there's no moon."

"I've heard of it." She gasped another breath and shook
the water out of her eyes and ears. "It's caused by phosphorescent organisms in the water that glow like fireflies
when something disturbs—"

He had come close enough to grab her. "Such a smart
woman, my golden professor," he said, laughing at her,
and silenced her with a kiss. They sank together in a
shower of sparks. Armand began kicking them to the surface, still holding her. They broke through and with a single thought swam together in a streak of light toward the
ghostly outline of *Cajun Pride Too*'s underwater hull.

Together they scrambled aboard, rolling over on the
deck. Armand wrapped his arms and legs around her and
began kissing her and teasing her with his lips, tasting the
musky salty water on them as he thrust his tongue into the
sweet warmth of her mouth.

He wanted to go slowly, to make their pleasure last as long as he could, but his desire had been caged too long. This was what he had been planning ever since he boarded that plane in New York—to take her on the deck of his boat—and it was too much for his control. He was suddenly a runaway train, plunging into her, cursing himself even in his ecstasy. *Dieu!* She was too much for him!

"I'm sorry, *chére*," he said with deep regret, when he could speak again.

He pushed himself to his knees and picked her up. Standing and carrying her wet body in his arms, with her hair dripping over his bare shoulder, he padded down the deck. He carried her through the galley and sat her on one of the two bunks in the cabin. Then he pulled a towel out of a cabinet and began gently drying her golden hair.

"Now, my sweet mermaid," he said tenderly, "we take our time, anh?"

She didn't say anything, but while he was separating her hair into strands and rubbing each lock dry, she began gently touching him, and in no time at all he felt himself hardening again.

"Anh!" he said, deep in his throat.

The towel moved more and more slowly. Soon it had dropped to the floor and his lips found her breasts. His hands moved sensuously over her body, and now she was the one who could not wait. "Love me! Love me!" she cried, and slowly and sweetly he made the narrow bunk a bed of ecstasy.

AFTERWARD, LYING STILL and warm and happy in his arms, Jessica asked him again about the proposed tour.

"It's only a possibility, but Gus said it's a strong possibility. He said there's a lot of interest in our Cajun music in France."

"Gus?"

"Fitzhugh. The agent."

So already he was Gus. High-powered, Russ had called him.

"I thought you were happy to be home," she reproached him. "You said you never wanted to leave the marsh."

His arms tightened around her. "This is where I want to be. Exactly. The question is," he said slowly, "if they all want to go, can I stand in their road?"

"And if this tour leads to another?" Jessica asked him. "And another?"

"Nance says they can get another guitar player easier after a successful tour."

"Oh, *Nance* says!"

"Nance says you're jealous," he teased her.

"Of course, I'm jealous!" she cried. "I've never in my life screamed at anyone the way I screamed at you over the phone, Armand! I couldn't believe it!"

Armand laughed. "You know w'at? I loved it." He raised himself on an elbow. "So we should maybe get married, anh?"

Jessica caught her breath and was stilled. Was she ready for this?

"When I can read a page from your book—the husband-and-wife book about the marshes—will you marry me?"

She couldn't speak, she was so moved, and yet still so confused.

The silence lengthened.

"W'y does love got to be so sad?" he asked resignedly. "Everybody chooses the wrong one to love, anh?"

"Don't say that," Jessica begged. "I do love you."

"Claire could have any one of a half dozen bayou boys and be happy, but she picks the one who wants to live half the world away, the one who will break her heart. And Nance Marie picks me."

Jessica thought, *So he admits she's in love with him!*

"And who do I fall in love with?" He rubbed his hand over the curve of her shoulder and down to touch her breast, and answered himself, "A woman who's read so many books that no matter how fast I read, she'll always be a thousand or two ahead of me. Funny, anh?"

"Armand..." She put her fingers into the fine curls of hair on his chest and twisted them.

"I went to that big library in New York," he told her. "The one you showed me, just a couple blocks from our hotel? I never knew there were that many books in the world! Do you expect me to read them all?"

It was hot in the cabin. The doors at each end of the sleeping compartment were open, but the night breeze entering through the open windows in the wheelhouse just forward of where they lay was almost as warm as the air in the cabin.

Jessica rolled away from him. "Let's go out on deck."

He reached for her, and held her lightly to prevent her rising from the bunk. "I want an answer, Professor. Are you going to marry me?"

"Armand, I can't answer you just like that!"

"W'y not?"

"I've got to think about it."

"What is there to t'ink?" he said roughly. "You say you love me. So w'y can't you answer me?"

"You haven't answered my question about going to France," she flung at him.

"You want to bargain?" he said, an edge of real anger in his voice. "Is that it? If I don't go on the tour, you'll marry me?"

"No," Jessica said, "I mean, no, I didn't say that. I'm not bargaining, Armand. I just want to be very sure."

"Of w'at? W'at's sure in life, except that some day we'll both die, anh? An' I hope it's together, me." There was still that hard edge to his voice. "W'at do you want, Jessica? W'at do you expect of me?"

When she did not answer at once, he said, "I tell you w'at. I'm gone take *Cajun Pride Too* offshore for a few days now when the fall season opens. I'm gone out and get me some five-inch white shrimps and make me enough money this year to buy us a house. So I'll wait 'til the end of the season for your answer."

He gave her a hard kiss, then pushed her up and sat up on the bunk beside her. "I'll tell you one thing for sure, my little mud hen, if your answer is still no when the season's over, I guarantee you I'll go to France wit' the band!"

Jessica had no answer. It was an ultimatum. Armand wanted a commitment, and she had been drifting, enjoying his love and his companionship, putting off a decision. The time had come to make her choice.

They went out on deck and retrieved their discarded clothing and silently put it on. A misshapen moon was rising in the east, and when Armand started up his engine and began moving the trawler through the water, there was no phosphorescence in it. The magic was gone.

THE NEXT EVENING Armand brought a CB radio to Jessica's house and told her what channel she could tune in to hear the shrimpers talk to one another. He also showed her how to reach him if she had a message for him.

"Remember I answer to 'Zydeco,'" he told her. "That's the radio name the other guys give me."

There was a tenseness about him that she recognized, the same tension he had shown before the spring opening. She sensed it in the very air along the bayou where the fishermen were mending their torn nets, fine-tuning their engines and trying to guess when the Fisheries and Wildlife people would declare the season open. It would depend partly on when the samples of white shrimp the state agency took were less than one hundred to the pound. Since the first boats out would get their loads more quickly and easily than the rest, all of them wanted to be primed to go the minute the word was out.

"I'm goin' to the Gulf, but just offshore," Armand told her, excitement brightening his eyes. "I've got me some fine new door boards for my trawl, and I'm gone sit out there in one of those passes through the offshore islands and scoop up a million or so of those pretty white shrimps that'll be travelin' through."

Jessica knew just what he was talking about, for she had studied the mysterious mass migration of both the brown and the white shrimps, still not fully understood by scientists. An adult female shrimp laid from half a million to a million eggs that developed, on their own, through eleven different stages of planktonlike creatures before becoming baby shrimps. Then they surged into the rich nourishing marshes where they were safe from the larger predators, and protected by law until they matured.

The cooling of the marsh water when fall came was the signal for the white shrimp, having matured during the summer months, to return to the place of their birth in the Gulf. They swam together, millions of them crowding the passes through the offshore islands that separated the bays from the Gulf. The trawlers waited in the passes to scoop them up through the wooden jaws of their nets that Armand called door boards.

"I suppose you're taking Steve out of school to go with you?"

"He can start late and make up."

When she frowned, he said, "Fishing is Louisiana's most important industry, Professor. I want Etienne—Steve to have a lot more schoolin' than I had, but he's gonna grow up knowin' how to handle a *paupière*, just like *Pépère* and Papa, just like me. He's a good hand, and I need him."

"Po-p-yee?" It was a new word to her.

"That's w'at we call the net. It means 'eyelid.'"

"Eyelid! Why on earth do you call it that?"

Armand shrugged, grinning. "W'y not?"

"It would make more sense to call them *papillons*, 'butterfly nets,' as they do in Mexico!"

"W'at Cajun has good sense?" Armand asked her, laughing. "Would I fall in love with a *jolie blon'* professor, if I had good sense?"

Once again the literacy workbook was forgotten in the excitement of getting ready for the opening. Once again the docks up and down the bayou gleamed with yellow mosquito lights as boats were readied to leave for inshore and offshore positions when trawling again became legal. Then the graceful small craft being loaded with ice and provisions would become groaning workhorses.

Jessica joined the LeBlanc family on their dock. She was not surprised to see Hugh Broussard there with Claire, helping the LeBlanc men ready the boat.

Claire was radiant. "Hugh's going to apply for a job that's opening up on an offshore rig," she confided to Jessica. "A friend told him about the opening, and he has an appointment in Houma at the oil company's office tomorrow morning. Isn't he lucky to have a friend who thought of him? Of course, he's an experienced roust-about. But there's not many rigs still operating, and so few openings."

"He's decided to stay in Louisiana, then?"

Claire's expression became defensive. "Well, he has to have a job. He's been out of work ever since he turned down the chance to go to Saudi Arabia."

So they had made up, Jessica guessed, but had still not solved the chief difference between them, the difference that had shattered their wedding plans. She wondered whether Hugh had relinquished his desire to see some-thing of the world beyond the bayous, or if Claire was willing to leave them. Neither seemed likely. How long would their reconciliation last?

Etienne was clearly happy to be leaving school for a few weeks of hard labor on the trawler, and Jessica surprised both Papa and *Pépère* looking wistful as the excitement of the evening's preparations intensified. They were not going with Armand this time, since he would be fishing in the passes and offshore, and staying longer.

Armand came up behind her and slipped an arm around her. "*Thh*ink of me when you go to bed tonight," he whispered. "And dream of those five-inch, thirty-to-the-pound whites that are gonna buy our house."

She kissed him goodbye, but made no promises. She was still warring with herself about a lifetime commitment with a man she admitted she would always love.

THE NEXT MORNING Jessica tuned in the CB band and lis-tened to the shrimp boat skippers talk to one another while she prepared breakfast and got ready to go to the lab.

"Where you at, Otter?"

"Over by the rig. You doin' any good, Pelican?"

"Purty good. But I don' like dat wind comin' up. It gone be choppy in the Gulf, no?"

"*Oui.* T'ink I stay right here. Ten-four."

Jessica poured another cup of coffee, and listened as the fishermen exchanged news and speculated on the weather and the availability of the shrimps, often in French. She jumped up when she heard Armand's voice.

"You listenin', Mud Hen? Zydeco here. Come in Mud Hen."

She scrambled for the controls and switched on the mike. "Mud Hen here. I'm getting you, Zydeco." Her voice trembled with excitement. "Over."

"Got ya, Mud Hen. Call home and tell them I'm gone be sittin' in Whiskey Pass today."

"Okay, will do. Is it windy where you are, Zydeco?"

"Not bad. Ten-four."

Jessica looked at her watch, and dialed Armand's house. The line was busy for several minutes, and she had to leave, or she would be late for work. She would have to call from the lab.

When she entered, the receptionist at the information desk greeted her with a message that Dr. Tarbell wanted her to call his office. As soon as she reached her desk, she picked up her phone.

"Good morning, Jessica," he said, when she reached him. "I'm canceling all field trips today. The weather picture is too uncertain."

"I thought the storm was heading for Mexico?"

"The picture could change. We can't take risks with the students."

"The fishing boats all went out this morning," she told him.

"They had to go out the first day of the season, but I expect they'll come in early. They'll be listening to the

Weather Service. They have to deal with hurricane threats every fall season."

She knew by the hint of assurance in his voice that he was thinking of Armand, too. She supposed everybody in the lab knew by now that they were an item, as the Hollywood gossip columnists loved to say.

It was not until her coffee break that she was able to call the LeBlancs' number again. Claire answered. She sounded vibrant as she thanked Jessica for calling.

"If you talk to Armand again, tell him that Hugh has an interview scheduled at the rig this afternoon. He's going out on the company helicopter with the man who interviewed him here. An employee was taken off ill, and they need someone in a hurry."

"That sounds promising, doesn't it?" Jessica said. "Wish him luck for me."

"Thanks!" Claire caroled.

So what if Hugh got a job on an offshore rig again? Did that mean he was willing to stay in the parish for Claire's sake? She hoped Claire's happiness would last.

Jessica couldn't wait to get home that evening to turn on the CB again. If the storm stayed on course to Mexico, Armand would unload his catch at a plant in Dulac on Bayou Dularge, which was closer to the Gulf than Houma. If the trawling was good, he would head right back offshore. She might not see him again until the season was over. And what was she going to tell him when he came back to stay?

She was still teetering between a reckless plunge into happiness today, letting tomorrow bring disaster, if it would—or a deliberate choice of abject misery today, and getting over it tomorrow.

If she could.

It seemed impossible for her to make a move in either direction.

Her mother had trained her too well to view every problem objectively. Her objectivity in trying to make this most important decision of her life was paralyzing her.

CHAPTER SEVENTEEN

WHISKEY PASS WAS DOTTED with trawlers of all sizes and shapes, and the air crackled with their excited talk. Armand could hear it from where he stood at the stern of *Cajun Pride Too*, feeding out his trawl while Etienne held the wheel steady.

"You hear me, Peewee? This here's Otter."

"Got ya, Otter."

"Ah'm over by the point. They's shrimps on the surface over here, a pretty sight. I'm puttin' down now."

Armand found the physical exertion of paying out the fine mesh net deeply satisfying. Nothing could beat a fisherman's life when the shrimps were plentiful, like now. He'd wager life held nothing finer than a calm night in the pass under a full moon when the feathery shrimps were crowding through. It would be especially fine if one knew one's woman was waiting, within reach on the CB, to hear if the catch was good.

But this morning the moon overhead, paling in the early daylight, was not even half full, and it was hassled by scudding clouds. The day looked as if it was going to be anything but calm. It seemed to him that the wind was freshening, although the Weather Service had said the storm two hundred miles south that had been moving west toward Mexico was now stationary. And while Jessica had her CB, he might not know for days yet whether or not she was his woman.

But he couldn't afford to think of that while the shrimps were running. The worry that she might say no was like a black mud hole waiting to devour him if he stepped into it.

His net was payed out. He threw out the tickler, a chain that dragged the bottom just ahead of the trawl. It was contrived to disturb the shrimps that might be feeding on the bottom. It wasn't needed today, he thought exultantly. The pass was so crowded with migrating shrimp that they were boiling up to the surface.

No question about a good catch this time! He was going to make a bundle today. Enough for a down payment on a house pretty enough for the professor, and large enough for the little LeBlancs they would bring into the world. Picture that, he told himself. Only that. He opened his door board so the shrimps the tickler stirred up could flip themselves right up into the net's mouth.

Normally it took two to three hours of trawling to fill the net, but here in the pass the shrimps were as closely packed as the noonday crowd on a New York street, so the trawl filled fast. It took experience to judge when to drag it in. With his motorized winch he pulled it up and dumped the catch into the sorting box.

As he expected, he had picked up a variety of sea creatures: a lot of crabs, one greedy gar who was still feeding on the shrimps as he thrashed about among the croakers and redfish and sea trout. It would take him and Etienne another couple hours to sort out the "trash" and throw it back into the sea.

"The faster we get our trawl back in the water, the more shrimps we'll catch," he told his brother as they worked. "We'll keep the crabs, anh? If the storm drives us in tonight, we'll have a nice crab feed."

He estimated the fine shrimps they had left could maybe be worth several thousand dollars. "This is gone be our lucky day, Et—Steve. *Eef* we don't pick up a turtle heavy enough to open the TED—and dump the shrimps wit' the turtle!''

If that storm stayed out in the Gulf, he would stay out, he thought, until his ice chests were filled.

By afternoon, trawling had carried the *Cajun Pride Too* through the pass and about five miles offshore. When they finished sorting the last haul, the wind had shifted and freshened, and the swells were higher.

"It's a good catch!" Etienne exclaimed as they dumped the last of the trash overboard.

"Time to go in, anh?" Armand glanced up, hearing an intrusive throbbing roar above his engine noise.

A helicopter was hovering above the trawler, coming lower. He could see the pilot for he was sitting in a clear plastic bubble mounted on pontoons. He was looking down at Armand and he lifted his hand, but not to wave. Instead, his urgent gesture seemed to say, "Come on!"

"That's the coast guard insignia," Etienne said.

"Somebody in trouble." Armand waved in acknowledgment and went into his wheelhouse. As soon as he was behind the wheel, the helicopter turned and headed out into the Gulf.

"I don' like this," Armand muttered to Etienne, who stood just outside the open window of the wheelhouse. "Look how high the sea's gettin'? This could be bad trouble." For us, too, he added to himself, but he was changing his course anyway.

The helicopter was moving steadily southeast, and he followed it, in spite of the chatter he was hearing on his CB.

"This is Pelican. Did you get the weather report? Me, ah'm gone in."

"Me, too, man. This sea's gettin' too heavy for me."

"I hear you, Pelican," another voice said. "This is Lucky Dog. Storm's changed directions. West northwest. Red Eye's done left. I'm goin' in now. Ten-four."

The others were running for the quieter waters of the bays and bayous, Armand knew. In a lull, he grabbed his mike. "You there, Mud Hen? Come in, Mud Hen."

There was no answer. It was too early. She was still at the lab.

"Geez," Etienne said. "West northwest, and we're headed into it."

The CB crackled. "Come in, Zydeco. You hearin' me, Zydeco?"

"I hear you, Pelican."

"Where you headin', man? Didn't you get that weather report? You headin' right into the storm."

"Somebody is in trouble out there. I'm followin' the coast guard chopper."

"Who is it, man?"

"I don't know, me, but it's a hell of a time to be in trouble, anh?"

"W'at's wrong wit' his CB? Me, ah don' hear no cry of help."

A half dozen voices were trying to get in with questions.

"Quiet, you guys!" Armand shouted. "This is Zydeco. You still there, Pelican?"

"Got ya, Zydeco."

"Call my house when you get to the bank. Tell 'em I'm headin' out on a rescue mission. I don't know when I'll be in. Got that, Pelican?"

"Got ya, Zydeco. Good luck."

"*Merci*. Ten-four."

Somebody at his house, Claire or Papa, would call Jessica, he hoped. And he hoped she would stay at her CB. He might need her help.

The sky was lowering with dark clouds, and *Cajun Pride Too* was wallowing in deep swells. They had chugged out of the shallows into deeper water. The coast guard chopper moved steadily southwest, above and slightly ahead of them.

JESSICA REACHED her house at about five-thirty. She turned on the television as she passed it, to get the weather news, and flipped on the CB when she entered her kitchen. In spite of the brisk wind that had tangled her hair on her way in from the car, she felt hot and sticky. The storm was not a cooling "norther," but was moving in off the Gulf, where hurricanes were spawned. Its breath was warm and moist on the skin.

While she watched for the radar weather picture, she listened to the fishermen chatting in French, occasionally exchanging notes in English on their catches and talking about the storm off the coast of Mexico. Apparently it had changed direction and was now heading northwest. She heard enough to surmise that the boats were all coming in, and with full ice chests.

The radar picture showed the swirl of clouds that was now being swept up toward the Louisiana coast. It was somewhat diffuse, not yet a hurricane, but it looked dangerous.

"—winds of thirty-five to forty-five miles per hour are making the Gulf choppy with swells as high as ten feet—"

Armand would have moved into the calmer waters by now, she thought. He might even have reached the bayou that would carry him up to Dulac, where he would sell his catch.

She desperately wanted a shower, but she stopped long enough to pick up the CB mike and flip it on. "Are you there, Zydeco? This is Mud Hen calling Zydeco. Do you hear me, Zydeco?"

There was a sudden silence on the band. Before she could repeat her message, her telephone began ringing. With a muttered "Darn," she put down the mike and picked up the phone. It was Claire.

"Jessica?" The shrillness of her tone caused a strange prickling along Jessica's arms, a quick flash of presentiment in her brain. "We've had a call from a friend of Armand's, a fisherman who lives down in Dulac. He had a message from Armand."

Jessica gasped. "Something's happened? He's—is he all right?"

"Yes, but he sent word he'll be late coming in. Somebody's in trouble and he's going out to help."

Out? "Where is he, exactly?"

"He's still offshore." Claire hesitated. "His friend said he was following a coast guard helicopter, and heading out into the Gulf."

Jessica stood with the telephone receiver in her hand, looking at the television screen, which was showing a radar picture of the storm again. The weather reporter was saying, "Fishermen are leaving the offshore fishing grounds, most of them, it's said, with a full catch. But they won't be going back to that rich fishing grounds in the morning."

She experienced a hard panicky leap of her heart. "Nothing can happen to Armand," she told Claire staunchly. "He's strong, he knows the sea and he knows his boat."

As intimately as he knows my body, she told herself, filled with love for him. He'd said he knew every board that went into it.

"It's the best-built trawler in the bayous. He told me so himself."

Ordinarily that remark would have brought one of Claire's giggles. But Armand's sister said uncertainly,

"Papa lost his boat, you know, and it was a good boat. But he got home because another shrimper picked him up."

And then he'd had a heart attack, Jessica remembered, brought on no doubt by fighting that terrible storm. And now Armand was on his way to rescue someone else. This was a taste of what the life of a shrimper's wife could be.

Jessica said staunchly, "Tell your mother from me not to worry about Armand. He can take care of himself." And he must. Oh, he must! "Did Hugh get the job?"

"I haven't heard from him yet. Papa says he must be on his way home, because they send everyone off the offshore rig when a storm like this blows up in the Gulf. So I should hear from him soon."

"I just got home, Claire, and I'm on my way to the shower." She tried to keep her voice flat and normal. "But I'll keep trying to reach Armand on the CB. I'll call you when I find out what's happening."

"Okay."

Jessica went into her bathroom and hurriedly stripped. She stood under a cool shower until she felt refreshed and more optimistic. Then she slipped into what was her hot weather uniform since she had come to the bayous, a fresh pair of shorts and a T-shirt.

She went back to the CB. "Come in, Zydeco. Do you hear me, Zydeco? This is Mud Hen." There was not much chatter on the band now but a lot of static, and it did nothing to allay her anxiety.

It was the storm she was hearing, and Armand was out there somewhere in *Cajun Pride Too*, battling it.

ARMAND FIGURED he had followed the helicopter about five miles when he saw the curious floating object ahead of him sticking up out of the water. A lone man had scrambled to his feet on it and waved wildly before a large swell obscured him. Overhead the helicopter pilot looked down, made a thumbs-up sign when Armand raised his head, and signaled he was returning to shore because of the high wind.

While the chopper was turning back, Jessica's voice burst out of the CB speaker with an urgency that startled Armand. "Come in, Zydeco. Can you hear me, Zydeco?"

He picked up his mike. "Got ya, Mud Hen."

"Where are you, Zydeco? Are you all right?"

"About ten miles offshore. Just sighted a man on somet'ing sticking up out of the water. Looks like a pontoon on one of them bubble choppers. We're gone in to pick him off it. Ten-four."

"Wait!" Her voice was almost a scream. "Hugh Broussard is on his way back from the rig on a helicopter!"

"This guy ain't Hugh. Gotta go. Ten-four!"

He dropped the mike and concentrated on maneuvering his trawler through the swells to the pontoon. "Get ready to throw him a rope," he ordered Etienne. "I'll get close as I can."

The man, who was wearing an inflated life jacket, looked to be in good shape. He caught the rope Etienne threw and expertly tied it around himself under his arms. Armand locked the wheel and went to help his brother pull the guy in. When he signaled, the man jumped into the sea and began swimming strongly toward the boat.

When they pulled him aboard, he was shivering with cold, but otherwise seemed okay.

"How long you been in the water?" Armand asked, and at the same time, Etienne demanded, "What happened?"

"Almost two hours, mostly on the pontoon. My helicopter burned." He was tall and rangy and his voice had a twang of Texas in it.

"You a pilot?"

"Pour some coffee, Etienne."

But the pilot waved the offer away. "There's two more guys out there in the water. My passengers. One of 'ems life jacket failed to inflate, and the other one can't swim."

"Mon Dieu!" Armand swore, thinking *Hugh!* Broussard could swim, so it must have been his life jacket that failed to inflate. Damn! His next thought was of Claire. This couldn't happen to her, not after all she'd been through because of loving Hugh! "How can I fin' me a man in a ten-foot sea?"

"Give me your binoculars," said the pilot. He took them and boosted himself up to stand, legs wide for balance, on the wheelhouse roof. He raised the binoculars to scan the seas. "There's an orange life jacket over there. That's one of 'em."

Armand jumped up to stand beside him. The pilot slowly scanned the horizon again, as *Cajun Pride Too* rose and fell with the swells. As they rose again, he pointed and handed the binoculars to Armand. "At least his dye marker worked. See that patch of color on the swell rising over there?"

"Anh! I see his head now." It wasn't easy to see a man's head when just the eyes and nose were above water. In the next instant it disappeared again as the swell washed over it. Was it Hugh?

"Better get to him first, hadn't we?"

"I guarantee!" Armand jumped down, and as the pilot followed him into the wheelhouse, said, "You handle yourself damn well on the water for an airman, anh?"

"Mike Kester," the pilot said, extending his hand with a grin. "I was a Navy pilot, and in the Navy I had survivor training for just such accidents as this one."

"Armand LeBlanc."

The pilot was still shivering, but his handshake was firm. "I'll take that cup of coffee now, Etienne, is it?"

"Steve," Etienne said. His dark look reproached Armand for never remembering, but Armand could not think of that now.

"Get the blankets off those bunks," he instructed as he steered for the patch of color on the gray water of the Gulf.

It was Hugh, all right, trying to keep his head above water in the dye slick. Every time a wave rolled over him, he sank a foot or so, then bobbed up again. He was a good swimmer and he was fighting, but he looked all in.

Armand gave the wheel to Etienne and told him to hold it steady. Then he took the rope and threw it to Hugh. Hugh grabbed for it but missed, and went under again. On the second throw, he caught it and they drew him up to the boat. His fists were white with strain, holding the rope, but he looked barely conscious and blue as ink.

Armand went over the side into the water and with difficulty pried the rope from Hugh's hands and tied it around his waist. Then he boosted him as Mike and Etienne hauled him over the side. They laid him on the deck, sprawled out on his stomach, and Mike worked on him to get the water out of his lungs and stomach, while Armand took the boat to the nonswimmer, who was floating in his life jacket. He was able to catch the rope and tie it around himself. As soon as they had him on board, Armand headed *Cajun Pride Too* homeward.

The strong wind was behind him now, and they fairly flew toward the bank. When he could, he picked up his CB mike and began calling Mud Hen.

JESSICA LEAPED for the mike as soon as she heard Armand's voice. "This is Mud Hen. I hear you, Zydeco, but there's a lot of static."

"A thirty-five-knot wind is blowing us to the bank. Storm's following—" For seconds his voice was blown away, then she heard, "Got Hugh and his oil company boss and the pilot of the oil company's chopper. It caught fire and burned. Nobody hurt. Got that, Mud Hen?''

"Got it, Zydeco." She was feeling a wave of horror. A fire? In a flying helicopter?

"Call the oil company." His voice was drowned in a crackle of static. Screech. Crackle. Then, "...ambulance to meet us at the lab dock, anh?"

"An ambulance?" Her sense of horror and unreality increased. A helicopter fire—nobody hurt—but an ambulance? She didn't know whether she could believe him. Her heart ached for Claire, knowing she must call her within minutes with this news. "Confirm, Zydeco."

"Get an ambulance to the lab dock, Mud Hen." Pop. Pop. "...be there in under an hour..." A prolonged crackle. "...exposure and shock."

"Are you all right, Armand?"

"I guarantee!" Suddenly his voice was as clear as if he were in the room with her, and she felt a rush of warm emotion. "But we're all wet as divin' ducks, 'cept Eti—I mean Steve. Tell Claire, Hugh's gonna be fine."

"Yes. Got you clear and loud. God bring you home safe!" A crash that sounded like an explosion of thunder and that she hoped was only static drowned out her last words. She wished he had been able to hear them.

She put down the mike and the silence on the band haunted her. All the other fishermen must be in, being greeted by their families. Everybody but Armand, who was out there being blown to shore by the oncoming storm. Biting her lip, she went to the telephone, but she stood unmoving for a few moments to compose herself. An ambulance. Then the oil company, who would call their employee's family. But would they call Hugh's? She'd better call Hugh's father, too. But first on her list after the ambulance was Claire.

Claire answered on the first ring. "Jessica?"

"Yes. I finally reached Armand. They're all right. They've got Hugh. He's going to be all right."

"*Hugh?*" Claire almost screamed. "Ah, *mon Dieu*! What's happened? Was there a fire on the rig?" It was the nightmare of all those who had loved ones working on the oil wells offshore. It had happened, with tragic consequences. Claire's wrenching sob twisted Jessica's insides.

"No, no, Claire, not on the rig...Hugh's all right!" she said loudly. "The helicopter went into the water. Armand turned back to pick them up." She decided not to repeat what Armand had said, since Claire was already near hysteria imagining a fire on the rig. She herself couldn't even imagine a helicopter burning. The vision of three men in a flaming object flying over the Gulf was too terrible to think about.

"He called to let us know they're okay, except for being in the water a while. That's why he wants an ambulance for them."

"An ambulance?" Claire shrieked. "He is hurt!"

"He's been in the water," she repeated patiently. "The helicopter ditched. He must have been wearing a life jacket. I'm going to drive down to the lab dock to meet them. Are you listening, Claire?" Armand's sister was sobbing hysterically. "Do you want to go with me?"

"Oh, yes! Are you *sure* he's all right?"

Jessica was not sure of anything at that moment except that she was going to be at the dock when *Cajun Pride Too* came in.

"Get over here, then," she said crisply. "Now I've got to make some other calls."

CLAIRE ARRIVED in Armand's car just as Jessica was locking her front door. The overcast sky was dark, bringing an early dusk, and the wild wind blew her dark hair across her face as she ran to Jessica's Rabbit. She climbed into the passenger seat and Jessica started driving toward the laboratory. The younger woman was clutching her rosary and her lips moved silently.

When they were about halfway there, the clouds darkening the sky opened up, and water poured out of them as if out of an overturned bucket. It was blown against the windshield in such quantities that Jessica had the fantasy that her little car was swimming underwater.

She could scarcely see where she was going, but she had driven the road along the bayou twice a day for so many months now that her memory of driving was in her hands, and she went doggedly on. Claire sat beside her, rigid with terror.

"*Dieu,*" she whispered. "It's a hurricane! All my life I've been terrified of them. I'm a basket of jitters until hurricane season's over."

"It can't be, Claire, they'd have warned us. If the storm offshore was of hurricane force, you know everyone would be out in it boarding up windows."

"Yes, that's true," Claire admitted. "But boats have been lost in storms that were not hurricanes."

"Armand will make it in," Jessica said with confidence. She had to believe that. She cared too much for him to allow any doubt to creep in. Anything else was unthinkable.

She could see him in her mind's eye, standing on his deck with his shirt off and his bare feet wide apart, and he was laughing at the rain that ran down his face and over his bronzed shoulders.

But even as she visualized him, she knew that was another fantasy. Actually, he must be in his wheelhouse, trying to see through his windshield, which was streaming with water like hers. And his boat was rising and falling on a stormy sea and perhaps rolling from side to side, as well.

He was wet, not from the rain, but because he had gone into that sea to get Claire's Hugh.

Armand would have been safe now, if he had not deliberately turned into the gale that was whipping rain in cutting sheets across the marches and must be making a hell of the Gulf, in order to try to rescue someone in trouble.

But his boat was strong, and so was he. He was a man you couldn't lose in the wetlands. Dr. Chris had said so. Young as he was, he had the respect of the other shrimpers. So naturally he would go to the aid of some unfortunate stranger, even if he was offshore in a storm, and every other boat was running for cover.

"He didn't even know it was Hugh who was in trouble," she told Claire. "He didn't know Hugh went out to the rig today until I told him. He—he just *went*."

"Yes," Claire said. "He thought it was another fisherman, probably a friend. Any other fisherman would have done the same for him."

Jessica thought that over as she fought to see the road ahead of them. Water was standing under the stilt houses and around the lab pilings when they reached the dock, but the downpour had lessened from a cloudburst to a steady rain. She drove carefully through it and parked on the dock near the lateral waterway through the marsh that connected the lab's harbor with the navigational canal. The canal was the route that Armand would take to the lab since it was the fastest way to connect with the end of a well-traveled road.

They sat in the car, looking out through the water running down the windshield. There was no boat in sight, nothing but the desolate marsh landscape mostly hidden behind a gray curtain of driven rain.

"I don't know how I could go on living if something happened to Hugh," Claire said. "Could you go on, without Armand? You do love him, don't you?"

"Yes, but I would go on," Jessica said slowly. "We can do lots of things when we have to. But I don't want that. I want to go on *with* him."

"I want Hugh to come back to me whole and well. It would be too cruel to lose him now, when I'm finally growing up enough to see what's important. For me, it's being with Hugh, not where we live or whether we're with family. I know that now. I would still rather be here, both for myself and for our children, but I would never again force my choice on Hugh the way I did. If he can forgive me for costing him the job he wanted so badly in Saudi Arabia—"

"Would you go there with him now?" Jessica asked her. She wanted Claire to go on talking, because it kept her from thinking of how dismal her life would be if she lost Armand.

"Yes, if that's what he really wants. It wouldn't be forever, you know. He told me that he would have thirty days' home leave every summer and money for air tickets. That wasn't good enough for me. Even the thought of leaving scared me out of my wits." She laughed shakily at herself, and added, "Of course, if he gets this job and is back on an offshore rig, and we get married, I can still hope he'll be satisfied enough to stay here. But I'm ready to promise him I won't stand in his way if he wants to travel. I love him so much, Jessica!"

Jessica looked ahead at the gray empty horizon, worry knotting her stomach. She was thinking it was time for Armand's trawler to appear. And she was remembering that scene of violence on the dance floor at the *fais-do-do* Armand had taken her to.

"What about that hot temper of Hugh's? Does it ever worry you that he might turn his violence on you, or your children?"

Claire straightened. "Hugh is *not* a violent man," she said indignantly. "You didn't see René's knife? He threatened Hugh first. That's why Hugh carried a knife that night! It was all my fault, Jessica. I knew I shouldn't play games with René. He can be ugly if he's crossed. Hugh knows that. It made him wild to see me with René. I could have got him killed. I've been so unhappy with myself over that."

"I didn't know," Jessica said. "Armand didn't tell me."

"That brought me to my senses, but by that time Hugh was so angry with me, he wouldn't even speak to me. I love him so much! I—" Her voice broke. "I want him back safe, Jessica!"

And I want Armand, Jessica thought, her eyes desperately searching the curtain of rain shadowing the marsh. She wanted his joie de vivre, his teasing laughter, his tenderness and his passionate love.

"Then pray with me," she told Claire, and they sat in a silence broken only by the noise of rain on the roof of the car.

A siren's wail came thinly to Jessica's ears, and presently a white ambulance pulled up beside them. She waved to the two young men who sat in its front seat, but remained in her car. Behind them the lab and the houses across the road, veiled in the rain, seemed deserted, although she knew they were not. She could see no other living creature out in the storm.

They waited.

CHAPTER EIGHTEEN

AT LAST the *Cajun Pride Too* came into sight, its running lights ghostly ringed moons in the early dusk, its engine scarcely audible over the roar of the storm. It moved steadily toward them, sturdy yet graceful. Jessica hugged Claire, impulsively in what was for her a rare demonstrative moment, and Claire clung to her as they savored their relief.

They saw Etienne in his rain gear jump to the dock to secure the boat. The medics were out of the ambulance with a gurney, wearing plastic raincoats over their white pants and T-shirts. When Hugh came out of the cabin, wrapped in blankets and supported between Armand and another man, both dripping wet, Claire leaped out of the car and ran down to the boat, heedless of the rain drenching her hair. Jessica ran after her, joy at seeing Armand whole and well almost bursting her heart.

Hugh was blue with cold but at least he was on his feet. Claire had her arms outstretched for him, but one of the medics gently warned her aside and they helped him onto the gurney.

He looked up at Claire and his blue lips moved. "I got the job," he whispered hoarsely.

"I'm glad," she said, and from her expression Jessica knew tears were mingling with the rain on her face.

The two medics pushed the gurney to the ambulance. Claire ran after them, saying, "I want to go with him."

"Sorry, miss, there isn't room. We've got three patients to take to the hospital."

The medic indicated the man who had helped Armand support Hugh and an older man who had followed them out of the cabin, clutching a blanket around himself. Both were shivering. The medics loaded Hugh's gurney, then helped the other two men into the ambulance, where they sat on a fold-down bench. The medics jumped in after them, and the driver closed the doors.

Jessica took Claire's arm. "We'll follow them to the hospital." She turned to Armand and for a long moment he held her close, their wet cheeks pressed together, the communication between their bodies making words unnecessary.

He held her tenderly but in a special way that told her he, too, had wondered if they would ever be together again. But he was here, solid and real and safe, and the icy fear that had frozen her heart was melting in the warmth that poured into her body from his touch.

Claire threw her arms around his neck and one of his arms stretched to encircle her.

"Are you and Etienne—I mean Steve—coming with us?" Jessica asked, when he released them.

"*Non.* We've got to unload our shrimps. I'll take 'em all the way to Houma. It won't take but two, t'ree hours. I'll find you at the hospital."

"You're drenched!" she protested.

He smiled, pleased by her concern. "I've got dry clothes on the boat. I couldn't take time to change. But we're near home now, anh?"

Home. The word was taking on a new meaning. Something was happening inside her. She suspected her objectivity was in shreds. But her emotions were still too raw to be tested. The ambulance was pulling out. She concentrated her thoughts on getting Claire to the hospital. From the force and direction of the wind, it seemed that the storm would be following them all the way to Houma.

AT THE HOSPITAL they were told they would have to wait to see Hugh. He was being given tests and treated for exposure and hypothermia. "He's suffering from exhaustion," the nurse explained.

Claire went to a phone to call home and tell the family Armand and Hugh were safe and that she and Jessica were going to wait at the hospital until they could see Hugh.

"I said it was no use for anyone to come now," she told Jessica when she returned.

Jessica was glad of that when the waiting stretched into an hour, and then two. Hugh's father had met the ambulance and was in the room with him when Claire and Jessica were finally admitted.

Hugh lay on his back, his color almost normal against the white pillows. He looked sleepy, but his eyes brightened when he saw Claire.

Mr. Broussard stood and offered Jessica his hand when Claire introduced her. "Thank you for calling me. Hugh's fine," he told them. "They've completed the tests and the doctor said what he needs now is rest. They want to keep him overnight, but he'll be going home tomorrow. Thanks to your brother, Claire. Armand saved Hugh's life by going after him."

Claire made the sign of the cross, and murmured something inaudible. A prayer of thanksgiving, Jessica thought, sharing her emotion. The young woman went to sit beside Hugh's bed, and took his hand. They had eyes only for each other.

"Hugh's mother is visiting her sister in New Orleans," Mr. Broussard told Jessica. "I'm going to bring her home this evening."

"Can you tell us what happened?" Claire asked Hugh.

"The helicopter caught fire."

Claire gasped. "*Eh, mon Dieu!* Jessica didn't tell me!"

"I was afraid to tell you what I knew, because it was so little," Jessica explained.

"At first I thought the pilot must have a cigar." His voice was still hoarse. "Then my new boss said, 'Do you think we're going to make it to the bank?' and the pilot said, 'No, we're not going to make it.'

"Pretty soon that plastic bubble we were in was full of smoke. The pilot, he kept on steering us toward the bank, but I could tell we were going lower and lower. The pilot was on his radio, calling the coast guard for help. Then I looked up and saw flames."

Claire shuddered. "Were you scared, Hugh?"

"Scared? I was frozen to my seat." Two spots of color showed on Hugh's cheeks as he relived his experience. His father was listening intently.

"The heat of the flames just melted that plastic bubble! The fifty-mile-an-hour wind was blowing right through us. We didn't even smell the fumes! And the pilot, I don't know how he did it, but the next thing I knew he'd set us right down on that water between swells. By that time, one of the pontoons was burning. The pilot told us to get out on the other pontoon and inflate our life jackets."

He took a deep breath, and his voice rasped, as he said, "Well, my life jacket didn't inflate. They jumped off, but I just stayed on that pontoon. They kept yelling to me to jump. 'It's gonna blow!' my boss yelled. Finally I went into the water. I kept pulling the cord, trying to inflate my life jacket."

His father said, "Didn't they tell you about the two little tubes, one on each side, that you can blow into if it fails to inflate when you pull the cord?"

"Armand reminded me of that after he got me on his boat," Hugh said, with a faint, sheepish smile, "but I was just too busy fighting the waves to think. I was pulling everything I could get hold of, and I pulled the cord that released the dye marker. That saved my life.''

A nurse entered the room and said, ''Mr Broussard, Hugh is here to rest. I'll give you five minutes and then you'll all have to leave.''

''Have a heart, nurse!'' Hugh protested, clinging to Claire's hand. He was looking better by the minute.

The nurse laughed, but warned, ''Five minutes!''

He looked at Claire, his face sobering, and continued his story. ''When the pontoon was half-burned, the helicopter just turned over and the sea put out the fire. It was still floating. The one good pontoon was sticking up and the pilot got to it, and yelled to us to come on, and hang on to it until they picked us up. He'd radioed the coast guard that we were ditching. Well, I tried to get back to the pontoon, but I just couldn't make it in that sea.

''Then a helicopter came out, but it circled over us and took off again.''

''A 'copter couldn't pick you up from a sea as rough as today's,'' Mr. Broussard said.

''I just about gave up then,'' Hugh admitted.

Claire made a low sound of sympathy in her throat.

That was the helicopter that found Armand and led him to the survivors, Jessica thought, her hands clenched into fists as she thought of the risks he had taken. But she didn't speak. She could see that the young lovers were oblivious of anyone but each other.

Hugh put his other hand over Claire's and said, ''Well, that's it, chére. After what seemed like forever, the helicopter came back with Armand.''

''You were in the water without a life jacket all that time!''

"By then I'd swallowed enough saltwater that I was throwing it up the whole hour it took Armand to get us to the bank!"

The nurse put her head in the doorway and announced, "Time's up."

"We're leaving," Hugh's father said. "*Le bon Dieu* was with you, Hugh. I'll be around in the morning to pick you up." He nodded to Jessica and they went out, leaving Claire and Hugh alone for a moment of privacy.

ARMAND WAS SITTING in the waiting area, talking to a young man Jessica had never seen before. She thought he must be a reporter, because he had a notebook on his knee and a pen in his hand.

Mr. Broussard walked up to them and offered his hand. "I owe you, Armand. Hugh couldn't have held out much longer."

Armand stood up to shake hands. "How is he?" He had changed into dry clothes, obviously the kind of working clothes he wore on his boat. He looked strong and resourceful and self-confident in them, and just as impressively handsome as he'd been the night he wore his white linen suit to meet her parents.

"Suffering from exhaustion, but he'll get over that. The doctor said another twenty minutes and he'd probably have gone under. You saved my son's life."

"No," Armand said easily, "the fella saved Hugh's life, he's here in the hospital—if they haven't already sent him home. He's the pilot of the chopper that burned. He's your man."

"If you hadn't turned back when you did, none of them—"

"He's an ex-navy pilot, trained by the Navy how to survive a ditching, anh?" Armand said. "We pick' him off that pontoon, and when we got him aboard, he said

'There's two men in the water.' *He* spotted the dye marker Hugh spilled and knew what it was. If he hadn't, we'd never found Hugh!''

The reporter was busily taking notes. ''That isn't the way the coast guard told it,'' he said, ''when I phoned to see if they'd had any calls for help during the storm. They said their helicopter had no communication with you, LeBlanc, and that you were pretty damn savvy to turn around and follow their man with nothing but a crooked finger for a message.''

Armand said good-naturedly, ''Anybody knows a chopper wouldn't be out in that wind unless somebody was havin' trouble, anh? An' there was no way he could safely set down on a ten-foot sea. You go talk to that Navy pilot before they let him out of here. I don't think they'll keep that fella overnight. You'd think he jus' took a little swim! *He's* your hero.''

''Thanks, LeBlanc!'' The reporter put his pen into his coat pocket and went over to the nurse's station.

Jessica looked at Armand, knowing her heart was in her eyes. For some reason, his words had made everything fall into place for her. Education didn't teach bravery or tenderness or the kind of caring that made a man risk his life for others. She not only loved the man Armand was, she knew that she wanted to spend the rest of her life with him.

She couldn't think now why she had tried to be objective in arriving at her decision. She could never be objective about Armand! She was totally subjective about him, and that was as it should be. She loved him! And love was *not* objective.

I must remember to tell my mother that, she thought.

Claire came out of Hugh's room smiling and holding her head at a familiar pert angle, her eyes suspiciously bright. In Jessica's judgment, she'd been thoroughly kissed.

''Shall we brave the storm again, Mud Hen?''

"Watch it," Armand growled. "That's *my* name for the professor, anh?"

Claire laughed, and the sound was good to hear.

It was still raining when they left the hospital, but the brunt of the storm had moved over Houma and northward. The wind was gusty but no longer as strong. They got into Jessica's car and Jessica drove down the bayou to the LeBlancs' house.

"Was it a good catch?" Jessica asked Armand.

"A pretty one." She knew he must be very tired, but his voice was deep and rich with satisfaction. The catch meant much to him, but she knew some of his satisfaction must come from the knowledge that he had succeeded in finding Hugh and getting him out of that dangerous sea.

He was a complex man, this man she loved, glorying in the hard work of trawling as well as in the complicated rhythms the black Creoles had added to the traditional folk songs he loved. He was also a caring man—and unhesitating in taking chances when he cared.

Claire jumped out of the car and ran up onto the veranda, but Armand held Jessica back. He pulled her into his arms and kissed her with hard passion.

She felt his kiss not only in her mouth as his tongue teased her, but in the tingling of her breasts and a warm flame that moved through her blood all the way down to her womb.

"Are you my woman?" he demanded.

"I'm your woman," she said, feeling the deep truth of the words, "and you are my man. I know that now."

"An' you'll marry me?"

"I'll be proud to marry you, Armand."

He lifted a finger and gently tucked a strand of hair behind her ear. "I've waited a long time to hear that. We'll go and talk to Père Naquin tomorrow, anh?"

"Yes."

"A Catholic wedding after the trawling season's over. But not in New York, anh? We'll marry in Père Naquin's church?"

"If you wish, Armand. But I want my family here, too."

"Will they come?"

"Of course! They love me. But what about that tour in France? What about Nance Marie's tour?"

"Oh, Papa can go with Nance Marie. He's always wanted to see Brittany and Normandy. That's where his ancestors lived before they emigrated to Nova Scotia. He can take Mama with him. An' Etienne!" he said, and laughed in delight. "Etienne can go and play the *fer*."

"You'll take Steve out of school again? Armand, are you really serious about learning to read?"

"I'm very serious," he said soberly. "I'm gone read bedtime stories to our *bébés, chére*. But maybe you're right about Steve. He must return to school, but after the season, no?"

"You have an answer for everything, don't you, Armand? Do you expect your Papa to play zydeco? What will Nance Marie say?"

"Listen to me, Professor. Papa is the best accordion player in the parish. He played for all the *fais-do-dos* when I was a kid. He taught me everything I know. And he can pick up the zydeco rhythm from Jocko in a jam session, jus' like that! Ask Nance Marie, anh? She'll arrange for another recording for Gus. The don' need me, an' I don' need them. This is what I need."

He kissed her again, then said, "Let's go in and tell everybody, so I can take you home. Me, I want to show you how happy I am, and it's gone take a long, long time. Prob'ly all night."

His kisses had stirred her to a singing joy. She was as eager to make love as he was. "Yes," she said. "Oh, yes!"

Inside, they found everybody gathered in the kitchen, as usual—Armand's parents, *Mémère* and *Pépère* and Danielle and Marie and their husbands with the children, all listening to Claire's dramatic account of Hugh's adventure, and Armand's part in it. Claire's eyes were bright and her voice was full of a deep thrilling emotion that Jessica had never heard in it before. It was clear that she and Hugh had reached a new understanding.

"We can surprise them with our news tomorrow," Jessica whispered. "Tonight belongs to Claire."

"I t'ink Mama's not gone *be* surprised," he whispered back.

He and Jessica were hugged and made much over, then Claire continued her recital, with Etienne supplying bits and pieces of how he and Armand became involved in the rescue.

At last Armand said, "Good night, everybody. Steve can tell you everything, anh? I'm gone home with Jessica now. Claire left my car at her place."

They slipped away while Claire, still high with happiness, kept the family's attention. Jessica drove the short distance to her little house. The rain had tapered off to a mere drizzle, and the wind had dwindled, but the air was still heavy with moisture.

"Don' you think you should get out of those damp clothes?" Armand asked, as soon as she had closed and locked the door.

"What an excellent idea!"

No matter how he tried, his "th" would always faintly resemble a "d", she thought fondly, as he began undressing her. Then he had her breasts exposed, and was kissing them, and she could think of nothing but the sweet sensations he was arousing, and the way tiny raindrops sparkled in his dark curly hair.

She buried her fingers in it, loving its crisp vitality, learning through her hands the shape of his handsome head.

Abruptly he bent his knees slightly to pick her up and carry her, still half-clad, to the bedroom where he finished stripping off her clothes. She began unbuttoning his shirt, caressing his solid chest and muscular shoulders as they were revealed.

When she let his shirt drop to the floor, he picked her up again and laid her on her bed. Swiftly, he unbuckled his belt and stepped out of the rest of his clothing and stood over her, his desire for her plainly evident.

He was a magnificent man. She gloried in his masculine beauty and in knowing his passion was for her. He lowered himself beside her and began a slow adoration of her body with his hands and his lips.

"You are such a beautiful little mud hen," he murmured. "Your eyes are so blue, so cool, and your lips are so warm with love. And your breasts, anh! Someday maybe your books will give me words to tell you how wonderful I t'ink you are?"

"Tell me in other ways, Armand," she begged him. "Love me."

Still he teased her with his lips and his tongue, caressing her with his hands and exploring the secret places of her body until she was wild for him, and she took the initiative, pleasuring him as he had her.

When at last he entered her, they were perfectly in tune and rose together as one being to a crescendo of shared ecstasy. For long moments they held each other, enjoying their closeness, enveloped in the same warm lassitude as their heartbeats slowed.

"Me, I can't imagine anything more wonderful than loving you," Armand said.

"I'll never have enough of your love," Jessica murmured.

After a moment he said, "I've got a house to show you, *chére*, a house I can buy if you like it. It's big, big, room for a dozen kids."

Her eyes opened wide. "A dozen?"

"An' maybe one more for *lagniappe*?" he teased slyly. "Say a baker's dozen?"

"Armand! You're kidding, of course."

"But you want a family, anh?" he asked innocently. "Eight's a good round number."

He was having his fun with her, she realized, relishing a private joke in the same way he'd teased her ex-roommate about fencing.

"Be serious, Armand! Will you settle for four or five? I'm keeping my job, you know."

He kissed her and said soberly, "I expect that, *chére*. You wouldn't be happy without it. I want w'at makes you happy. So long as I've got a couple of boys to help me on my boat, and a little *jolie blon'* like her mother."

"It sounds like heaven," she said, sighing.

A moment later she thought he was asleep, and resolved that tonight she was not going to wake him and send him home. What a day it had been! And how wonderful it would be to wake up together in the morning.

She was almost asleep herself when he said, "I don' like to bring this up, but I'm very hungry, *chére*. I haven't had much time to eat today."

"Darling!" she exclaimed in remorse. "None of us thought to ask! What would you like?"

"Oh, a little hot chocolate," he said. "With maybe a few things to go with it, like gumbo, or oyster spaghetti, or whatever else you've got in that chester-freeze of yours." He added, bemused, "It's nice being called 'darling,' anh?"

She laughed and got out of bed and slipped a cotton shift over her head. "I'll see what I can find, *darling*. Come out when you're decent."

She was whipping up an omelet when he came into the kitchen. He went into her living room and when she looked in to see what he was doing, he had her personal telephone directory open and was dialing a number. She soon recognized from the short spins of the dial that the area code was for New York.

"'Allo, Miz Patricia!" he said. "W'at you *thh*ink? Your little mud hen's gone marry me."

"Armand?" Jessica could hear her mother's shriek through the phone. "Let me talk to Jessica!"

She set down the bowl of eggs she was whisking on the coffee table, and took the instrument from him. "Hello, Mother. Yes, it's true. We're going to be married."

"Phil, get on the extension!" her mother said. "Jessica's getting married! Dear girl, I want to say one thing, only one, and then I'll give you my blessing."

"Yes, Mother?"

"Consider this, my dear. You're not marrying a person, you're marrying a family."

"Yes, isn't it wonderful?" Jessica cried. "I can't wait for you to meet them all! You'll love Danielle's babies!"

"We wish you and Armand all the happiness in the world," her father said. "Since you love him, I'm sure we will. He's a very lucky man."

"Oh, Daddy!" she cried, all her love for him welling up and for a few seconds making her feel like a little girl again. "Will you give me a wedding out here, please? We want to be married in the little church where Armand was christened."

"Of course we will, if that's what you want. Won't we, Patricia?"

"Of course," her mother said gamely.

"It will be a very large wedding," Jessica warned them. "There are hordes of relatives."

"Then I'd better call Herb Tarbell and see if he can help me arrange for a reception at the country club. Put Armand on," her father ordered.

Jessica picked up her bowl of eggs and went back to the kitchen, but then she set it down again. She listened carefully, but all she heard Armand say was, "Yes, sir, t'anks, sir." And then, for a long time, she heard only, "Yes, sir...yes, sir...yes, sir...I'm very lucky, sir."

"What was all that about," she asked when he came back into the kitchen.

"A warning," Armand said with a straight face. "He told me what a stubborn little cabbage you are and all about your terrible temper, and that you'd do anything to get your way, and—"

"Are you sure you're hungry?" she asked. "Because I'm about to pour these eggs either down the sink or over your head!"

He laughed and made a show of dodging. He felt so much love and bubbling happiness that he wished he had some way to express it besides grabbing her and squeezing the breath out of her. He had promised himself that when he mastered reading, he would read her a page from her wonderful book about the marshes, but in his view he was not quite that good yet.

He spotted the newspaper lying on the kitchen table, and recalled how she had advised him once to practice reading it, especially advertisements like those for fishing supplies in which he would recognize words he constantly heard. At least he could show her that he was making progress, that he could read passably well, if slowly.

He picked up the paper and unfolded it to an inside page. A small ad with large, very black type caught his eye.

He began puzzling out the boldface type phonetically, aloud. "Help kids—kidneys," he read, "pass—" With an explosive laugh, he shouted, "*One pint!* Ah, Professor, it's for *this* I'm learning to read?"

Jessica turned with the whisk she had picked up in her hand, her eyes bright with startled mirth, her lips breaking into a wide smile.

Armand grabbed and held her, and they rocked with laughter.

Virginia Nielsen

Several of my historical novels were set in early Louisiana, but for my fifth Superromance, I chose the town to which the U.S. Navy sent my husband a few years after we were married. It was deep in the bayou country of Louisiana where French was spoken as commonly as English, but it was not the French I had studied in school. It was Cajun talk.

The moss-draped oaks, the mysterious shadowy cypress swamps and the tropical birds and flowers seemed intensely romantic. To one who had grown up in Idaho, with its long winters and brief summers, it was like going to a foreign country.

I loved the people I met there—their style, their sense of fun, their ability to laugh at themselves and life and to give themselves to love. I've tried to give those qualities to my characters.

When we returned to Houma, visiting friends and researching Louisiana history, I saw many changes in the town, a commercial center for the fishing and oil industries. Its former isolation from mainstream America had vanished, but the marks its heritage left were there. It was still different, a fascinating background for a contemporary story. So I planned *Jessica's Song*.

Last April my husband and I went back to the bayous of Louisiana for a week I will never forget. Helpful friends took us on trips into the marsh and introduced us to the trappers and fishermen. We visited the marine biological laboratory where Jessica would work and went aboard a shrimp trawler like my hero's. At an oil rig in the swamp we found the ending scene for the book in a personal experience the "company man" in charge of the rig shared with us.

I came home filled with ideas and enthusiasm for finishing the book. I think it's one of the best I've written. Certainly it was the most fun!

SHRIMP GUMBO

Gumbo is a nutritious soup thickened with filé (powdered sassafras leaf) or okra and served over a mound of hot rice. There are many variations, but gumbo is most often made with seafood. A popular variety uses both shrimp and oysters, but there is also a chicken gumbo, and chicken and turkey carcasses and ham bones may be boiled for the stock. Some cooks add pureed boiled vegetables. It is a great dish for using leftovers and can be enriched in many creative ways.

Gumbo originated in South Louisiana, and the name is derived, depending on whom you ask, from *kombo*, the Choctaw Indian name for sassafras, or from the Bantu word for okra, *ngumbo*. Both filé and okra gumbos have their devotees.

Almost every Cajun recipe begins with "First make a roux..." and gumbo is no exception. A roux is made by browning flour in butter or oil. Many cooks sauté chopped vegetables such as onions, celery and green peppers and perhaps a clove or two of garlic in the butter or oil until transparent, and then add the flour and stir over medium heat until the flour is well browned before adding a liquid.

This basic recipe for Shrimp Gumbo is from *River Road Recipes*, published by the Junior League of Baton Rouge.

3 pods garlic (optional)
2 onions, chopped
1 bay leaf
2 lbs uncooked shrimp, peeled and deveined
1 can tomatoes
2 qts water

3 cups okra, chopped or *1 tbsp filé*
4 tbsp oil
2 tbsp flour
1 tsp salt
pepper to taste

In a large skillet, make a dark roux of flour and 2 tbsp oil. Add shrimp and stir constantly for a few minutes. Set aside.

In a 4-quart pot, smother okra and onions in oil. Add tomatoes when okra is nearly cooked. Add water, bay leaf, garlic, salt and pepper. Add shrimp and roux. Cover and cook slowly for 30 minutes.

If okra is not used, remove from heat and add filé.

Serve with rice. Serves 6 to 8.

Harlequin
Superromance.

COMING NEXT MONTH

#398 BEHIND EVERY CLOUD • Peg Sutherland
Kellie Adams loved her position as head pilot of
Birmingham Memorial's air ambulance service. But
when VP Dan Brennan put the service and Kellie
under scrutiny, she knew she might lose her
job... and her heart.

#399 WHITE LIES AND ALIBIS • Tracy Hughes
Luke Wade had only touched her in a brotherly
fashion, but even as a young teen, Kristen's pulse
had raced whenever he was near. He'd been oblivious
to her undeclared emotions, too caught up in the
task of protecting her virtue to ever recognize her
desire. Now she was a grown woman and fate had
thrown them together again in a way that made any
secret between them impossible....

#400 A GENTLEMAN'S HONOR • Ruth Alana Smith
They were from different worlds. But the cotton
farmer-turned-model and the Madison Avenue
advertising executive seemed destined to be
together—until their worlds crashed. To Joe Dillon
Mahue, honor always came first—though Virginia
Vandiver-Rice was steadily gaining in importance....

#401 UNDER PRAIRIE SKIES • Margot Dalton
Kindergarten teacher Mara Steen sometimes
fantasized that she could marry Allan Williamson
and live with him and his young son on his Alberta
farm. But reality always intruded. She could never
abandon the grandmother who'd raised her, even
though her decision meant she'd never have a life of
her own....

Harlequin Superromance®

LET THE GOOD TIMES ROLL . . .

Add some Cajun spice to liven up your New Year's celebrations and join Superromance for a romantic tour of the rich Acadian marshlands and the legendary Louisiana bayous.

CAJUN MELODIES, starting in January 1990, is a three-book tribute to the fun-loving people who've enriched America by introducing us to crawfish étouffé and gumbo, zydeco music and the Saturday night party, the *fais-dodo*. And learn about loving, Cajun-style, as you meet the tall, dark, handsome men who win their ladies' hearts with a beautiful, haunting melody. . . .

Book One: *Julianne's Song*, January 1990
Book Two: *Catherine's Song*, February 1990
Book Three: *Jessica's Song*, March 1990

Have You Ever Wondered If You Could Write A Harlequin Novel?

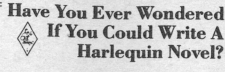

Here's great news—Harlequin is offering a series of cassette tapes to help you do just that. Written by Harlequin editors, these tapes give practical advice on how to make your characters—and your story—come alive. There's a tape for each contemporary romance series Harlequin publishes.

Mail order only

All sales final
